BLUSH

ALSO BY LAUREN JAMESON

Surrender to Temptation

BLUSH

Lauren Jameson

 NEW AMERICAN LIBRARY

New American Library
Published by the Penguin Group
Penguin Group (USA) Inc., 375 Hudson Street,
New York, New York 10014, USA

USA | Canada | UK | Ireland | Australia | New Zealand | India | South Africa | China

Penguin Books Ltd., Registered Offices: 80 Strand, London WC2R 0RL, England
For more information about the Penguin Group visit penguin.com.

First published by New American Library,
a division of Penguin Group (USA) Inc.

First Printing, May 2013

 REGISTERED TRADEMARK—MARCA REGISTRADA

LIBRARY OF CONGRESS CATALOGING-IN-PUBLICATION DATA:

Jameson, Lauren.
Blush/Lauren Jameson.
p.   cm
ISBN 978-0-451-41972-9
I. Title.
PS3610.A464B58 2013
813'.6—DC23   2013002168

Printed in the United States of America
10 9 8 7 6 5 4 3 2 1

Set in Arno Pro
Designed by Sabrina Bowers

PUBLISHER'S NOTE

This is a work of fiction. Names, characters, places, and incidents either are the product of the author's imagination or are used fictitiously, and any resemblance to actual persons, living or dead, business establishments, events, or locales is entirely coincidental.

The publisher does not have any control over and does not assume any responsibility for author or third-party Web sites or their content..

This one is very enthusiastically for Kerry, aka Super Editor.

ACKNOWLEDGMENTS

As always, there are a million people who take part in the creation of a book, and who as such deserve thanks. For this book, however, there are three biggies—Deidre Knight, Kerry Donovan, and my own dear husband, Rob. Deidre— thank you for being so careful with the book of my heart. You're not only the best agent in existence, but you're a dear friend, and I value you more than I can say. Kerry—where to start? Thank you for believing in this book to begin with, and for pushing me (a wee bit mercilessly at times, if I may say so, ha ha!) to make this book more than I'd ever imagined it could be. This story truly would never have happened without your hard work. You've made one of my biggest dreams come true. Rob—what can I say? When I was swamped with this project, on our vacation no less, you kept me fed and watered and made sure I didn't burn in the sun. That's love right there. Thank you to all of the others who worked on this book, many of whom I don't even know. Penguin rocks! To the rest of my family, particularly my mom, thank you for watching the kid when I needed to work and for supporting my dreams. Thank you to my Ravelry buds for the yarn-y inspiration for the club name in this book. Thank you to the Sirens and Scribes (Nini Angell, Grace Conley, Sara Fawkes, Barbara J. Hancock, Elle Ricci, Suzanne Rock, D. L. Snow, Juliana Stone, Amanda Vyne, and Cora Zane)—the never-ending group of awesome who critiques, celebrates, and holds hands—I love you guys. A special thank-you to Sara Fawkes, for answering my random questions and discussing erotica and BDSM with me ad nauseum. And, as always, a massive thank-you to my girl Suzanne Rock, who listens to me whine, kicks me in the butt, whips my plots into shape, and sends me knitting books. I adore you!

BLUSH

CHAPTER ONE

Someone is watching me.

Aware of his eyes on her, Madeline Stone drew her finger down the side of the glass, tracing a fat stripe in the condensation while resisting the urge to sneak a peek through her eyelashes at the man seated down the bar from her, to her right.

She hadn't turned her head, hadn't looked at his face. But a feeling had alerted her to his attention, that prickling of the skin at the back of her neck—the primordial human sense of being watched.

Though she was curious—men didn't often take much note of her—she resisted looking. She had a purpose there tonight, a goal.

She had to focus on that. It was a small goal, to be sure, but it was a giant step on the road to getting her life back.

She felt jittery and drummed her fingers on the sticky surface of the bar to release some nerves. The clicking of her nails on the wood was an irritant as it scraped across her ears. Having wiped her soda glass clean of its chilled fog, she lifted it to her lips for a sip. The straw was bent at an awkward angle, and she had to open her mouth wide to catch it between her lips.

"You seem nervous." The voice was low, velvety, and unexpected.

Maddy jolted, forcing syrupy sweet cola to splash from her cup. "Damn it." She reached for a napkin to mop the spill from her hand. Embarrassed and grumpy now, she swiveled on her bar stool to face the person to whom the voice belonged.

She very nearly choked when she raised the glass. Her breath caught in her throat, and she felt a jolt of adrenaline go straight to her gut when she raised her eyes to the person who had startled her so. This was the man who had been seated down the bar from her, and she had been drawn to his presence, though she couldn't have explained *why*, exactly. Maybe because he radiated a powerful . . . aura, for lack of a better word. One that was impossible to ignore.

His hair was dark, the color of black licorice. His eyes were blue, deep blue, like the sea. He appeared to be maybe a few years older than her, which put him in his early thirties. His face . . . well, he looked like a wicked fallen angel. But there was a hint of concern etched in the fine lines around his lips.

His body . . . oh, his body. Though he wore expensive-looking clothing—a soft button-down shirt and neatly pressed black slacks—the strength of someone who used his muscles hard couldn't be hidden. An unfamiliar desire ran through her.

"Are you all right? I didn't mean to frighten you." There was that voice again, smooth and hot, like the burn of whiskey on the throat.

Maddy caught herself staring and saw the resultant smirk on his lips. Pursing her lips, she reminded herself that it didn't matter what he looked like.

He couldn't possibly be interested in her. After the events of the past year, Maddy knew that she radiated enough fragility, enough neediness, that most men would give her a wide berth, not bothering to search for a reserve of strength underneath.

She had one. That was why she was there—trying to again channel the strength that she had once had.

He seemed to be waiting for an answer, though, so she shuffled through the last few minutes in her mind and came across the question he had asked.

"Yes. Yes, I'm fine." She needed something to do with her

hands. She picked up her abandoned cola, sucked hard on the straw. The wetness eased the discomfort of her mouth, which was suddenly dry as the desert dust outside.

Maddy dared another glance. His eyes were fixed on her mouth, his expression entranced, and he watched her watching him. Instead of trying to pretend that he hadn't been looking at her mouth, he drew his stare lazily up to her eyes, not caring that she knew.

His utter confidence made something unfurl deep in her belly.

"I'm fine." Maddy repeated the words to break the silence that was growing uncomfortable . . . uncomfortable for her, at least. "I just . . . You startled me."

Most people—at least, most people she knew—would have apologized for it, whether the apology was sincere or not. This man pinched his lips together in irritation and, as if she were a child, removed the nearly empty glass from her hand.

"You should never be startled. Be in control of your surroundings." He reached behind her to set the glass on the bar. The ice rattled against the glass walls. As he leaned, he moved in very close to her, just for a moment. The intense heat that he gave off reminded her of the sun at midday in Nevada, glowing golden and hot enough to incinerate.

Maddy narrowed her eyes as she studied him—she was certain that she'd never met him before. Yet his words struck a chord deep within her, a meaning that he may not have meant layered underneath the simple sentence.

Always know where I am. Well, there was her problem in a nutshell, wasn't it? In the last year, she had lost all sense of where she was—of *who* she was, really. It was almost enough to bring her to tears in front of him.

She bit her tongue until she tasted blood, not willing to tear up in front of this man. He couldn't have known how lost she'd been feeling. He didn't know anything about her. Really, she should have been irritated with him for scolding her like he had.

She was a grown woman, after all—no matter how much she may have felt like a lost child in recent memory.

Many people would have felt uncomfortable under the intense scrutiny that she had been directing his way, Maddy mused. This man didn't flinch, didn't blush, didn't toss her a cocky smile. Instead, he continued to return her stare, unabashed, stoic even, letting her look her fill. He didn't touch her, either, but after he set the glass down, she felt as if his hands had been all over her.

"Let me get you something else to drink." She thought he gave a flash of a smile then, just the smallest upturn of his lips, but the expression was gone before she could be certain.

He waved the bartender over; Maddy wasn't listening and didn't hear what they said. She was busy focusing intently on not making a fool of herself—that and wondering why on earth this creature was there, talking to her. What could have drawn his interest to her?

"There." The man eased himself up onto the stool beside her and turned to face her. Their knees bumped together, and Maddy got the impression that he had done it on purpose.

"I'm Alex Fraser. Now, why are you so nervous, so uptight, that my hello made you spill your drink?" He steepled his fingers, rested his chin on them, and looked right into her eyes. As if he cared intensely about her answer. Rather than luxuriating in the attention, Maddy felt like a bug pinned on the wall.

"I . . . I . . ." She couldn't tell him why. It was stupid. No, it wasn't stupid, but it would *seem* stupid to someone who didn't know her, who didn't know what she'd been through or what had brought her there.

The man frowned when Maddy didn't reply, and she felt,

again, a bit like a child being scolded. Then he smiled again, a seductive smile right at her, and the sun seemed to shine.

"Let's start with something easier, then." The bartender arrived at that moment, setting down a bottle of wine with an elongated neck and two stemmed glasses. The man paid it not a whit of attention, keeping his eyes on hers.

Maddy found herself growing very warm.

"You know my name. Want to tell me yours?"

Why on earth did he care? Why did she care why he cared? "Maddy. Maddy Stone."

He nodded as if he had never heard anything so interesting. "And is Maddy short for anything?"

"Madeline." Maddy's voice was soft, but she couldn't seem to speak any louder.

"Well, then." Enormously pleased, the man she now knew as Alex Fraser turned and poured two small glasses from the bottle, which was already uncorked. He handed her one, and though she could feel the heat of his hand as she wrapped her own around the glass stem, he didn't touch her.

Maddy found herself oddly disappointed.

"Please share a drink with me, Maddy." Instead of raising his own glass, he watched her expectantly. She lifted hers, studied its ruby contents, then lowered it again. As she returned her gaze to him, she knew her eyes must have been wide and befuddled by this inexplicable encounter.

"I usually stick to cola." Maddy had learned the hard way that too much alcohol unlocked the grief that she tried so hard to keep pent up. She became another person entirely when she drank, a stranger who was wild, emotional, and above all, angry. Since she liked alcohol, it was just easier not to start.

"This is much better than cola." He was watching her lips again, expecting her to sip.

She knew better than to accept drinks from strangers in

bars, but she had watched this one's journey from the bartender's hands. Alex seemed to want so badly for her to taste it.

"You'll like it." The promise sounded sultry, and Maddy warned herself to settle down, knowing that his hormones were probably much calmer than hers in that moment.

"How do you know what I'll like?" Her voice was breathy and so very unlike how she normally sounded. She had a sneaking suspicion that she would like anything he told her to like. Still, she couldn't resist pushing, just a little.

She couldn't remember the last time she'd flirted. She had so much on her mind that no man had seemed worth the bother. Until this one. And the small smirk that curled his lips told her he knew just how attractive she found him.

Smiling a bit to herself at the strange rush that was filling her, Maddy lifted the glass to her lips and took a sip. Heaven poured over her tongue and down her throat, and she surprised herself by taking a second sip.

"It's lovely." Alex was watching her with pleasure, and she felt absurdly happy that her enjoyment of the wine pleased him. "What is it?"

"Mouton Rothschild, Bordeaux Red—1943 was an excellent vintage." The flirtatious smile froze on her lips for a moment.

1943? This wine was seventy years old?

Her face displayed her shock, and Alex laughed—a sound unexpected from someone who looked like he did. There was no malice in the sound—he seemed to be genuinely enjoying her.

She couldn't help it—she laughed along with him. "You know, a rum and Coke would have done the trick." She eyed him through the lowered fringe of her lashes. She knew that she wasn't imagining the sexual pull between them, but still her rational mind tried to reason with her. What on earth was he going to expect in return for two sips of something this outrageously expensive?

"Why not?" Alex sipped again, not breaking eye contact with her. "I think you deserve it. If you feel the need to alleviate some ridiculously misplaced sense of give-and-take, then tell me why you are so nervous."

Maddy's jaw dropped a fraction at his supercilious words, her sudden irritation lashing through the haze of the spell for a quick moment. Misplaced sense of give-and-take? *Excuse me?* But in the same breath he had told her that he—a stranger—thought she deserved wine that was over twice as old as she was. Flustered, she took another deep sip from her glass, buying time as she tried to figure out what had happened between them.

She wasn't naive. She knew what men generally had in mind when they approached women in bars, when they bought them drinks. And she'd have had to be blind, deaf, and dumb not to pick up on the sexual tension that misted the air like heat rising from the sand, making her nipples pucker and the space between her legs ache.

But he hadn't said anything overtly sexual, hadn't asked her to go to his room, his car, his hotel room.

She was confused, attracted, and turned on as hell. Since she'd long ago learned that there was nothing very exciting about sex, the feelings this stranger was rousing in her were odd indeed.

Trying to cool off the internal heat that she felt rising, Maddy took one more small sip of the wine. Since she no longer really drank, she already felt a buzz humming through her veins from the potent liquid, but to her surprise, she found it pleasant. Relaxing.

It loosened her tongue enough to answer his question.

"I want to play a game of blackjack." Oh, it sounded so lame outside her head. She was sitting in the bar of the El Diablo Casino in Las Vegas. Every other person wanted to play a game of blackjack. "I . . . I know how to play, but I've never done it in a casino."

"Why haven't you?" Alex's voice wasn't derisive; nor did he seem anything but genuinely interested. As he spoke, he reached out and toyed with the fingers of one of Maddy's hands, making her breath catch.

She'd driven to the El Diablo rather than going to the smaller casino in Paradise on a whim. Right at that moment, she couldn't have been happier with her decision.

"I—" Something about him made Maddy want to confide. At the last moment, she bit her lower lip, swallowing the words back down. "I just do. I never have, and it's about time."

Alex didn't speak. When she dared to glance up, he had pursed his lips, regarding her as if she were an exotic animal that he had come upon unexpectedly. Yet no one had ever seen her as exotic before.

The look in his eyes told her that he wasn't fooled by her answer. Her heart beginning to beat a rapid tattoo, Maddy looked away quickly, before the strange, sexy man could coax the answer out of her with one of those dark smiles.

"Then you should do it." For reasons she didn't quite understand, her spirits lifted at his words. "And don't be afraid. Most of the people at the tables are there only because of greed. You aren't, and that will give you an edge."

Maddy shivered at the sincerity shining in those blue eyes, looking down at their intertwined fingers hastily. She felt like Alex could read her, could see right into her soul, and it made her uncomfortable.

Uncomfortable, but . . . she kind of liked it.

"It's not that easy for me." Maddy didn't know why she felt the need to explain—she knew she'd never see the man again.

The realization sent her heart crashing down to her toes. Wildly, she realized that she wanted more time with Alex.

He hadn't asked her for more. He hadn't asked her the expected questions, hadn't done what she'd thought he would.

He was a puzzle, one that she was suddenly dying to try to put together.

"Tell me, Maddy." He wasn't asking a question. His tone demanded a response from her. She raised her head to look at him, her mouth opening to tell him everything. She only just managed to stop herself. She dropped her head again bashfully, unwilling to look him in the eye, and shook her head.

When she looked up again, both of their wineglasses were full. Refusal was on her lips before hers was even offered to her, refusal coated with relief that he didn't push.

"Oh, no. You've given me enough of a treat." Not to mention her fear that a second drink would lead to a third, then a fourth and then into oblivion.

Though Alex looked disappointed at her refusal, making Maddy kick herself for her lack of social graces, he nodded, then gracefully slid off of his stool. He was tall, well over six feet, and for the first time in her life, Maddy felt small as she stood beside him.

She was a woman of average height and build, but she had always felt as though she took up more space than she should have.

"Well, thank you." What else was there to say? It had been a strange encounter all around, and though she was still breathless from it, if she wanted to do what she'd come there to do—and she knew that she needed to—then she had to go. Besides, he hadn't made that final move that she'd been expecting, hadn't asked her to go home with him.

She would have said yes.

The man was silent for a moment, studying her. Nervously,

Maddy twisted a strand of her mahogany hair around a finger as she was assessed, shifting her weight from foot to foot, feeling awkward as the handsome man nodded in acknowledgment of her thanks but said nothing.

Then he leaned in, close enough that his breath tickled her ear.

Maddy felt a small shudder pass through her as she turned her head and found his lips a whisper away from her own.

"It was nice meeting you, Maddy Stone."

She closed her eyes, certain that he was going to kiss her— wanting him to. The touch didn't come. Her eyes flew open to find him studying her face intently. She flushed a brilliant shade of scarlet as she realized her error. Before she could say something stupid, sticking her foot so far into her mouth that it hit her gag reflex, she booked it across the marble tiled floor of the bar.

The entrance to the casino itself was on the other side. Inhaling deeply, Maddy tried to will her feet to move her into the room.

"Would you accept a piece of advice?"

He must have followed her, because there was that voice again, low and sultry, whispering against her ear. This time she was irritated. She whirled and found Alex standing right there, right in her personal space.

While part of her noted how delicious he smelled— expensive cologne, musky soap, and something else primal and male—it did nothing to dispel her irritation.

If she was honest with herself, she was mad that he had turned her on, made her desire him, and then not followed through, but she wasn't planning on admitting that to *him*. It was hard enough to admit to herself.

"Will you stop sneaking up on me, please?" A look of shock

crossed over his face. Maddy wondered if he wasn't used to being snapped at.

As he continued to examine her without speaking, she felt her drive to enter the gaming floor of the casino dissolving.

"Well?" Maddy tapped her foot, her high-heeled sandal clicking on the tile.

Alex looked down at her feet, then slowly back up to her face, his stare caressing her body on its way back up.

"Well?" he echoed, and she noticed that his right hand fisted and unclenched several times in rapid succession.

"Your advice. What is it?"

He raised an eyebrow, at her tone, she thought, before speaking.

"Have another drink. Just one." His words sounded cautionary. She looked over his shoulder, at the half-full bottle of wine and the two glasses, where they still sat on the bar.

She had indulged in one drink tonight . . . She wasn't likely to have another. But she was curious nonetheless.

It seemed like odd advice for someone to receive before a card game.

"Why?" Maddy intended for the word to be blunt, but he was still looking at her in that way, and it was making the nerves in her skin skitter around like someone was tickling her. Alex leaned in close and, irritation aside, she basked in that heat again, though he still didn't actually touch her.

When his mouth was a mere whisper from her ear, he paused, and her heart stopped, then began to beat again, double time. She very nearly arched her neck toward him, wishing for his lips to brush her ear, for his teeth to nip at it.

"One drink has brought some color to your cheeks. Two will make you flush. This will keep the other players from knowing when you have a good hand . . . because your blush is very telling." And after dropping that bomb on her, he walked away, leaving Maddy gaping after him.

She also drank in the sight of his spectacular ass, but that was neither here nor there.

Stupefied, Maddy watched as several people greeted him. It seemed odd to her, but maybe he was a regular there.

It certainly seemed that he could afford to be.

Your blush is very telling. Well, she was blushing for real now, the ruddy tones painting her skin all the way to the roots of her tawny hair, she was sure.

What was *that*? Her body felt electrified, her heart was pounding, and that flush had spread over every inch of her skin. She had never reacted so intensely to a person in such a short time, and she was thoroughly flustered by it.

But in the end, it was the nudge that she needed. She stopped gaping after the gorgeous man who had whirled into her life and then just as quickly whirled out of it. Before he made her spill her cola, she had been on target to play a game of blackjack.

Having gained his attention, even if just for a brief twenty minutes, had given Maddy a surge of confidence.

She wasn't leaving until she played that game.

It wasn't until she took a deep breath and stepped onto the casino floor that the worry began to trickle back in. With a start, she realized that she hadn't thought of her nerves, her angst, for nearly half an hour.

Alex, with his gorgeous smile and inquisitive nature, had made her forget all about it.

Alex entered the casino floor through the far entrance with the express purpose of catching another glimpse of the little doe who had so captured his attention. In the drab floral skirt and cheap knit top, she was hard to spot, effectively camouflaged among the flash of bright satin, the glare of multicolored sequins, the glitter of sparkly baubles.

There . . . there she was. He watched as she wound her way through aisles of slot machines, pausing to peek over the shoulder of a tiny, elderly woman with purple hair who was playing one involving shirtless firefighters. He watched that rosy flush spread over her cheeks as she stared, seemingly fascinated, at what Alex knew was a rotating stream of very nearly lewd images that the cheeky machine featured.

He watched as she wavered, lured by the ease and relative anonymity of feeding quarters into a slot machine. Her fingers reached tentatively for the handle of the neighboring machine, and when she drew the length of one finger down the shaft of the handle, his eyebrows rose to his hairline at the seemingly suggestive gesture that he knew was actually entirely innocent.

"That's a good girl." Alex watched as Maddy squared her shoulders, then, with a deep, shuddering breath, deliberately marched her way to the card tables.

He could see her anxiety riding her like a monkey weighing heavily on her back.

"What has you so worried about a card game, babe?" He watched as Maddy, with little to no idea of what she was doing, headed for a table full of cardsharks who would eat her alive in one tasty bite.

"Dylan." Alex caught the eye of his pit boss. He gestured to Maddy and shook his head just the slightest bit. The capable manager spoke a few words into his Bluetooth, and then the dealer—a new kid named Milo who was bright enough to count cards if he wanted to—looked up, around, and finding Alex, nodded at him. When Maddy approached the table, Milo shook his head, gesturing that the game was full, then pointed her in the direction of a blackjack table that might be more her speed.

Alex watched as her body tensed, poised to argue—he smiled that she had noticed there was still an empty chair at the shark table. He liked that she wasn't pleased at being given the runaround. But when she looked across at the indicated table, the one that held a preppy-looking young executive type and an older woman draped in jewels, he could almost hear her sigh of relief.

"Damn." The withering look that Maddy cast Milo was hot. Alex wasn't usually drawn to brats, but something about the steel under the fragile exterior of this woman had pulled at him since he'd first looked down the bar and seen her sitting there.

At first glance, her downcast eyes and reservations called him in the way that a Dominant was drawn to a submissive— he wanted to protect, to take control so that she could stop worrying. Heaven knew the Dominant in him was rearing for *something* to control, ever since the call he'd gotten from Lydia earlier in the day.

He had never once been late in a payment to her. It was a point of honor for him. Still, she called every month, like clockwork, to remind him and to trowel on the guilt.

She wasn't trying for more money; no, he gave her plenty, and didn't miss it. Alex knew that she did it because it satisfied something inside of her to make him bleed.

Some months he was able to shrug it off. This time the woman had gotten under his skin, stuck there like an intravenous needle, feeding him a never-ending stream of poison.

Then he'd looked down the bar, had seen the sweet, intriguing face of Maddy Stone. The first look at her had wiped all of his negative thoughts away. Even if she hadn't appealed to him on a gut-deep sexual level, he would have been intrigued by her simply because of that.

And *then* he'd seen that blush, the color of a perfect rosé wine, spreading over her creamy skin, and he'd had to clench his hands to keep from fisting them in her hair, lowering his mouth to hers, and claiming her in the most basic of ways.

The attraction between himself and the sweet, cheaply dressed woman had had a tangible pulse—a connection that was rare to find and, in his experience, had the potential for mind-blowing satisfaction for them both.

"What's your secret, babe?" Fixing a scowl on his face that would discourage all but the bravest of souls from approaching him, Alex skirted the edge of the casino floor, searching for a vantage point that would let him see her face.

There—*there.* Maddy was settling herself at the table that Milo had indicated for her. The steel in her expression had him second-guessing his assumption that she was a natural submissive.

He hadn't been able to resist buying her the wine, simply to see that blush spread over her cheeks again. When her skin heated, she radiated the faintest scent of freesia, and he'd have bet a good chunk of his empire that that was the smell of a body cream, activated by the warmth of her flushed skin. It had been intoxicating, clouding his senses.

But now he forced himself to turn away from the fascinating creature, made himself walk away.

Madeline Stone was a delicious temptation, but if she had any idea of what he wanted to do with her, to do *to* her, she'd run screaming into the night. He knew what he needed, and sweet women with visible baggage weren't it, no matter how delectable they seemed.

Steeling himself, Alex headed back toward the exit of the casino. Just before he left—he needed to get back upstairs, for he'd left Rae for far too long already—he succumbed to desire and cast one more look back over his shoulder at Miss Madeline Stone.

Her lower lip was clamped between her teeth, and her features were set with concentration. She'd refused to tell him why playing a game of blackjack scared her, but he couldn't help admiring the way that she was bulldozing through her nerves with steely determination.

Again catching his pit boss's attention, Alex pressed his hand to the buttons of his Bluetooth, which he always strapped on when he entered the casino floor area. He was very tempted to arrange for Maddy to win her game.

He watched a flush of pleasure paint her face as she received a good hand. After a long moment, he released his Bluetooth and, turning back, continued on his way.

He wasn't going to cheapen the reward of whatever triumph she so clearly needed. He couldn't bring himself to darken the innocence that seemed to hover around her like a cloud.

"And that counts for more than just the game, Fraser." No matter that watching her bite her lip had made his cock swell in the trousers of his made-to-order Italian suit, no matter that he wasn't used to denying himself anything.

He knew he'd have to refrain from watching her from the balcony of his private office until he left, the one from which he could see the entire casino.

He didn't know if he could, but Madeline Stone wasn't for him, not on any level.

That was just the way it was going to have to be.

CHAPTER TWO

Maddy had decided to ignore Alex's advice to have another drink—she wasn't willing to risk it. But the sips of Alex's expensive Bordeaux had warmed her stomach, giving her a flush of courage . . . and so had his words. Now she was seated at a blackjack table, and her fear was very nearly gone, replaced instead with the fizz of anticipation.

"Chips in." Maddy slid a small black chip across the table. It seemed like such an insignificant token, yet it represented one hundred dollars, the minimum buy-in for the table. It may not have been much money to the health-club-fit thirty-something on her left, the one who was handsome and dressed well yet still left her cold. It might have been pennies to the predatory-looking woman to the left of him, the one wearing gold sequins and an expression of hawklike intensity.

The sharp suit on the man next to her, black wool accented with a deep purple tie, drew Maddy's mind back to Alex and to the hardness of his frame beneath his expensive clothes. She must have looked drab in comparison, her floral skirt, black shell, and sandals all from Walmart.

She reminded herself that it didn't matter. She'd never see him again. She had to focus on the game, or risk losing money that she really couldn't afford to part with.

The dealer placed Maddy's two cards in front of her. They weren't very good, a six and a seven compared to the dealer's ten. Anxiety blossomed in her gut. The man to her left had a jack and an ace, and the woman a seven and an eight.

The woman won the hand, and Maddy watched her hundred dollars slide away across the green table.

She had played a hand now—she could go. She *should* go. But Maddy found that she'd caught the bug . . . She wanted to win.

Reluctantly, she slid another black hundred-dollar chip across the table. She'd purchased more chips than she could really afford. She watched the woman slide forward two rounds of orange plastic, which Maddy had learned were called "pumpkins"—each represented one thousand dollars. Her knees quivered at the thought of losing so much money in a game. The man offered up a pumpkin and a barney, a purple token worth five hundred.

Maddy looked at her lonely black chip. As if possessed by someone else, her hand slid four more little black pieces across the table. Five hundred dollars, and she had already lost a hundred.

She blanched when she realized what she'd done, but it was too late. And even though the idea of losing that much money made her feel sick, the risk was . . . exciting. Yes, exciting.

It washed over everything else that she felt, tinting those thoughts a vivid, rosy pink.

The dealer placed a card faceup in front of her, then repeated the gesture for the man, the woman, and himself, though his faced down. The circuit went around once more.

When he gestured to Maddy, she was distracted looking at her cards and working out her hand.

She didn't immediately understand when the dealer said the magical word. "Blackjack."

She very nearly groaned aloud, thinking that he must have meant one of the other two. But wait . . . the woman had a four and a seven. The man had a jack and a queen—a great hand, but not an automatic blackjack.

Slowly Maddy looked down at her cards. Lying on the felt before her were the glossy faces of a jack and an ace. A jack was ten, and an ace could be an eleven or a one.

Holy shit. She had hit blackjack.

The dealer slid Maddy's five hundred in chips back to her, plus another five hundred on top of those. She had won four hundred dollars, as well as winning back the five hundred that she had bet to begin with. The dealer said she got a bonus on top of that. It wasn't a large amount, not at all, but the win felt absolutely glorious.

"Congratulations, sweetheart." The suited man grinned at her salaciously. She smiled back, too excited to care about his leer, and contemplated playing again, just once more.

She couldn't quite have explained why, but her gaze was drawn up from the table. Across the casino floor, way up high, was an ornate balcony, almost like what she imagined she would see in an opera house. It offered an unfettered view of the entire casino floor.

Standing up there, his arms braced on the balcony, was Alex Fraser. He was watching her intently, and when her eyes connected with his, she could feel her heart skip a beat.

His shirtsleeves were rolled up, his tie loosened. It was like getting a look at the more casual side of him, the one who had let that controlling persona, the one with the answers, slip just a bit.

He nodded at her solemnly, the whisper of a smile around his lips. Flustered, Maddy looked back at the chips that she had clutched in her suddenly sweaty palms. Moments later, she narrowed her eyes back up at the alluring man. Alex appeared to wink, just the tiniest movement, before his face returned to normal, as if they had just shared a joke that no one else knew.

"Do you know who that is?" Maddy hated to draw the man at the table, who had leaned in closer than she would have liked, into conversation, but at the moment she found she needed an-swers. She gestured with her head toward the balcony. She had hoped he would be subtle, but her seat-side companion turned and stared, unabashed.

Maddy could feel herself blushing furiously, well aware that Alex Fraser must have known that she'd asked about him.

The man beside her leaned back in, far too close. Maddy could smell scotch on his breath, one with extra peat, as well as the stench of cigarette smoke and sweat.

"That's Alex Fraser. Bloody Irishman. Owns the place."

Her mouth fell open as the enormity of the statement hit her. He owned the casino? Alex Fraser owned the whole entire casino?

The health club man chose that moment to place his hand over hers. It was clammy and pulled at her skin. She barely hid a shudder.

"I can take care of you just as well as that fucker."

Maddy was repulsed by the man's choice of language and couldn't help reeling a bit at the knowledge that Alex owned the casino. No wonder he could afford to buy a seventy-year-old bottle of wine. Hell, he could probably afford to buy the entire vineyard.

"Thanks. I'm going to go freshen up." Maddy extracted her hand from beneath the other man's and knew that the first thing she would do in the ladies' room was scour the flesh that he touched with soap and hot water. She gathered her chips, the little stack a satisfying weight in her hand. As she stepped away from the table, she dared to take another look up at the balcony, to see if Alex was still there.

He was there all right, and he was scowling at her. No, not scowling, glowering. After a faltering step—what had she done?—she realized that he wasn't glaring at her at all, but at the man whose sweat felt like it still stained her palm.

Surely ... Could he be ... ? He wasn't mad that the man had touched her ... ? She shook the thought out of her head as soon as it made itself known.

She didn't really know Alex Fraser at all, nor did he know her. She still didn't know why he had introduced himself to her in the casino bar, and she probably wouldn't ever know. But she did know that he couldn't possibly have cared who touched her.

As she scurried across the casino floor to the door marked *Ladies*, Maddy reflected that even if he did care, he really didn't have anything to worry about.

She hadn't been touched, not in that way, for a very long time.

She thought of the wink as she walked, and it hit her out of nowhere. Had he arranged for her to win?

The suspicion made her angry, furiously so. How dare he? He might have been thinking that he was doing her a favor, but he had just undermined her entire experience. She didn't feel as if she could cross this item off of her bucket list anymore—it wasn't real.

Maddy wanted to go up there and yell, which was strange, because she never yelled. No, she swallowed her feelings, burying them inside.

She looked over her shoulder, one more glance at the balcony before she entered the ladies' room. She wondered if she could signal somehow that she needed to talk to him, that what he had just done had upset her. Not that he'd care, but Maddy felt driven to do so anyway.

Also, she wanted just one more look at him, the sexy male who had aroused lust that she hadn't even known she was capable of.

She caught sight of the back of him, walking away from the balcony. She also saw a wisp of golden hair, shades paler than her own, vanishing from the balcony in front of him. Someone else was up in that balcony with him, someone she couldn't see. He followed that person back inside.

Then he was gone, and she would never see him again.

To shake off the overwhelming disappointment that hit her when she thought of never seeing such an alluring man again, she patted herself on the back for her blackjack win.

She'd moved to Paradise, Nevada, a year ago. She'd started seeing a new therapist a year ago, too—a clean break from her old therapist, who, while perfectly adequate, was a tie to her old life. Dr. Gill, her new doc, had taken great interest in her reluctance to try new things, and together they'd constructed a list of activities that scared her, ones that she nevertheless wanted to conquer her irrational fear of.

This had been number one, urging herself to enter a casino. Urging herself to have the courage to walk up to a table and play a game. Since she knew how to play blackjack, this had been the game that she'd put on her list.

For the woman who would drive ten extra miles on empty simply to go to the same gas station, it was a huge step.

She was thankful she hadn't spilled her secrets to Alex when he had pressed her.

She didn't need to explain it to Alex. She didn't need to explain it to anyone, and she certainly didn't need the distraction of a gorgeous, enigmatic billionaire casino owner. Doing things that pushed her out of her comfort zone was small steps that added together would give her some measure of control over her life back.

"Alex, Massimo Santorini is on the phone." Alex's indispensable personal assistant, Kylie Anderson, stuck her head into the inner sanctum of his office without asking. It wasn't an uncommon practice for her, so she took a full step back when she noted the expression on his face.

"Whoa. What's got your panties in such a knot?"

Alex simply glowered in response, and Kylie raised an eyebrow at him. Though the curls of her red hair were wild, and the pink silk of her floaty gypsy skirt gave her the look of someone who was laid-back and ready to kick off her sandals at any moment, he knew that she was anything but.

"Don't you have something better to do?" The scowl that intimidated the heads of international corporations had long ago ceased to even register with the scarily efficient Kylie. "Surely it's been at least half an hour since you drove Declan crazy?"

Kylie raised an eyebrow archly; then, twisting her hair back, she secured it with the pencil she'd had in her hand.

"As a matter of fact." Tapping away on her iPad, she made a note of something, then looked straight at Alex. "But seriously. A, what should I tell Santorini? Are we still trying to sweeten the deal? And B, do I dare hope that it's a female who has finally gotten underneath your skin?"

Alex growled. It should have bothered her—it was a sound that scared every one of his employees besides Kylie and Declan and the sound that warned every submissive he'd ever been with that they were pushing him a bit too far.

Kylie leaned against the open door, tapping her bright blue nails on the screen of her iPad. She gave no reaction to his intimidations.

Feeling a headache coming on, one induced by relentless thoughts of Maddy Stone and that delicate pink blush, he frowned in the direction of the sparkly nail polish.

If Kylie weren't so good at her job, he'd have insisted she make her appearance a little more professional. Instead, he'd found that her bohemian style was useful at disarming the business tycoons, distracting them while he went in and made the kill.

Unfortunately, that wouldn't work on the phone.

"Put him through." Alex pressed his lips together tightly. When Massimo had first approached him about purchasing A Casino in Paradise—the day that he'd met Maddy, in fact—something had seemed off about the man. But when he'd done his due diligence, he'd uncovered nothing incriminating.

Santorini liked to gamble, particularly in high-stakes horse games, and had made some poor choices starting a few years earlier, around the time his wife had died. He owed a lot of money to some bad people, and that was why he was quickly trying to liquidate one of his businesses. But everything on the casino had checked out clean, though Alex knew that he could get a better price, which was why he was trying to draw things out with the man, to make him anxious for the sale to conclude.

He had nothing but a gut sense that the man wasn't telling him everything. Still, it strengthened his need to stall, both to make sure he'd examined every nook and cranny of the deal, as well as to put the squeeze on the seller.

He hadn't become as rich as he was, as successful, by being a nice man. It was just another reason that he was all wrong for Maddy Stone.

"Hey, boss?" Unlike Declan, Alex had an almost never-ending supply of patience when it came to Kylie. But when she stuck that red head of hair back into his office one last time, he couldn't hold back the snarl.

Thinking about Maddy—specifically, thinking about how he should stay far, far away from her—had put him on edge.

"I've never seen you worked up over a woman. That alone makes me like her. I'm just saying." Her expression was serious, and she held his gaze for a second before she was off and run-

ning again, a whirlwind of movement. "Transferring the call in
two!"

Alex's hand hovered over the phone, waiting for Kylie to put
the call from Santorini through. He wasn't good at denying himself what he wanted, and Kylie's words had just given him a push.

The report he'd had Declan prepare on the woman the day
after he'd met her, while the memory of her heady fragrance
still lingered in his nostrils, had told him that Miss Maddy lived
in Paradise, Nevada, which was where Santorini's casino was
located.

Perhaps just seeing her again would help purge her from his
system. Perhaps she wasn't nearly as alluring as he'd remembered.

Yes. Certainly that was it.

The phone beneath his fingers rang, and Alex made up his
mind. After he concluded his call with Santorini, he would take
a drive to Paradise, Nevada, where he could check out A Casino
in Paradise personally.

And maybe he'd stop for breakfast at Joe's Diner on the
way, in hopes that a certain sweet little waitress would be
working.

"Maddy, can you take this to table twelve for me?" Susannah
Phillips, the closest thing Maddy had to a friend in Paradise,
had beaten Maddy to work the next morning, a rarity for her. As
Maddy looked the other woman over, she noted that she was
having a crazy bad hair day, and her face was devoid of makeup.
But the other woman's cheeks were rosy and her eyes sparkled.

Somebody had had a good night, and that somebody was
not Maddy.

"Sure." Methodically, Maddy turned to the warmer and retrieved the plate. Her eyebrows rose slightly at what the plain

white ceramic dish held—whole-wheat pancakes with fruit and cottage cheese, no syrup, no whipped cream, no ice cream. Not a common order for Joe's Diner, a greasy spoon in Paradise, Nevada, aka her place of employment.

She'd been back at work for a week and had obsessed over Alex Fraser for every one of those seven days. She should have been congratulating herself on crossing an item off of her bucket list, but the thrill had been lost in her angst-ridden desire.

"Table twelve is smokin'." Susannah winked at Maddy as she scurried past her with two glasses full of fizzing soda. Maddy rolled her eyes in return. Her shift started a half hour after Susannah's did, and from the look on the other woman's face, Maddy had very nearly missed the best thing since sliced bread.

"You think everyone is smokin'." Maddy whispered this back before hefting the plate and a coffeepot. She felt a lock of hair fall into her eyes as soon as her hands were full and flipped it back with the ease of long practice.

There wasn't much that she couldn't handle there, in comfortable surroundings.

"By the way, someone called for you this morning. Ned maybe—or Nathan? Anyway, he said he'd try your cell later." Susannah scurried away with her drinks, leaving Maddy glued to the floor, conflicting feelings rioting around inside of her.

It wasn't unusual for her brother-in-law to call. It wasn't even unusual for her to feel sickness and guilt every time that he did, though she knew he'd die before deliberately making her feel that way.

It wasn't his fault that she didn't want him to call. She'd pushed him out of her life for a reason.

Back home, everything had reminded her of Erin, especially Nathan. Maddy's grief clung to him like a shroud, and she couldn't function when it, and he, were around.

Grimacing, Maddy took a second to force her way through the painful sensations. Gradually, her surroundings filtered back in, and as they did, her muscles began to warm, a hot bath of familiarity.

Her name was Maddy Stone. She was twenty-eight years old. She lived alone in Paradise, Nevada. She was a waitress at Joe's Diner.

She had survived the worst thing that could ever have happened to her.

She was okay.

Inhaling deeply, Maddy swallowed her feelings down deep. She was at work. She needed to do her job, and to do that, she couldn't stand there and ruminate on her past—she needed to move on, just as she had struggled to do for the last year.

She could almost—almost—convince herself that she had.

Eyes carefully trained on the plate and pot in her hands, she arrived at table twelve. It was a man; that much she could tell without a good look and with hair in her eyes.

"Here you go. Careful—the plate is hot." Maddy leaned over the table to place the plate in front of the customer. His potency hit her before she raised her eyes to that wicked face—expensive cologne, musky soap, and pure man.

She straightened back up and brushed her hair out of her eyes. Smoky blue eyes regarded her with amusement from a face that was too beautiful to be real. "Hello again, Miss Stone."

Maddy couldn't force any words out of her mouth, she was so stunned. What on earth was Alex Fraser, casino owner, doing in Paradise, Nevada, let alone in Joe's Diner?

"Mr. Fraser. I—uh—enjoy your breakfast." Like an idiot—a shell-shocked idiot—Maddy spun on her heel and all but ran back to the kitchen, where she could at least put a counter between Alex Fraser and herself.

Behind the counter, she leaned over the ice bin, trying to

cool her flushed cheeks. What was he *doing* there? Part of her screamed that he couldn't possibly have been there to see her, and the other part was equally as certain that it wasn't a coincidence that he was in her place of work, in her little city, which was close enough to Vegas but still a bit of a drive.

Why was he there, in her safe zone? Hell, she wasn't stupid—she knew why. She'd felt that connection between them, a palpable thing in the air, drawing them together.

Still . . . this was her bubble, the place where things were always the same. If she stepped out and forced herself to do something uncomfortable, well, that was her prerogative—but *she* chose the place; *she* chose the time.

This wasn't her choice, at all. And following on the heels of the news that she should be expecting a call from Nathan, she felt nauseous.

"Are you okay?" Joe was the owner of the diner. He was tall and lanky, with reddish gold hair that was scraggly and the barest hint of a matching beard. His eyes were startlingly green and full of concern as he spoke to her.

"I'm . . . I'm fine." Maddy struggled for the words, though she was unable to muster up an accompanying smile. How did Alex Fraser have such an effect on her? For the entire year that she'd lived in Paradise, she had been indifferent to the opposite sex. Changing that was something she might consider putting on her bucket list at some point . . . just not yet. She wasn't ready.

Could a woman ever really be ready for Alex Fraser?

"You don't look fine."

Maddy liked Joe. She really did. But right at that moment she wanted him to leave her the hell alone. Mustering the shreds of her composure—and again marveling at Alex Fraser's ability to turn her into a witless idiot—she straightened and smiled at Joe.

"I'm good, Joe. Just warm."

"Take care." Joe reached out for a strand of her hair before jerking his hand back. Maddy studied the hand hovering awkwardly in the air, puzzled.

"Right." With that, Joe retreated hastily into the kitchen, leaving her staring after him.

She couldn't even contemplate his gesture at that moment, not with Alex Fraser eating whole-wheat pancakes that weren't even on the menu across the room. Joe did the majority of the cooking at the diner, and he specialized in grease. It was no surprise that Susannah had likely fallen all over herself to assure Alex that his special order would be taken care of, but she must have had to bat her eyelashes extra hard to convince Joe to follow through.

She'd have to think about Joe's strange actions later, when her mind had space for it. Right now she had her hands full with worry and excitement over Alex, who took priority because Joe's near touch didn't bring butterflies and nerves and want and need all rolled into one tangled ball in her stomach the way Alex's did.

Maddy looked across the room to where he was sitting. He was watching her intently, his coffee cup hiding his lips, but she got the impression that he was amused.

Right. She wasn't the first woman to work herself into a state over him, of that she was quite certain.

Ducking back out of sight, Maddy considered her options. She could hide in the kitchen until he left, begging Susannah to take his table. Or she could be an adult and warm up his coffee, make small talk, and present him his bill.

In her heart she knew that the latter was the only option that she would really consider. No matter that she'd embarrassed herself in front of him with her awkwardness, as with the first time they'd met, she felt the strange connection between them pulling tight, drawing her to him like a moth to the light.

She wanted to be around him, wanted to spend time with him, whatever she had to do.

Mumbling as she grabbed the coffeepot, Maddy chanted to herself.

I will not do anything dumb.

I will not do anything dumb.

I will not do anything dumb.

Then he looked up and smiled at her, and she felt herself blush.

Alex sat back, watching intently as Maddy approached his table with a smile on her face. He suspected she was going for friendly, but the look she had achieved was closer to hysteria topped with a forced smile.

He didn't mind making her nervous—a little bit. It was a heady feeling for a Dominant, knowing that he had an effect on the woman in his sights. However, he'd also been told by a past lover—or several—that he was scarily intense at times.

He didn't want to scare the little doe, so he made a concerted effort to appear relaxed. Not an easy feat when every muscle in his body tensed up the moment she and her delectable little body got near him.

"Coffee, Mr. Fraser?" Alex nodded without speaking, trying to repress the images of her naked and bound under him. His cock swelled as he caught a whiff of that amazing floral scent that seemed stamped into her very skin.

Clearing his throat, he shifted his napkin on his lap, suddenly appreciating the stiffness of the cheap paper. In any other situation, he wouldn't have been the least bit shy about letting a woman know the effect she had on him.

This woman, though—if Maddy knew that he'd gotten hard just watching her denim-clad hips walking across the diner to him, he was pretty sure that she'd freak out and run.

It was that attitude exactly, combined with the faded blue jeans that molded to her thighs and ass, the simple white T-shirt through which he could see the barest hint of her lace bra, the skin he wanted to touch, open entirely to his stare on a face that was free of makeup . . .

Maddy Stone seemed to lack pretense, and Alex found it incredibly refreshing. Even though her insistence on playing a game of blackjack when it clearly terrified her was still a puzzle, he didn't think she was the game-playing type.

He thought of Lydia, of so many of the women who had come after, and shuddered inwardly. Never again.

"Ouch! Fu—mmm."

Alex looked up sharply as Maddy started to cuss, swallowing the expletive before she shouted it out in front of the entire diner. He had been vastly pleased to catch her sneaking a look at his face as she refilled his coffee, but the result was that she hadn't watched what she was doing, and now coffee had overflowed from his cup onto her hand. She hissed as it burned, scalding the skin, her free hand barely catching the pot before she upended the entire thing in his lap.

He was momentarily sidetracked when she sucked the burned fingers between her full, rosy lips, trying to soothe the skin. When he realized that she'd hurt herself, his expression darkened, and he had to hold himself back, wanting to pull her into his lap, to soothe the burn with his own tongue.

Since he was pretty sure it would scare the hell out of her, he refrained, though he couldn't vanquish his frown.

Nothing should mar that beautiful skin of hers. Nothing.

"I'm sorry." Maddy cringed, probably realizing that she'd shouted a profanity halfway across the diner.

Alex furrowed his brow at her. "You need to be more careful. You can look at me anytime, babe, so pay attention when you're doing something where you could hurt yourself."

Though irritation flashed over her features, Maddy opened her mouth, probably to reiterate her apologies, he thought. Unable to resist touching her any longer, he shook his head and held out his hand. "Let me see."

Warily, Maddy let him take her injured hand in his own. *Interesting.* Alex felt an electric jolt travel up his arm as his fingers closed over the soft, fragrant skin.

Alex owned a lot of things. One of them was a wine bar with a dark side—a BDSM club. Though he preferred private scenes to public, he'd go when the urge struck him and as such had had the opportunity to touch plenty of eager submissives.

Some, though attractive, had left him cold. Some had turned him on.

None had made him feel this kind of slow, wicked burn.

"It's a shame to injure skin like this." Slowly he lifted her fingers to his lips and brushed one soft, soft kiss over the top of them. He placed the hand that he'd touched back on the smooth surface of the table gently. "That cream does look beautiful with a touch of pink, though."

Her mouth fell open completely, her eyes wide as marbles to match. Alex felt a frisson of pleasure slip into his veins at his ability to affect her.

"Are . . . are you in town on business?" Ignoring the burn on her hand, though it had to be painful, Maddy pulled a bar cloth from her apron and mopped at the spill in front of Alex as if she needed something to do. As she lifted the coffeepot to refill his cup, she looked over her shoulder and winced.

Alex followed her glance and caught the eye of a man from behind the counter. The man was tall, on the rangy side, with messily spiked red hair and stubble.

He also seemed pissed off. Alex glared right back, none too impressed.

The guy had better not be pissed with Maddy about spilling the coffee, or anything else, for that matter. Sure, he didn't know the woman well, but the way she appealed to the Dominant inside of him . . . well, he knew that he'd go to great lengths to make sure she became his. When it came to Maddy, he was starting to feel just obsessed enough to pick a fight over another man looking at her the wrong way.

Maddy turned her attention back to Alex's cup, making sure that she stopped pouring well below its white porcelain rim. His attention pulled immediately back to her, Alex waited until she was done to answer her question.

When her eyes met his own, Alex could almost hear the air between them sizzle. He flexed his fingers, craving the touch of her skin, soft and warm.

"I'm thinking about buying A Casino in Paradise." He assumed she'd heard of it—Paradise was a small city. He took a sip of his coffee, smirking a bit when he caught her watching the bob of his Adam's apple as he swallowed.

She looked at him with confusion clear in her eyes. "Why would you want to buy a casino here? You already have one."

Alex snorted into his coffee, laughing. He couldn't help it.

The women who constantly surrounded him like piranhas knew, without him ever having told them, which businesses he owned, where his homes were scattered throughout the world— one had even known the amount in his checking account, with scary accuracy.

He swallowed his laughter when he saw that she was asking a serious question. He wanted to crush her lips beneath his own for her sweetness.

"I own a lot of things, Miss Stone." Alex studied her face, trying to discern whether he should go into more detail or not.

Considering how nervous she'd been when she'd found him sitting at one of her tables, he opted for not.

Her face studied him nervously, searching for a clue as to how she should act . . . wanting to please him.

She did please him, immensely, just as she was. He didn't want her nervous about it.

Well . . . not *too* nervous.

To lighten the mood, he winked at her. Her face registered surprise, a hint of pleasure, then, as if she'd just remembered something, irritation.

"Why did you let me win that game?"

Taken aback as he so very rarely was, Alex schooled his face into an expressionless mask. "Letting you win a game in a casino would be illegal, Miss Stone. Surely you know that." How had she known that, against his own sense of morals, he'd considered it, just for her?

He could see that she didn't believe him, that she was still angry. He wasn't used to explaining his actions, and it felt strange to try to convince a woman of something.

"I thought about it." Maddy eyed him narrowly, and Alex very nearly squirmed in his chair under the penetrating gaze. Clearly she wasn't the type of woman to hold with actions that registered in shades of gray. "But then I decided that I couldn't rob you of the victory of whatever it was you'd set out to prove that night. You won fair and square, babe, all on your own."

Maddy blinked, weighing his words. Her anger seemed to evaporate into thin wisps that floated away softly, replaced with pleasure and pride.

She was so damn cute. Just looking at her, he saw why he would have risked setting up the game for a woman who was a stranger.

Maddy opened her mouth, looking like she was about to say something—what, Alex would never know. She was interrupted.

"Here's your table's bill, Maddy." From over her shoulder came the vinyl folder with the slip of white paper sticking out. The person behind her was the pissed-off man from behind the counter.

He placed a protective hand on her shoulder—he was marking his territory. Irritation washed through Alex as Maddy shrugged uncomfortably, trying to dislodge the touch.

The other man's message was all too clear—run along now.

"Thanks, Joe." Maddy's voice was calm, but Alex picked up on the thread of irritation. "I've got it."

From behind her, the man named Joe huffed out a sigh, hesitated, then stomped away, muttering under his breath. Maddy exhaled slowly, then slid the vinyl folder over the table.

She didn't seem to want him to go any more than he wanted to. She also still wasn't ready for him to make a move. The woman was nervous, as if she might take flight at any moment.

Though he wasn't at all accustomed to delaying his gratification, Maddy appealed to him on so many levels that he swallowed his desire down and pushed back his chair.

Not bothering to look at the total, Alex meticulously placed a twenty-dollar bill with five hundred-dollar bills hidden beneath inside the vinyl folder. From the corner of his eye, he saw Maddy shake her head a bit, probably at his lack of concern with money.

Alex ignored it. He had more money than he could spend in his lifetime, and every day he made more. He found that he wanted to lavish it all on this woman, if only she'd let him.

"As I was saying." Alex handed Maddy the billfold. Though

he was tempted to brush his fingers over hers, he needed to cool down in order to leave, rather than heat up.

"Yes. You're looking at a casino in Paradise." Maddy tucked an errant lock of hair behind her ear, gaze flickering quickly away and then coming back to rest on his.

Alex stood, though the look in her eyes made him want to nibble on her lower lip. Deliberately, he kept his next words light, trying his best not to scare her off.

"I could use a local's opinion." He shrugged on his jacket, his favorite, made of well-worn chocolate-brown leather.

He saw Maddy eyeing it, and unbidden, an image of her wearing nothing but the jacket flashed through his mind.

He swallowed his groan.

"I don't know if I count as a local. I haven't been here for all that long." Though he could see on her face that she thought she'd stuck her foot in her mouth, Alex still felt a whisper of exasperation. It figured that the one female who intrigued the hell out of him was the one who would make him work for it.

From the pocket of his coat he withdrew a business card and a pen and proceeded to write his cell number, the pen digging deep into the pristine white paper.

When he handed it to her, Maddy's fingers brushed tentatively over his. He felt the light sensation like a full, heated kiss, making the air around them sizzle.

He looked into her eyes as he handed her the card, enjoying the flicker reflected in the blue depths.

"In case you change your mind." Alex cocked his head, studying her, then reached out and brushed his fingers through that loose lock of hair that kept escaping her ponytail.

"Damn." His voice was a whisper, and he felt perplexed.

He couldn't remember the last time he'd felt unsure around a woman. It was a strange sensation, and one that he wasn't entirely certain that he liked. His brow furrowing over the notion, he nodded, breaking the spell of the moment.

The dry air of the desert outside didn't help him clear his head.

He wanted Madeline Stone.

He would do whatever it took to have her.

CHAPTER THREE

Maddy wouldn't have told anyone about the five-hundred-and-ten-dollar tip that Alex had left her on a ten-dollar meal, would have just called him and tried to give it back, but Susannah had spied it peeking out of her apron pocket late in the afternoon and had pestered her until Maddy spilled the entire story. Her friend had urged, "He's interested. He's so interested. Call him."

The five hundred-dollar bills now sat in the middle of her coffee table, the visage of Benjamin Franklin staring sternly up at her.

Having never come across the situation before, Maddy had also contemplated telling Joe. But then she'd thought about the pissing contest the two men had gotten into in front of her, and she'd sealed her lips shut, though she felt incredibly strange about it.

Obviously five hundred dollars was less than pennies to Alex. But it didn't feel right to take it.

Something told her that Alex would be less than thrilled if she tried to give it back.

"Make a date and then go shop for something sexy with that money."

"Susannah." Maddy filled her name with as much exasperation as she could muster, which wasn't much, because she was still stunned.

He was interested. She had to agree.

But *why*?

She was a little apprehensive wondering what he was expecting with his big "tip."

"Do men like him even date?" Maddy couldn't picture Alex Fraser at the movies, eating soggy popcorn, his Italian leather shoes sticking to discarded bubble gum on the floor.

"What, you think the man's a monk?" Susannah snorted out a laugh, then continued to rummage through Maddy's closet. She had insisted on helping Maddy decide what to wear on the date that Maddy didn't even yet have.

From the size of the pile of "no" clothing in Maddy's lap, she was pretty sure that she'd be attending the so-called date naked.

An image of Alex Fraser naked, his muscled body offered up for her exploration, popped into her mind unbidden. Her mouth suddenly felt cottony, and she reached for the water that was set on her bedside table.

She thought that she might not mind a naked date if it meant that he was naked, too.

"Of course I don't think he's celibate." No, Maddy thought that he probably had a harem ... or a supermodel for a girl-friend, or maybe even a wife.

No, not a wife. Though she didn't really know the man at all, something about him—she couldn't quite put her finger on what—told her that there was no wife waiting at home.

Maybe it was the concern he'd displayed when she'd burned her hand. Maybe it was the way that he looked at her, as if she were the only woman on the face of the planet. Maybe it was the way he'd purchased a hideously expensive bottle of wine for a woman he didn't know, when plenty of other women in that same room wouldn't have even needed a bottle of beer before sucking his cock.

The image *that* brought to mind made her blush. She knew her red cheeks would give her away to Susannah, and she didn't think she could stand another inquisition. The only way to beat her friend at her game was to play along.

"Fine. I'll call him." Susannah squealed with delight and tossed the bright blue blouse she was holding to the floor. With record speed, she threw Maddy her cell phone—Maddy didn't have a landline—and flopped on the bed alongside her, preparing to lean in close enough to hear Alex's side of the conversation, Maddy was sure.

"Clean up that mess you made." Maddy pointed back to her closet. When Susannah pouted, Maddy froze for a second, wondering if she'd gone too far.

It had been a long time since she'd hung out with a girlfriend. She was out of practice. She and Susannah had always gotten along well enough, but they'd never spent any time together outside of work until that afternoon.

The pout turned to an exaggerated grimace, Susannah sticking her tongue out at Maddy in a way that made startled laughter bark from her throat. Seeming completely unoffended, Susannah shifted over maybe an inch on the bed and then started folding the things that she'd piled on Maddy's lap.

"I know your game. Over there." Maddy pointed again. Calling Alex Fraser was a big enough deal to make her heart race on its own. If Susannah were in her face, hanging on her every word, she would never even hit send.

Maddy went one step further and locked herself in the tiny bathroom down the hall. It was small, the only bathroom in the cramped apartment. Perching on the closed lid of the toilet, she bit her lip, then speedily dialed the number that she now had memorized and hit send.

One ring. Two.

"Fraser."

Holy shit. He answered. The sexy billionaire answers his own phone. Somehow Maddy hadn't counted on him actually answering—she'd thought she would get an answering machine or an underling, or something.

"Hello?" His voice was a bark, and the nerves in her stomach intensified.

"Um, yes. Mr. Fraser? This is Maddy—er, Madeline Stone. The . . . uh . . . the waitress? From the diner?" Suddenly she was certain that he would have no idea who she was.

"Miss Stone." His voice softened and warmed, sliding over the syllables of her name, making them sound as tasty as melted chocolate.

There was a pause, one that she knew he and his charm and people skills could have filled effortlessly. Instead he waited, pressing her to say something else.

"You . . . you mentioned you could use some company? To look at a casino?" Maddy grimaced as she spoke, feeling as though she'd been transported back to junior high school.

"What are you asking, Miss Stone?" He knew exactly what she was asking—she was sure of it—but for some reason he wanted her to say it.

Maddy squirmed.

"Would you still like company while you look at a new casino?" She felt a bit like she was asking for permission.

"If that is what you want." His voice was still warm, practically oozing sexiness, but his words confused her.

If it's what she wanted? So . . . what did he want?

"Um . . . yes. I'd like to see you." She didn't know what else to say, or even what she was answering, exactly. There was a minute's pause, and she heard him murmuring in lilting tones to someone at the other end, and she wondered whom he was with.

"Tomorrow afternoon. Four p.m. I will send my driver for you. Wear jeans." It sounded like he was taking the phone away from his ear, and she was left reeling again.

It all sounded fine, except for one thing.

"Wait!" There, he was back. She could hear his breath.

"Yes, Miss Stone?"

Maddy couldn't tell if he was exasperated or amused. "I'll meet you there." The number one thing that her older sister had always taught her about dating was to take her own transportation. She knew better than to find herself alone in the car with a boy—a man—if she didn't know without a doubt that she could trust him.

Well, Alex Fraser was no boy—he was most definitely all man. But though her gut told her she could trust him, really, she didn't know anything about him.

Driving her own car was a smart decision.

On the other end of the line, she could hear Alex sigh. This time she was fully aware that it was a noise of irritation.

"I would like to extend to you the courtesy of my driver and car." Although his voice was deep and sexy, in this stilted conversation he sounded like someone straight out of the pages of *Pride and Prejudice*, and Maddy briefly pictured him in tight pants like those worn by Colin Firth.

Bad Maddy. Bad. Pay attention. You're not going anywhere if he insists on his car. It was enough that she was agreeing to go see him, something that had the potential to throw her into a tizzy if she obsessed about it too much.

"Thank you, but it's not necessary. I'll drive myself there."

There was another pause, and when he replied, his voice was clipped. Was he angry? Surely she hadn't done anything to make him angry. She'd thought maybe he would be attracted to her more confident self, rather than the awkward version he'd met at the diner. "Very well, Miss Stone." He *did* sound angry. Maybe he thought she'd been rude, refusing his generous offer.

His demeanor was disconcerting. Did she even want to

spend time with someone who would get upset over something so small?

"You owe me one, Maddy." His voice had softened as well, and it was low and full of promise.

She shivered, in a very good way.

"The rest, however, is nonnegotiable. Four o'clock. A Casino in Paradise. Wear jeans." And then he was gone, having reverted back to his formidable self with his parting words.

Maddy hugged herself with glee, though she didn't quite understand why. Oh, that was a lie; she did know. Something about Alex inexplicably drew her to him, magnet to metal. What she didn't understand was why, after she had become so comfortable in her own little cocoon. He'd stirred a part of her that she almost didn't recognize after so long.

Well, she would take the happy feelings where they came. Heaven knew they'd been in short supply over the last year. Maddy did a little booty shake in the privacy of her bathroom, enjoying the moment, as she put the phone down on the counter and rose from her seat on the lid of the toilet.

Then she realized something.

Shit.

Four o'clock at a casino in Paradise? He didn't say which one.

Shit.

"A Casino in Paradise. Very funny." Maddy was a little irritated when she marched up to Alex in the lobby of the casino. Her spirits had hit rock bottom when she'd thought that he had perhaps not wanted her to tag along with him after all and had deliberately not given her the name. Before calling him like a lovesick schoolgirl, though, she at least had the presence of mind to hit the Internet connection on her phone.

She'd searched on the Internet for "casinos in Paradise, Nevada." The only hit was for the tacky joint in which she now stood.

Alex appeared to be entertained. He was wearing the kind of blue jeans that she just knew were from some high-end department store, a white T-shirt, and that battered leather jacket. His eyes were hidden by dark aviator sunglasses, the name of some French brand that she'd never heard of emblazoned on the temple.

She imagined that this was his idea of blending in. If only he understood that with his fallen-angel face, his ridiculously toned body, his sexy-as-hell smirk, he would *never* look like he belonged with the tourists, the showgirls, the sweaty businessmen who frequented this kind of place.

Maddy pulled her stare forcibly away from his face. She couldn't see his eyes behind the dark glasses, but she was sure he was looking straight at her.

It was unnerving not having even a clue to what he was thinking, and she was unnerved enough just being there. She'd gotten lost on her way there, and though it turned out she was only a block away, it had been enough to send panic coursing through her veins.

She told him about none of that, though. She wanted to show her best self to him.

"Hello, Miss Stone." His voice was low and husky. "You look sexy in heels."

What?

"I'm wearing jeans, as you requested," Maddy remarked as she stared at her feet. She'd painted her toenails so that they would look nice in her sandals, but the glossy red now seemed ridiculous, like she was trying too hard. She should have stuck with her usual pale pink.

Alex followed her stare down. She squirmed under what

she assumed was scrutiny—she still couldn't tell, because he had those damn sunglasses on.

He looked back up to her face, and suddenly she felt hot, though she couldn't see his eyes.

"What?" Maddy stuffed her fingers into her pockets, then took them out again.

Before she could form a reply, he was moving, finally removing those sunglasses, but now his face was carefully blank.

"Let's go." He replaced the shades with spectacles and started to walk toward the entrance to the gaming floor.

Maddy felt her insides melt. She had *such* a thing for a good-looking man in glasses.

Trying not to drool, she glanced at him from the corner of her eye. It had been two years since she'd worked as an optician, but she was pretty sure that his glasses weren't real. There was a glare from the lights shining off of the clear plastic, which most prescription lenses—especially lenses belonging to someone who could afford all the bells and whistles—no longer had.

"Are you nearsighted?" Startled, Alex stopped in his tracks next to her, his sexy mouth frowning. Maddy couldn't help the small wash of satisfaction, that she'd managed to catch him off guard, something she didn't think many people managed to do.

"As a matter of fact." He studied her intently.

"But those aren't real." Maddy was confident she was right.

"They don't look good?" And there it was, a first thread of vulnerability that made him seem like a real human instead of a god.

Maddy was quiet for a moment before telling him the truth. "They look great." Well, it wasn't actually the entire truth. If she told him *that*, then she would have to let it slip that those little wire-rimmed frames perched on his nose made her hot in a way that she'd never been before.

She still didn't understand it. All she knew was that she wanted him and that the wanting couldn't be good for her.

Maddy caught him studying her face for a long moment, as if to ascertain some truth there, one that she wasn't sure she knew herself. Eventually, he took her hand and led her across the lobby. His palm was warm and dry against her own clammy one, and he rubbed the base of her thumb absently with his own as they walked.

A rush of nerves and excitement nearly knocked her to her knees. She hadn't been touched with such simple pleasure in . . . oh, it had been so long. And there was something between them that was getting harder and harder to ignore, something intense, something intoxicating.

Maddy snuck a sidelong glance at Alex. He was looking at her straight on—no sneaky glances for him. His lips were frowning, just a slight bit, but his eyes told her that his mind was just as far into the gutter as her own.

A squeak escaped her lips. Her words got stuck in her throat at the intensity of that gaze. Mortified, she felt herself turning red and stared at the ground as they walked.

He tugged at her arm just before they entered the casino floor. She hadn't realized that she'd pulled away slightly, resisting entering the area—she'd grown somewhat comfortable where she was already, next to Alex in the lobby. She wasn't eager to change. But he insisted, pulling her along gently. When she got the nerve to again meet his eyes, she thought, for a moment, that he was going to kiss her.

He reached out, ran a finger over her heated cheek, then looked puzzled, as if he didn't know why he'd done that.

"That blush." He raised an eyebrow, then said no more about it. Instead he transformed in front of her eyes, moving from the more approachable man who let a small vulnerability show to Alex Fraser, the smooth, suave businessman she'd met the other night. Even in blue jeans, he exuded confidence—the young billionaire with the world at his feet.

Maybe that was why Maddy was so drawn to him. He had enough confidence for the both of them.

"We are a young couple here on our honeymoon. Just tourists looking for a fun afternoon gambling at a casino. Okay?" Ah. So that explained the denim and glasses. Maddy didn't want to be the one to tell him that even dressed down, he didn't fit in. He was too handsome, too self-assured.

Too damn sexy.

"All right." What else was she going to say? She certainly couldn't tell him that his words had sent her mood crashing, or that the entire experience had her on pins and needles.

That was why she was here, then. That's why he'd asked her here—to help him make a business decision. She shouldn't have cared, but she did.

"I want to see what the casino is really like, from a consumer's point of view. What I get shown is often what the current owners want me to see." His thumb moved absently over the mound of Maddy's palm. It was not an erogenous zone, but still she felt a thrill throughout her entire body, one that she fought.

This would never lead anywhere. Even if he weren't a gorgeous gazillionaire, she was a waitress with more baggage than he could ever possibly imagine.

"Do you do that for every place that you buy?" Maddy was pretty sure that Alex owned more businesses, more buildings, more *things* than her mind could fathom.

"Yes." His voice was curt. "I didn't become wealthy by being careless. Though this deal . . ." His voice trailed off as he studied the casino around him, his eyes finally coming to rest on Maddy.

"I'd like to have your impression of the man who wants to sell this to me."

Maddy nodded. She would have agreed to just about anything, just to keep enjoying the feel of his hand in hers.

They walked around the casino slowly, looking carefully at
the slot machines, the blackjack tables, the poker games. At least,
Alex looked carefully—Maddy was consumed with awareness of
his presence. It was a weird sensation for her, one that took the
place of the ever-running stream of consciousness that usually
clouded her mind.

She liked it. She really, really liked it.

"Would you care for a drink?" Maddy was looking a little overwhelmed by either the casino, Alex's hand holding hers, or
maybe a little bit of both. He steered her to the bar in the center
of the room.

A drink would do her good. He would have been lying if
he'd said that he didn't hope it might also bring that color back
into her skin.

He led her to a small, round table by the bar. The waitress
asked for his drink order first, and Alex interrupted her, not
impressed.

"The lady will have a gin and tonic, with a lime wedge. I will
have a golden tequila . . . in a highball glass, with a lemon
wedge."

Maddy blinked, probably wondering how he knew what
kind of alcohol she liked to drink, since she hadn't been drinking it the other night. He wasn't about to tell her that he em-
ployed people who could find out all kinds of things about
anyone . . . or that he'd wanted to find out just such things about
her.

He was pretty sure that she wouldn't appreciate it. Still,
he'd felt like he had to know—he'd wanted to know everything
about her.

No, he would just keep that little detail to himself.

The waitress flushed, nodded, babbled a little, and retreated. Maddy cast a sympathetic smile after her, and Alex frowned.

He was used to the effect he had on women, though he never really thought about it. It was his looks, which he'd had no part in, and his money, which he couldn't blame them for being attracted to. It was just how it was.

Still, he'd rather elicit the kind of reaction in Maddy that had her snarling at any woman who came near her man.

Not that he was her man, but he had hope.

"What if I don't like gin?" Maddy seemed to be a little more relaxed around him today—relaxed enough to question him a bit.

He liked that she didn't just smile and nod along with whatever he said. Though once inside his club, the term for her behavior would be "brat," outside of sex, he found that he was enjoying the hints of spunk that blazed out of her sweet personality from time to time.

Alex didn't crack, merely arched an eyebrow in her direction. She did it right back, and he found the small movement to be sexy as hell.

"Do you?" He sounded sure of himself, which was the entire reason that he liked having information on people.

He liked knowing what he was dealing with. He liked being in control.

Maddy muttered a reply that he couldn't quite make out and sipped at the drink that the waitress had just placed in front of her. The gin must have been strong, since she made a face as she swallowed, but then again, if he'd guessed correctly, she wasn't much of a drinker.

He watched as she licked her lips, which started a slow burn in his gut.

"Do you see the man to your left?" Indicating with his head,

Alex didn't shoot the tequila that he'd ordered, instead squeezing the lemon over the glass, then sipping, running his tongue over his lips to savor the liquor.

From the corner of his eye, he caught Maddy watching him, her stare fixed on his mouth. Gratified to find that she was feeling the heat as much as he was, he smirked, enjoying the way her skin flushed when she realized that she'd been caught.

"The man in the blue suit, with the three big men. The ones standing behind me." Alex had zeroed in on the man he'd seen only in pictures as he'd guided Maddy to the bar. The man stood out like a sore thumb among the brightly adorned tourists, both because of the lack of color in his attire and also because of the desperation that Alex could feel radiating from him, even from across the room. "That is Massimo Santorini. He purchased this casino ten years ago and is looking to sell quickly. He is offering a good price, because he needs the cash fast to pay off a gambling debt. What I don't understand is why he would target me, a complete stranger, for a cash deal." It wasn't unheard of, but Alex would have thought that the people he owed the money to might have been interested in taking the casino over as payment, or in purchasing it themselves against the debt. It was what he would have done.

That said, he was still the head of a successful empire, and Massimo was liquidating to get out of trouble. Perhaps they just had entirely different points of view.

Still, something didn't sit right. He just couldn't put his finger on what.

"What do you think of this place?" Alex hadn't lied—he was interested in Maddy's point of view, as someone who hadn't actually spent much time in casinos and therefore had no expectations. She looked a bit unnerved by the question, and Alex sat back in his chair, giving her a moment, still aware of Santorini and his goons behind him.

"Well, I ... I don't really have anything to compare it to, but ... it's kind of garish, isn't it?" Her cheeks heated as she spoke, and Alex couldn't smother his grin of enjoyment.

"Casinos tend to be, babe. That's what Vegas is all about." He grinned as he thought back to his first sight of the city, way back when he was a kid, on vacation with his family. They'd done a long road trip, down from their home in Washington, along the California coast, into Nevada, Arizona, Mexico.

His world had opened up on that trip, but the thing that had fascinated him the most had been Las Vegas. He'd been overwhelmed by the lights, the opulence, the excess. He'd never forgotten, and that was where he'd headed, right after his business degree was hot in his hand.

The never-ending crowds made him feel a little bit less alone, too, since that once carefree family had disowned him for his "immoral" lifestyle. It still hurt, but he had to give them credit for sticking to their guns—and their beliefs. They'd never once tried to make nice, begging for a handout.

He hadn't talked to them in years, and so apart from a few staff members, like Declan and Kylie, and of course, Rae, he had very few people who could comfort him when he needed it.

The lights of the city that never slept, though, kept him from feeling quite so alone.

Shaking away the heavy thoughts, Alex looked down at Maddy. She had been watching him think—watching the emotions play out over his face—and she looked thoughtful.

To please himself as well as to distract her, he took her hand in his and lifted it to his lips for a kiss.

She gasped, then froze, her eyes fixed over his shoulder.

"What is it?" Alex shifted abruptly, leaning on the table with his arm, partially blocking his face. "Did he see us?"

Maddy nodded, and Alex cursed. Reaching around her, he splayed his hand flat on her back and drew her in. The skin beneath his hand heated, and he eyed the long, graceful curve of her neck, wanting to plant his lips there.

He wanted to kiss her everywhere.

"Is he coming over here?" When Maddy nodded, Alex felt disgust wash over him, though he followed it with a reassuring smile for Maddy. There was no way that he could have missed her breathy little sigh of pleasure, since they were now practically nose to nose. He could feel her exhalation, warm on his cheeks. "Prepare yourself for his version of the VIP treatment." From what he'd dug up, Alex knew it was nothing he wanted.

He also knew that there was no way that the man would not come over to introduce himself in person, now that he'd seen him.

"What is his version of the VIP treatment?" Maddy whispered, though Santorini could not have heard her from across the crowded casino.

"Expensive liquor and even more expensive whores." Alex eyed Maddy speculatively, curious to see if she thought that was what he was used to anyway.

He smiled slowly, possessively when her cute little lips pursed with displeasure. Unless he was very much mistaken, she was getting to the point where she wasn't thrilled at the idea of another woman's hands on him.

That was good, because the only woman whose hands he wanted on him was the one sitting so close that her freesia scent clouded his brain.

Alex got one hell of a surprise when, after inhaling deeply, Maddy placed her hand on his thigh and leaned in closer, until her hair brushed over his shoulder. If Massimo hadn't been heading toward them, he might have taken that moment to thread his fingers through her hair, to finally possess her mouth with his own. Still, with the muscles of his leg hard beneath the flat of her palm, he found himself loath to move. He wanted to nip at her neck, to inhale her scent.

Swallowing thickly, he tried to shake off the lust that was riding him. He needed a clear head to gauge Santorini.

"What are you doing?" Alex's words were a warning, but he wasn't sure if the warning was for Maddy or for himself.

"You don't want to be noticed. Maybe he didn't actually see you. Now you're hidden. We look like a couple stopping for a drink during their day of gambling." Alex turned his head to find her lips close, so close.

Unable to resist, though it went against every bit of business sense that he had, Alex leaned in and brushed his lips over Maddy's in the briefest but sexiest kiss he'd ever had in his life. Her mouth was hot, wet, and tasted ever so faintly of strawberries.

He wanted to drag her upstairs, to fist his hands in that wealth of golden brown hair, and to slide inside of her waiting heat until he forgot his own name.

Unfortunately, right at the moment, it wasn't an option.

Pulling back a fraction, Alex saw the rejection run over Maddy's face. He shook his head, needing to explain that he wasn't pulling away because he wanted to.

The women he knew wouldn't have felt rejected—they would have slid onto his lap, grasped his cock in long, greedy fingers, and continued right on with what they were doing.

Maddy wasn't like those women. He had to remember that.

Desperate for one more taste, he nipped at her ear before whispering into it, "You're playing a dangerous game, Miss Stone. If you knew what I truly wanted to do to you, you would run screaming into the night."

She inhaled slowly, as if trying to offset the rise in temperature that surrounded them.

"Don't look at me like that." Again, he didn't hold back that warning tone.

"I don't know what I'm doing," she protested, and he withdrew fully. He was a whisper away from clearing the table where they sat with one arm and sliding his fingers into her liquid heat after laying her on it.

He could breathe a bit more easily when her sweet floral scent wasn't invading his every sense.

"Mr. Fraser!" The name was shouted from halfway across the room, yet was still discernible over the noise. The man speaking was loud and had a heavy accent. Wincing—he had indeed been made—Alex and Maddy turned as one to find the man Alex recognized from his research as Massimo Santorini bearing down on them, his beefy black-clad bodyguards following closely in his wake.

"Shit." Alex felt his muscles stiffen underneath Maddy's fingers. Though he wanted to wrap her away where she couldn't be touched by this man—what the hell had he been thinking, bringing her here?—he did the next best thing he could think of, stepping into his ruthless tycoon suit so fully that when Santorini reached their table, it was the eyes and smile of a shark that waited for him.

"Mr. Fraser, why didn't you tell me you would be here?" Massimo took Alex's hand before it was offered and shook it vigorously. Alex didn't stand, but stayed seated.

It was deliberate, a tactic Alex often used to tip dealings in his favor. Make yourself seem larger, more important than your opponent. It makes them want to please you.

"Massimo." Alex used the other man's first name, which was again deliberate. He watched Santorini's lips pinch together briefly at the perceived slight.

For all of Santorini's exuberance, Alex's instincts, which were finely honed after so many years, told him that the man was a wolf in sheep's clothing.

The wolf had to be smart to get as far as he had . . . so why was he turning to a stranger to bail him out of trouble with a cash deal?

Maybe Alex had simply been too suspicious for far too long. After all, it was only his gut telling him that something was off. Everything else about the deal checked out.

"Why didn't you tell us you were coming, Mr. Fraser?" Santorini emphasized the *mister*.

"I wasn't aware that I needed to inform you that I would be on the premises." Alex's voice was low, layered with steel. He couldn't quite understand his own hostility, only that he was responding to something that the other man was giving off.

"Of course. Of course." Again, the wolf gave every impression of being genial, but the tension radiating from him was palpable. "But if I had known, I would have arranged for you to be treated like a king. In fact, can I get you anything now? Something to drink that's better than this swill? Some . . . entertainment?"

In his peripheral vision, Alex saw Maddy's glare. She swallowed it down, probably not wanting to interfere in his business, but rage washed over Alex that she felt put down at all.

He stood abruptly, and deliberately taking Maddy's hand, pulled her with him. His arm wrapped around her shoulders, his arm sliding down, down, until his hand came to rest on her waist. It was an intimate touch, a possessive one.

"It is in incredibly bad taste to offer me a whore in front of Miss Stone." Alex barely suppressed the anger in his voice, and Santorini blinked at its intensity.

Alex had half a mind to walk out of there with Maddy right then, deal be damned. The only thing stopping him was the idea that had taken root when he'd analyzed the profit of turning around Massimo's casino.

He'd been wanting to start up a charitable foundation for years, a philanthropic side to his empire. The clear profit he'd projected he would make could fund whatever it was he wanted to do on that end.

Plus, he thought as he looked into the other man's eyes, given the strange undercurrents of hostility from Santorini that he didn't appreciate, given that he was here to bail the man out, it might prove somewhat satisfying to play the bigger man.

"I do apologize, Mr. Fraser. I didn't realize that this young lady was . . . with you." Those cold black eyes finally looked at Maddy, though they had pointedly ignored her before. Santorini looked her up and then down, slowly, and Alex clung to the last shred of his civility.

He didn't like the way Santorini looked at her. She was *his*, damn it.

"Watch yourself." Alex waited, satisfied, as Santorini took a physical step back, though he didn't look happy to do so.

As if he'd only just realized that he'd overstepped, Santorini assumed the demeanor of contrition, and he was good enough that Alex would have believed him, if it weren't for that gut feeling.

That instinctive feeling that kept getting canceled out by his desire to build a foundation for teens and young adults who needed support when their families rejected them for their lifestyles.

"I assure you, Mr. Fraser, I meant no ill will." Santorini held up his hands in a pleading gesture, though there was still a malicious spark in his eye. "I will treat your . . . companion . . . as if she were as precious as a child."

For a moment Alex was taken aback, something that didn't happen often. Why had Santorini chosen those precise words?

He decided that he didn't care as his puzzlement was replaced with the red flare of horrible, hideous rage. Though he rarely lost his temper, preferring to channel it into the discipline of tae kwon do, he wasn't entirely certain that he wasn't about to strike the other man.

When he felt the soft fingers of the woman beside him curl into his arm, he knew why. It was Maddy. He wanted her so badly that his reactions were on the far side of extreme.

Knowing it didn't help to ease the reaction. Alex tightened his grip on Maddy's hips, his fingers kneading her flesh. "We are leaving."

She reached hastily for her purse before he all but carried her out the door. "Thank you for sticking up for me . . ." Maddy's voice was tentative as they stepped out the front doors, into the late-afternoon sunlight, and walked the short distance to the dilapidated hunk of junk that was her car. Alex shook his head at it.

Surely that thing wasn't safe. That was something that needed to be taken care of right away.

There it was again, that need to protect this woman. It went far beyond what he normally felt for a submissive.

He had no idea what he was doing. He didn't date—he couldn't date. Lydia had made damn sure of that.

Maddy looked up at him questioningly as he exhaled with frustration. The way that she worked her lower lip between her teeth when she was uncertain drove him crazy.

He couldn't resist anymore.

Yet he had to. His life couldn't offer her any more than a place as a lover, and this kind of woman wasn't cut out for that.

With one hand still on her hip, he nudged her backward until she was pressed against the driver's door of her car. The searing heat of the metal pressed into Alex's palms, and he worked his hands between her body and the car so that she didn't get burned.

He fit his body against her front, delighting in her curves, the feel of his hard angles against her softer flesh, another layer of heat.

I have to have her. He'd never wanted a woman so much, and he wasn't in the habit of denying himself. He was going to kiss her again, was finally going to let himself sample those lips that had haunted his dreams. Beneath him, her lips parted in anticipation. Alex pressed the hard ridge of his erection into the curve of her belly, and he moaned with something near pain as she arched against him.

"You should run, Madeline." He wasn't an altruistic kind of man, but somehow he found that he didn't want to hurt this perfect creature. And he would—he wouldn't be able to help it. His lifestyle, which was a need ingrained deep within him, wouldn't hold any appeal to an innocent like Madeline Stone.

One hand still cupping her hip possessively, Alex used the index finger of his other hand to trace Maddy's lips slowly, first the upper and then the lower. He felt her knees quiver. He was so close that he could have kissed her without moving at all. His body was pressed in to hers, and the heat surrounding them burned away thoughts of anything beyond her. "Or maybe I am the one who should run. A woman who can make me drive this far to see her must be a witch, casting a spell over me."

With supreme effort, Alex took his hands from her body, stepped back away from her.

Maddy was too much of an innocent to do the things he wanted to do with her, no matter how much he craved her. And his life was too much of a shit show for a woman clearly dealing with her own issues.

He hadn't spoken to his family in years. He worked all the time, except for when Rae was with him, and she wasn't someone he was willing to share.

No, he could see no part for Maddy Stone in all of that. It was nearly painful for him to take yet another step back, unable to take his eyes off of her as she stood openmouthed at his words.

"You drove out here to see me? But ... the casino ..." Maddy's words trailed off, and Alex shook his head with wry amusement.

That she truly had no idea of her appeal was an absolute mystery to him.

"Did you really think it was a coincidence that I showed up at your diner?" Reaching out, unable to resist, he rubbed a thumb over her cheekbone, his expression fading from amusement to something darker. Then he stepped back yet again, putting space between them.

To his surprise, sweet Maddy growled, showing her anger. She narrowed her eyes and stepped toward him, her hands fisted at her sides. Though he found her spunky attitude sexy as hell, he realized with a sinking heart that, if he were a halfway decent guy, he wouldn't have come out to Paradise in the first place.

So as she stepped away from the car, he opened the driver's side door for her, smooth as can be, and coaxed her in with a nudge of his hand on her hip again. Leaning in, he buckled her into her seat as if she were a child, then tucked a loose strand of hair behind her ear.

He had to end it, despite the palpable heat between them. It was what a decent man would do.

"Why?" Maddy was quick to speak, and her narrowed glance at him told him that she knew exactly what he was doing. He didn't bother to feign ignorance.

"There are secrets in my life that would scare you, and there are other secrets that I won't share. These secrets mean that this isn't going to work." Maddy's eyes widened as he spoke, and he forced himself to look away from the innocent stare.

"I don't date, Madeline." Alex made sure that his voice was firm as he summed it up. Even if she asked for an explanation, he wasn't going to give it.

Telling himself that he'd get over it in no time—he barely knew the woman, after all—Alex found that he was still bitterly disappointed.

"Goodbye, Miss Stone." When she bit her lip, hard, before he walked away, he very nearly changed his mind.

He couldn't. No matter that during the entire time he'd been with Maddy that day, he hadn't felt the least bit alone.

CHAPTER FOUR

The next day, when Maddy arrived home from work, there was a courier box on the ground in front of her door. Her mind immediately went to Alex . . . Well, actually, her mind had been on the man all day.

Though there was no return address, she knew, just knew that it was from him. Perversely, she set the thing on her tiny kitchen table and glared at it periodically as she made a grilled cheese sandwich and ate it standing at the counter, a folded paper towel as her plate. Though she told herself that she would just feel worse if she opened it, she finally couldn't take it any longer and attacked it with a kitchen knife, sawing through cardboard and packing tape.

Some men sent flowers when they'd been an ass. Some sent chocolates. Alex Fraser sent a bottle of Mouton Rothschild, the 1943 vintage—the same ridiculously expensive wine that he'd bought Maddy the evening they met. Attached to the neck of the bottle was an envelope, cut from thick, cream-colored paper.

The note inside said simply, "It is better this way." It was written by hand, on stationery monogrammed with his initials.

Of course he had monogrammed stationery. What other kind of man would send a bottle of wine like that, one that had meaning attached, no less, and a note like that to a woman he barely knew?

More money than sense. Maddy had heard the saying once,

and she was pretty sure that it had been coined with Alex Fraser in mind.

"Fuck you, Alex Fraser." Of course, the bottle of wine didn't respond, instead sitting where it was, mocking her with its intrusion into her life.

She was tempted to pack the thing back up, drive to Alex's casino in Vegas, and dump the box in the middle of one of his blackjack tables. He'd made her feel things that she hadn't even known she was capable of and then cut her off at the knees, insisting it was for her own good.

If she wanted to do something stupid, well, that was her decision, damn it.

So instead of returning the wine, she uncorked the bottle, grabbed a juice tumbler and her iPod, and headed for the bathroom.

As hot water poured into her worn porcelain bathtub, she poured her first glass of the delectable wine. It tasted just as good out of a cheap tumbler as it had out of a fancy wineglass. The first few slugs fortified her, and she wrapped herself in her bravado as she topped off her glass, added perfumed oil to her bath, and set her iPod to Adele. The singer lectured men about rumors as Maddy cranked the volume as loud as it could go and slid into the water and steam, careful to keep the device outside the water. The heat wrapped around her like a hug, and she snuggled into its embrace.

Half an hour later, she was warm, relaxed, and more than a little drunk. She also had to pee. As Maddy clambered out of the tub, she drained half the water, then topped it up again with more hot and more scented oil. She felt decadent—though it might have been the wine talking—and decided that she deserved another glass of wine.

As she stood dripping on the tile, Maddy noticed her phone sitting on the counter. She knew that she was drunk;

she knew that she shouldn't even pick up the thing, but she did anyway.

She wasn't quite brave enough to call him, but her fingers, fueled by wine, flew nimbly enough over the keys, as she quickly wrote out a text to Alex.

U R AN ASS.

The phone rang no more than a minute later. Surprise, surprise, it was Mr. Fraser. Though her brain had been drenched with wine, she was still coherent enough to wonder why he would bother replying to her drunken, texted insult, since he'd made it so clear that there couldn't be anything between them.

Maddy ignored the ringing and clambered back into the bath. She couldn't achieve the same manner of peace, though, and decided that it was Alex's fault.

Her phone rang again and then once more. Then all was silent, her iPod forgotten on the floor, nothing but the *drip, drip, drip* of water into the tub to distract her from her thoughts.

Maddy shifted uncomfortably in the bath. Alcohol removed the ability to keep her grief at bay, and she felt the sadness and pain creeping back in. *This* was why she didn't drink often. She felt panic choking her as she remembered what she'd lost, and layered on top of that were thoughts of Alex Fraser, the man who could have made her forget but wouldn't.

For once Maddy didn't cry. She just sat in the tub, exhausted and fighting back emotions that she didn't want to feel. It felt as if she sat there forever, but in reality it was probably no more than twenty minutes. The water started to cool, and Maddy began to shiver but was loath to move.

From down the hall, she heard the doorbell chime. Narrowing her eyes, she ignored it. She didn't know who it was, and she didn't much care. She didn't want to see anyone.

Seconds passed. Then there was a knock, a fist rapping repeatedly against the wood. The knocking continued as, finally curious, Maddy scrambled from the tub.

"Madeline! Open the door."

Holy shit. Alex. Hastily, Maddy wrapped her worn cotton robe around her dripping body, not bothering to dry herself off, and hustled down the hall. The looseness of her muscles from wine and the heat of the bath made walking harder than it normally was, her legs having turned to jelly.

She wrenched the door open, half in shock, and there stood Alex Fraser, ripped jeans hanging low on his hips, a black T-shirt hugging his muscles. The short sleeves revealed a tattoo that she hadn't seen before, a ring of something black and tribal around his right biceps.

She wanted to lick it.

She wanted to lick *him*.

"What do you want?" Maddy was too drunk to manage much more than the question and a frown in his direction. His eyes swept her over from head to toe and widened. The heated look came back into them, and he clenched his hands tightly at his sides.

"Why are you opening the door for a stranger at night? Don't you know better?" He looked angry and frustrated. Well, Maddy felt the same way and didn't appreciate the lecture.

"You're not a stranger." She eyed him as well, and though he looked taken aback, she rather thought that he liked it. "You don't send strangers seventy-year-old bottles of wine."

He raised an eyebrow at her, but didn't reply. Feeling like she'd won a minor battle, Maddy stepped back, giving him room to enter.

He stayed in the doorway, his fists still clenched tightly.

"Are you coming in?" At this point she no longer cared if he did or didn't.

A strangled noise issued from his throat.

"What's your problem?" Maddy would never have spoken to him like that if she were sober. She wasn't.

"It's better if I don't." His eyes raked her over from top to bottom, and she realized that she was all but naked, clad only in her short robe, the cotton of which had become nearly transparent from years of wear. She was still damp in places from her bath, and the thin material clung to her skin.

This was interesting. Despite the fact that he kept trying to push her away, it seemed that he still wanted her. How else could she explain him showing up at her door at night? If she'd been sober, she would never have believed it. In her inebriated state, though, she not only believed it, but wanted to do something about it.

"Suit yourself." Maddy shrugged nonchalantly, then let her fingers stray to the ties of her robe.

"Maddy. Don't." His voice was tight, tense.

Her fingers froze on the ties of her robe. "Why?" If she was going to put herself out there, then he had damn well better have the decency to respond the way that she wanted him to. "I want you; you want me. Why is this wrong?"

His eyes bored into hers, and she thought that she'd never seen such a bright blue. "You've been drinking. And if you knew what I wanted from you, you'd never want to see me again."

"Try me."

Heat washed over Alex's entire body. He wasn't entirely sure why he'd come to her apartment, other than the fact that she'd provoked him with her text message. It had warned him that she was irritated, but he'd never in a million years have anticipated that she'd channel her anger into desire.

Holding himself rigid, he stepped into the foyer as Maddy

sauntered toward him and closed the door. It brought her nearly flush with his body, a scant whisper of space between them.

"Madeline." His voice came out harsh, a last-ditch attempt to scare her away. If it had been any other woman, he was sure he would've had the strength to push her away for the good of both of them.

But it wasn't another woman; it was Maddy. Inexplicably, each time he saw her, she chipped away at his resistance a little more. And now a tipsy, scantily clad Maddy was pressing herself against him, arching up to stand on her toes. Alex steeled himself to resist her clumsy seduction attempts.

But the truth was, he wanted her. More than he'd ever desired any woman. This woman touched something deep inside him. He craved her submission.

She wasn't helping him save her.

"Alex, I want you." She repeated the words and brushed her lips over his chin. If he dipped his head just a bit, he could taste her lips, devour them the way he had outside the casino.

He found that he wanted her kiss more than he'd ever wanted anything in his life. There wasn't much that concerned Alex, but the depth of his desire for this woman counted.

Instead of succumbing to the kiss that she was begging for with her wide blue eyes, Alex drew on the last reserves of his inner strength and scooped her up over his shoulder. She squawked, one of the cutest sounds he'd ever heard, as he tipped her upside down, placing her eyes at a level with his ass.

His hand splayed over her inner thigh to brace her weight, and as he fought the need to slide his hand up higher, to the center of her heat, he felt her shudder at the touch.

She was so responsive to him. It was the hottest thing.

"What are you doing?" Maddy's body went tense as Alex searched for and easily found her bedroom—there were only two doors in her apartment, and one was clearly the bathroom.

The smell of her bath oil lingered in the air there, along with residual steam.

The thought of her, naked and in the bath, did nothing to help his blood pressure. Squeezing his eyes tightly shut for a moment, he tried to remember that she was drunk and didn't have a clue what she was doing.

That was the only reason he'd come over, he reminded himself—tried to convince himself. She was drunk, alone in her apartment, and it wasn't safe. He'd wanted to check on her.

That was all.

As he laid her gently on the bed, she squirmed and her robe fell open, treating his eyes to a slice of creamy white breast.

Alex looked away and counted to ten, but he couldn't tamp down his arousal. His cock had risen as soon as she'd answered the door in that see-through excuse for a robe.

"Maddy, if you're sure you want this . . . lie down." His voice was commanding and confident, far more so than he felt in the moment, though he felt that surge of power when she obliged.

Slowly, she moved backward on the bed, then lowered herself until her head was on her pillow. He watched the fabric of her robe hitching up with her movement, bunching around her hips.

"Put your hands behind your head."

She shivered, and her eyes cleared a bit. She might have had a lot to drink, but she knew exactly what she was doing, knew who she was with.

There was nothing better, in Alex's mind at least, than a woman willingly giving him her submission.

Especially this woman.

Beneath him, Maddy closed her eyes and sighed, opening herself to him.

Alex felt his heart stutter a bit, painfully. He bent over her, inhaling that seductive floral scent that was so uniquely hers.

He contemplated kissing her, placing his lips on her mouth, her neck, and elsewhere.

He couldn't resist her anymore, not when she wanted it, too. The connection between them was thick, full of heat, and wouldn't be denied.

She might have known what she was doing, but she was still not thinking clearly. So instead of sampling her lips, he lifted the cotton weave of her sheets, sliding them up over her legs. Her eyes flew open when the kiss she'd been asking him for with her body didn't come.

Alex cursed to himself, his cock throbbing with a near-painful arousal.

He caught the narrowed, determined expression in her eyes moments before she tugged at his arms, which were gently tucking a sheet around her waist. She caught him by surprise and he fell, his full weight splaying on top of her.

"Christ, Maddy." He should have stood right back up, but Maddy wound her arms around his shoulders, nipped at his neck, and rotated her hips slowly.

She'd been drinking. He needed to get up.

"Fuck." He was rock solid against the softness of her belly, and she purred with satisfaction.

"Alex. Please."

Groaning, he buried his face into her hair, savoring the scent. "You smell so fucking good."

Maddy slid her hands over his back and down to cup his ass. She was bolder than he'd thought she would be, fueled by the wine in part, but he was beginning to see there was a core of solid steel beneath her sweet exterior. It was a wonderful combination for a submissive. And her touch did absolutely nothing to quell his desire.

Rising onto his elbows, he studied her face intently for a long moment. He had no doubt that she was sexually submissive—

the way that she responded to him told him that. But had he been wrong? Was she strong enough to handle what he was dying to ask her to do?

He tucked a strand of her hair behind her ear, frowning as he had the day before, in the parking lot. He needed more time to think. This wasn't a woman he could play with without consequences.

She moaned when he slid off of her, the sound leaving him warm and aching.

"Why?" She wasn't whining—the question was matter-of-fact. He appreciated that about her, but he wasn't in the mood to answer, not when his body was a tight tangle of need.

He crossed the room. If he inhaled her intoxicating scent any longer, he wasn't sure he could trust himself.

"Sleep, Maddy. Go to sleep."

He'd stay until the next morning, to make sure that she was all right. But as Alex looked down at his rock-solid erection, he thought that he'd likely be seeing to his own pleasure that evening.

Sleep wasn't on the menu for him.

Maddy woke with the tantalizing aroma of bacon and coffee tickling the inside of her nose. Cautiously, she opened her eyes. She was in her bedroom, in her bed, and to judge by the brilliant white light streaming in stripes through her venetian blinds, it was morning.

Those were all normal things. The pile of sand in her mouth and the tenderness in her head were not; nor was the fact that she was in bed in her bathrobe, which had bunched uncomfortably around her waist.

As memories of the evening before started to filter into her waking mind, she wanted to pull the sheet over her head and hide.

She wasn't embarrassed at the amount that she'd had to drink, though she wasn't proud of herself, either. What made her want to lock herself in her bathroom for about a year was the knowledge that she'd thrown herself at Alex Fraser . . . and that he'd said no.

He said no. He said no. This caused panic to roil around in her gut. She had finally found someone around whom she felt safe, and she'd ruined it.

Fuck. In throwing herself at him, she'd reduced herself to one of the harem that she knew must follow him around everywhere. Whatever had caused him to single her out, her actions must surely have squashed any desire that he had.

Maddy felt a searing disappointment tighten her lungs. Well, what had she expected? Nothing good had ever come from overindulging in alcohol. The fact that Alex had sent her the alcohol just made her mad.

Her throbbing temples and dry mouth wanted to shift the blame from herself squarely to him, and, judging by the scents emanating from her tiny kitchenette, he was still there.

Maddy was halfway across the room with her mind set on yelling at the man who had turned her down yet was still in her house when she realized that she was half naked. Though she was fairly sure she'd given him quite a show the night before, there wasn't any point in offering up what he clearly didn't want. Quite out of sorts, Maddy exchanged the worn robe for an oversized T-shirt and cotton sleep shorts and made a quick detour to the bathroom. Her body was anxious to be rid of the previous night's toxins, and her mouth felt infinitely better with a refreshing wash of spearmint.

Her anger dissipated slightly when she finally, tentatively edged out of the bathroom, down the hallway and into the kitchen. She wasn't used to having someone else in her living space, especially not someone who seemed to take up as much space as Alex did.

Plus she'd behaved badly the night before, even if he had kind of deserved it. She owed him an apology.

"Good morning, Miss Stone." He was reading the *Wall Street Journal*. Of course he was. He lowered the paper, and Maddy felt a rush of heat when she saw that he was wearing glasses—wire-rimmed frames that sat halfway down his nose.

She had such a thing for a man in glasses.

Something niggled at her memory.

"Those glasses are real. The ones you wore in the casino weren't."

Alex tilted his head at her, curiosity on his face. "Very perceptive, Maddy."

He looked amused that she had remembered and questioned him on it. "I prefer to wear my contacts when I'm doing business. I prefer to not have a barrier between myself and others in those kinds of situations. But my eyes get tired sometimes, so I give them a rest with the glasses. I keep a spare pair in my car."

"Why didn't you just wear your real glasses at the casino?" She couldn't help but press him on it.

Alex raised an eyebrow at her. "I could have, I suppose. A superstition maybe, since technically I was still doing business. The ones I wore that day were cheap fakes that I picked up at a pharmacy on the way."

He smiled at her, and the smile made butterflies riot around in her stomach. "And good morning to you, too."

Maddy ducked her head, somewhat abashed. "Sorry for the inquisition. I used to be an optician. I still find it interesting." Her knees quivered a little bit as she looked at him, seeming at home in her shabby kitchen, watching her intently with those

spectacles perched on his nose. Knowing that he actually needed them, that he wasn't one hundred percent perfect as a physical specimen, made her mouth water.

"Ah . . . and good morning to you, too." This felt like the most awkward of morning afters, and they hadn't even done anything. She was so out of her comfort zone, it was incredible. What was she supposed to do? What should she say?

She was frozen in the doorway of her own kitchen, unable to move forward or back.

Something in Alex's stern expression softened a bit as he looked at her. "Come here."

Though she found it odd to be ordered around in her own home, she did as she was bid. The closer she came to the tiny card table that she'd covered with a cheerful, floral-printed oilcloth, the more tantalizing the smell of bacon and coffee became.

"Sit and eat." Leaning forward, Alex pulled out a chair for her and rested his hand comfortably on her shoulder as she complied. He was wearing his clothes from the night before, and there was a shadow dusting his cheeks. He looked delectable, and Maddy's mouth watered for him more than it did for the food.

Stop it. She had to stop; she knew it. He didn't want her. He'd made that perfectly clear.

"How do you feel?" Alex folded the paper neatly and laid it on the table, his eyes never leaving her. Maddy squirmed under his intense scrutiny.

"I . . . I've felt better." She was thirsty, so thirsty. She wanted to get up and get a glass of water, but for some absurd reason, she felt like she needed his permission.

"I would imagine so." Leaning forward, he tucked a strand of her hair behind her ear, a gesture he had performed before.

Maddy laced her fingers together tightly. She wouldn't press him for answers, not after last night, when she was afraid to make the situation even worse. He moved his gaze from her face and down over her body, and she became very aware of her traitorous body beneath the thin layers of cotton.

He said nothing, simply rose and moved to her kitchen counter.

"Here." Two small brown pills and a glass of pink grapefruit juice appeared before her. She had no idea where they'd come from—there had certainly not been any juice in her fridge or pills in her cupboard last night.

"What is it?" Maddy's voice was suspicious. She heard a huff of exasperation from somewhere behind her.

"It's Advil. Now take it."

She did, but only because she desperately wanted the juice.

"Good girl." Alex once again sat down across from her. This time he had a plate in one hand and a steaming paper cup of coffee in the other.

"Where did this come from?" Maddy was startled at the breakfast that had appeared before her—light, fluffy pancakes, crispy strips of bacon, and fresh, juicy wedges of melon. Again, she knew that none of it had been in her fridge—she rarely ate breakfast, and a good dinner for her involved throwing something into the microwave.

Erin had been the cook. Though she'd only been twenty when their parents had died, she'd learned from a need to take care of her eighteen-year-old sister. Some of her creations had been more edible than others, but all of them had been better than anything Maddy would have been able to come up with.

Alex didn't respond. Maddy shrugged and picked up her fork—she was hungry. Before the utensil was even halfway to her plate, Alex leaned over and wrapped his long fingers around her wrist, halting the movement.

Maddy look up at him in surprise.

"I should lay my hand on your naked ass for the stunt that

you pulled last night." His voice was angry, furiously so, and she was reminded of the anger that Alex had shown toward Massimo in the casino. Her mouth dried up, and her muscles tensed. She didn't feel like she was in danger—somehow she didn't think that Alex would ever hurt her.

No, she was aroused, aroused by the image of herself in his lap, her bare skin beneath his palm.

"I beg your pardon?" Her mouth opened and closed silently, and she was sure that she resembled nothing so much as a fish.

"You heard me." His anger faded slightly at her discomfiture. "You should never drink so much at home alone. What if you had passed out? Or got alcohol poisoning?" He flexed his fingers around her wrist, and she shivered. "You're not very big, and since the bottle is empty, I am assuming that you drank all of that wine yourself."

Maddy opened her mouth to argue—she felt like she should be angry with him for lecturing her. She was a grown woman, after all. She found that though she wanted to get mad, the sensation just wasn't there—he was only speaking the truth, after all. And it was nice . . . In a way, it was nice to find that someone cared.

"You're right." She muttered the words, then tried to move her hand. Her stomach was protesting its lack of solid food. She needed to eat.

Alex held firm.

"Do you want your breakfast?"

Maddy narrowed her eyes at him, then nodded. Of course she wanted her breakfast. What kind of question was that?

"Then promise you'll never put yourself in danger so stupidly again."

She was taken aback. Who demanded such a thing? And why did he care?

Her stomach growled. "Fine. I promise."

He released his grip on her wrist slowly, letting his fingers trail down the smooth skin on the inside of her forearm. She found that the pancakes had lost their appeal compared to the feeling of his hands on her skin.

Reclaiming his hand, he steepled his fingers and tucked them beneath his chin. Hesitantly, Maddy cut a bite of pancake and chewed slowly. At the moment, it was the best thing she'd ever eaten.

She swallowed and spoke. "I promise to try, anyway." She choked a bit on her grapefruit juice, surprised and amused to hear Alex Fraser hiss in frustration.

"You think it's funny?" His voice was silk covering steel, and she was suddenly wary. He stood, walked behind her. Grabbing the nape of her neck in his hand, he stroked lightly over her vertebrae.

"Eat." Yet she couldn't eat, not with his fingers on her. She tried to protest, but he hushed her with a soft sound. "Eat."

Maddy lifted a strip of bacon to her lips and bit. It was dry in her mouth, all of her senses focused on the touch of his hands on her neck. But she chewed, she swallowed, and she was rewarded with the movement of his hands. He rubbed her neck briefly, his fingers massaging her muscles. She arched into the touch, but it was brief, just a tease.

Eager for more of his touch, Maddy again bit, chewed, swallowed. This time he trailed his finger up the length of her spine.

They continued in that manner until she had emptied her plate. None of his touches were overtly sexual, but by the time her belly was full, she was a quivering mass of hot, needy nerves.

"Very good. Maddy . . ." His hands descended onto her shoulders, rubbing in slow circles down and out, coming very close to her breasts but not touching them.

She felt his breath on her earlobe, then the brush of his lips on her hair.

"What is it about you?" His voice was soft.

What was it about *her*? What was it about *him*? In the last twenty-four hours, he had resisted her drunken advances, tucked her chastely into bed, threatened to spank her, and fed her pancakes. She was confused, needy, and above all, heavily aroused.

His fingers moved lower, trailing from her neck and down over her spine, exploring the lump of each vertebrae. He leaned forward—she could tell because she could feel the warmth of his breath on the top of her head.

She felt the weight of his lips as he planted the lightest of kisses there. His lips traveled to the nape of her neck, and she stiffened, but it was with desire, not displeasure.

A sigh caught in her throat as the shrill automated sound of her cell phone ringing sliced through air that was thick with a delicious tension. She started, and Alex's fingers pressed into her neck.

Maddy leaned back against his touch. "I'll let it go to voice mail." She didn't care who was on the other end—she felt as if she would never be able to get enough of Alex's fingers on her skin.

He removed them—cruelly, she thought.

"It could be important." In his voice was a quiet reprimand, and she remembered that she hadn't answered the phone when he'd called the night before. His tone was harsher than she thought was strictly necessary. It reminded her that she didn't appreciate being scolded, and she narrowed her eyes as she considered letting the phone keep ringing, just because.

He did have a point, though. Heaving an exasperated sigh, Maddy reached for the cell that was sitting on the kitchen table, at the edge of her now empty plate.

She glanced at the caller ID before accepting the call. It was Dr. Gill's office—why would they be calling her?

Shit—*shit*! Her appointment. She'd forgotten all about her appointment yesterday.

"I'm so sorry!" Maddy tried to stand as she held the phone to her ear, but Alex pressed a hand to her shoulder, gently, and it held her in place. She twisted in the chair to cast an irritated glance at him.

She didn't really want him to hear this conversation. She didn't want him to know that she was in therapy. No matter how strong this feeling was, however, she felt the need to obey him. *That* confused her enough that she stopped struggling, just for a second. He seemed to be a dominant kind of guy, true enough, but it didn't explain why she wanted to do what he said when it went against what she wanted.

"Is everything all right, Madeline?" Dr. Gill's gentle voice echoed in the speaker of her cell phone. "It is not like you to miss an appointment."

"Yes, yes. Everything is fine." Alex's hand had stayed on her shoulder and was squeezing slightly. She wasn't sure if she was telling the truth or lying to the doctor, however.

Things had been different since Alex Fraser entered her world, but she wasn't yet sure of her feelings on the subject.

"Shall we reschedule, then?" Dr. Gill spoke after a pause, and Maddy sensed that the doctor was surprised Maddy hadn't brought the subject up by herself. "Tomorrow at five o'clock? I have had a cancellation."

Hurriedly, Maddy agreed to the appointment and ended the call. Right at that moment, she couldn't think of anything beyond Alex's touch.

"What appointment did you miss?" Alex removed his hands, and Maddy's first thought was to despair the loss of his caress.

"Just . . . an appointment with my therapist." It wasn't a shameful thing, seeing a therapist. In fact, she was proud of herself for taking control of her life, but she just didn't want to go into detail with this man, this beautiful man who had so unexpectedly entered her life.

Alex studied her for a long moment, nodding, but the look on his face was hard to decipher. "I see."

Alex's gut tightened as he examined Maddy's face for a long moment, then turned to cross the room.

All throughout breakfast, he'd been convinced that he'd gotten lucky, that Maddy might just be perfect for him.

Then, though she couldn't have known how he felt about the subject, she'd mentioned therapy, specifically *her* therapist.

If Alex believed in such things, he would have said that the universe was trying to tell him something.

I can't do this. Therapy might have been an unlikely sticking point, but it was a deal breaker for him.

"Will I see you again?" Maddy's voice was soft behind him, soft but strong. It stopped him in his tracks.

Most women would never have dared to ask him something so bold.

Madeline Stone was far stronger than most women.

No. Alex thought back to his own experience in therapy and shuddered. He'd been hardly more than a teenager, had been confused by his sexual need for control.

It hadn't gone well. And that was just a reminder that he was better off with one of the women from In Vino Veritas, one of the women who knew the score, even if it didn't fulfill him totally.

Steeling himself, Alex didn't reply.

The scrape of a chair told him that Maddy was now standing. He turned to face her—he owed her that.

"I'm not what you need, Maddy." His voice was a whisper.

Hesitantly, she crossed the floor to him. God, but he wanted to see her again, more than he'd wanted anything, ever.

She whispered, too. "Let me decide what I want."

"Therein lies the problem." Alex's lips quirked up in a smile that held no amusement.

Maddy looked puzzled in response. She reached out and traced a finger slowly over the ink of the tattoo that was peeking out from the sleeve of his shirt. He closed his eyes against the feeling of her soft, tentative fingers on his skin.

Yes, he wanted her, but he wouldn't take her.

"I have to go, Madeline." Her fingers clenched on his arm, her nails digging into his skin. They both looked down at where they were touching, her pale fingers with the neat oblong nails, his skin, tanned golden from the sun and stretched tightly over solid muscle.

"Fuck." Alex's body moved so fast that his brain didn't have a chance to catch up. Then his hands were fisted in the length of her hair and she was pinioned beneath him against the wall. His hips pressed into the soft curve of her belly as he kissed her with all the pent-up desire and frustration he'd felt since he'd met her.

His tongue parted her lips roughly, demanding entrance. He traced the pattern of her teeth, her tongue, staking his claim, nipping at her lip sharply. Then, as quickly as it had begun, it was over. Pulling his hands from the tangles of her hair, he released her, and Maddy leaned against the cool plaster of the wall, wide-eyed and panting.

"Fuck." Alex cursed as he watched her lift her hand tentatively to touch lips swollen from the assault. She moved her mouth, but nothing came out.

"Maddy. We can't do this." Alex choked out the words before turning and slamming the screen door behind him. He was furious with himself for losing control, for tasting her again.

No matter what his mind said, he knew that one taste was never going to be enough.

CHAPTER FIVE

At her appointment with Dr. Gill the next day, Maddy knew she was holding back. She was pretty sure that the doctor knew it, too, but Dr. Gill had never been one to press, instead preferring her patients to come to their own conclusions.

"Have you set any goals for the next week, Maddy? Anything off of your list?" Dr. Gill asked this as Maddy was slinging the strap of her purse over her shoulder. Maddy paused, not entirely sure of how to answer.

She had found something new that she wanted to explore—namely, Alex Fraser. However, he wasn't cooperating, and Maddy had no illusions about who was going to win the battle.

"I haven't quite decided yet, Dr. Gill. I'll think about it." The other woman smiled at her, her expression comforting as she gathered up her notes.

"Don't make it a hugely stressful event if you're already feeling uptight, Maddy. It can be as simple as filling up your car at a new gas station. The important thing is just to do something, to push yourself into taking forward steps."

Maddy sighed as she left the office. Her footsteps were muffled by the industrial carpeting.

Surprisingly, Alex calmed her nerves. His presence in her life had soothed her in a way she'd never expected. Around him, she could probably go to a new gas station every day of the damn week.

Buck up, Maddy. Alex had made his decision. Instead of

feeling wistful, wondering what had gone wrong, Maddy found that she was angry.

There was something between them. She had no idea why it was there, but it nevertheless existed. The fact that he was fighting it so hard pissed her off.

Maddy pushed through the glass door of the building, stepping out into the late-afternoon sunlight, where she found Alex leaning against the dinged metal of her car.

"Well, shit." It gave her a start, the juxtaposition of the magazine-perfect man and something that belonged to her.

"What are you doing here?" Nerves clung to her like static-charged fabric, neutralizing some of her anger. By showing up, Alex had thrown her off her game—well, more so than she'd already been—and she was having trouble telling which way was up.

She wasn't sad, though. This was new. Normally, an hour spent with Dr. Gill meant an hour spent crying, and she would emerge shaking and exhausted.

Alex waited a minute before responding, and it seemed as though he didn't quite know how to answer her question. "I couldn't stay away." His face was serious as he spoke, and Maddy knew that he was speaking the truth.

"Why?" She couldn't help but ask the question. She didn't think she had low self-esteem, but she was just an average woman—she was a waitress, she had average looks, she'd never done anything very special with her life. He was akin to a movie star—unnaturally beautiful, rich beyond her wildest dreams, and fascinating.

It just didn't match up, at least not in her head.

Alex shook his head in answer to her question, and Maddy knew that he wasn't going to answer. Instead he changed the subject.

"Why do you think you need to see a therapist?" His voice was flat, and Maddy understood immediately that he didn't approve.

She could deal with him not approving of her seeing a shrink, although she didn't think it was any of his concern and felt belligerent that he couldn't understand why someone would meet with a therapist. "It's none of your business." The words slipped from her mouth before she could stop them and she barely suppressed her cringe—she'd just told off Vegas's equivalent of Brad Pitt.

Maddy waited for him to leave. He didn't, though he did look a bit stunned that she hadn't acquiesced to his unspoken request to stop seeing Dr. Gill immediately. The stunned look gave way to severe irritation, and Maddy was gratified when he appeared to swallow it down.

She took courage in the fact that he hadn't left her standing alone on asphalt so hot that she could see the air shimmering directly above its sticky surface.

"How did you find me?"

Alex quirked an eyebrow, and Maddy realized that he wasn't used to being questioned. Nor, did she think, was he used to explaining himself, since he didn't look the least bit embarrassed at the fact that he'd done something rather stalker-like in waiting outside of her car, outside of her therapist's office.

"I have a PI on retainer." His tone was matter-of-fact—doesn't *everyone* have a private eye on call? Maddy shook her head slowly, bewildered.

"But why would you go to that trouble?" The look in his eyes told Maddy that he knew what she was asking—not why did he have a private eye on retainer, but why had he used his services on her? Why on earth would he go out of his way to track her down? After all, he had already turned her down.

Once again, he didn't answer what she'd asked, but instead asked her a question in turn.

"Would you accompany me to the casino tonight?" Alex stuffed his hands in the pockets of his jeans—nice ones again, not the worn ones of the night before, Maddy noticed. He looked young, cocky, powerful—it made her mouth dry.

The visage of Massimo, the owner of A Casino in Paradise, flashed through Maddy's head, and she shuddered. Something about him discomforted her, and she told Alex so.

He shook his head and pinned her with that cerulean stare again. "No. El Diablo—my casino. Come have dinner with me."

Heat washed over Maddy in a tidal wave, followed by the sensation of a million hummingbirds flocking through her veins. Did that mean what she thought it meant? She couldn't. She shouldn't.

Should she?

"Say yes." When he looked at her like that, she knew there was no way she would say anything else. She wanted to be with this man in a way that astounded her. Even though he ran hot and cold with her, she wanted to take this chance to spend more time with him.

Maddy nodded her assent—not speaking, afraid to break the spell between them, afraid that with another one of his lightning-quick mood changes, Alex would change his mind again.

Instead, pleasure enveloped his face, and Maddy felt inexorably pleased that she'd made him so happy.

"Maddy, there's something I want to tell you." Suddenly he was close to her, his hands lightly touching her waist. Her skin felt seared from the heat of his palms. "I've tried to stay away from you, but I just can't get you out of my mind."

Maddy smiled nervously. *He* couldn't get *her* out of his head? More like the other way around.

"Let me go home and change; then I'll meet you there." She felt a frisson of panic—what on earth was a woman supposed to wear to dinner with a man like Alex?

His next words left her mouth hanging open—and without much say in the matter. "Don't change. You look beautiful just as you are."

"Miss Stone." Maddy's door was opened for her, a man dressed in the sleek black of the casino staff holding out a hand for her as soon as she'd put her car in park. She scrambled for her purse, then allowed herself to be escorted gracefully from the low vehicle.

As the neon lights of the casino washed over her, she slung the vinyl strap of her purse over her shoulder and tugged uncomfortably at the hem of her shorts. She wished that Alex had given her a chance to run home to change clothing, but instead she was stuck wearing the cotton shorts and simple T-shirt that she had changed into after her shift at the diner, before her appointment with Dr. Gill.

She also would have appreciated a chance to pack a small overnight bag. It might have been wishful thinking, but she was *really* hoping that an adult sleepover would follow dinner.

She shook with nerves at the very thought. The idea both terrified and thrilled her.

Could she if he asked? Since he would know very well that she wouldn't have an overnight bag, it seemed unlikely that he would.

If something didn't happen to release some of the sexual tension that drew hot and tight between them, Maddy thought she might explode.

Pushing her thoughts away—she could go around about it forever—she focused on following her guide and on not becoming lost in a sea of sequins, lipstick, and silicone.

"This way please, Miss Stone." Another man dressed in sleek black took her by the elbow and steered her toward the front lobby of the casino. Alex couldn't have gotten there more than a few minutes before Maddy had, but it seemed that he had announced her arrival. She wasn't sure whether she was relieved or nervous to be in the company of a man built like a tank, a man who knew her name even though she didn't know his.

"Who are you?" The question sounded rude, though she hadn't meant it as such.

To her surprise, the giant in black dropped his dour expression and chuckled. "I'm Declan."

Maddy blinked when she realized that the man had a thick Irish accent. Thinking of how the man at her blackjack table that first night in the casino had called Alex an Irishman, she wondered if he was maybe a relative.

"I take care of things here." He resumed his serious expression as they reached a bank of elevators.

Maddy didn't ask any more questions, because she didn't think that she was going to get any more out of the man. He seemed to have shut down after that one brief flash of approachability.

He took care of things? Like her? Or Alex's business-related things?

As a gaggle of gaudily dressed young girls approached the elevator that had just opened for them, Declan caught Maddy by the elbow again and towed her inside, warning the girls off of the same lift with a scowling shake of his head.

Maddy raised an eyebrow at the head shake. The elevator was big enough to comfortably fit a crowd. There wasn't any need for them to hog it.

The doors closed, and Declan inserted a card into the slot below the keypad. What appeared to be an LED screen popped out, much in the manner that cash was dispensed from an

ATM. He pressed a thick index finger to the pad, and a light rolled down the screen from top to bottom.

"Declan St. Adams." An automated female voice filled the elevator, which then began to move. Maddy felt her mouth fall open a bit with astonishment. Declan caught her expression, then very nearly smiled again.

"Security." The word was a grunt.

Where on earth were they going? When Alex asked her to have dinner with him at the casino, Maddy had assumed that he'd meant one of the restaurants in the casino itself.

The elevator rose, then rose some more. Just when she started to wonder if the ride would ever end—the higher they rose, the more nervous she got—the elevator gently shuddered to a stop.

"Miss Stone." Declan gestured for Maddy to exit the elevator. She was rooted in place with wide eyes, staring at the elegant room that had opened up in front of her.

She swallowed thickly and turned back to Declan. She would have to ask him to take her back down. She couldn't do this. She was way, way, way out of her league.

Declan eyed her with calculation written over his face as Maddy battled her inner demons. Then his face softened, just the tiniest bit. "He'd never hurt you. Not unless you wanted him to." Then, with a hand on Maddy's elbow yet again, he urged her off of the lift. It swallowed the great big man back up, and she was left alone in what she assumed was the penthouse of the building, wondering what on earth his words had meant.

Holy shit.

The floor was intricately tiled, an array of blue, green, and white. The walls were tinted pale green, and the glass dewdrops of a chandelier that soared above her head cast light on the wall in a pattern that reminded Maddy of a flowing stream.

A polished mahogany table sat against the wall, holding

carved jade bookends and a bright stripe of leather-bound books. Her fingers itched to touch them—she loved to read—but she still couldn't quite bring herself to move.

"Welcome, Maddy." His voice parted the air softly, and she shivered as she looked up and saw Alex standing at the end of the hallway, watching her. He had unbuttoned the top two buttons of his black shirt, and Maddy's mouth watered at the sight of the tanned skin beneath.

She ran her tongue slowly over her lips without realizing that she was doing it. His eyes followed the movement hungrily.

"Hi, Alex." This was all that she could manage to say. He waited, presumably for her to come in. Nervously, she toed off her sandals and then flushed when he studied the action curiously.

"You're very sweet." Alex didn't come any closer as he spoke, seeming to want Maddy to come to him. Hesitantly, she took one step toward him, then another. Finally she reached the end of the long hall, and as she closed the distance separating them, she felt weak in the knees.

What am I doing here?

"Are you all right?" Alex smiled at Maddy's nervous nod before tucking her hand into his. He was suddenly transported back to junior high school, when just the touch of another's hand was exhilarating.

"Come with me." Alex led her a bit farther down the hall, until the corridor opened into a massive kitchen. The room gleamed with bright copper and polished wood and was kept neat as a pin.

He liked things in order, and though he'd never bothered himself wondering what others thought of his home, he suddenly found himself hoping that Maddy liked it.

Releasing her hand, Alex urged her into the kitchen with a gentle push at the small of her back. Warmth from her skin made him burn, and when he saw her shiver, he assumed that she felt the same way.

She gasped when she saw the spacious wooden island in the center of the room, loaded with dishes.

"What . . . Surely this isn't all for me?" Maddy turned to look at him, bewildered. She looked so cute, he wanted to kiss her nose.

That was a new one for him.

"I didn't know what you'd like, so I had the Bistro send one of everything." Her eyebrows rose to her hairline at his words, and he winced inwardly, following her line of thought.

"One of *everything*? From *the Bistro*?" Despite its casual name, the boutique restaurant located on the lower level of the casino was five star and ridiculously expensive.

He hadn't yet had cause to tell her how incredibly wealthy he was.

"Alex, really . . ." Maddy's words trailed off under his gaze, and his eyes narrowed further. He wanted her to understand that this was nothing compared to everything that he wanted to lavish on her.

As if plucking the thought from his head, she swallowed whatever she was going to say and instead replied simply, "Thank you."

Alex couldn't help it. He grinned and guided her closer to the island. Pulling out one of the high bar stools for her, he clasped her around the waist and seated her gently, then reached for the bottle of wine that sat nearby, open to breathe.

She squinted at the label, wincing when she saw that it was the Mouton Rothschild again. "Just water, please."

Alex couldn't help but chuckle. Clearly the memory of her binge was all too fresh in her mind.

Still, he couldn't complain. If she didn't need a drink to relax around him, then she was trusting him a bit more.

"Just a taste?" Alex poured himself a glass and offered it to Maddy. Warily she nodded, her eyes widening when he kept his fingers clasped on the stem, entwining them with hers. Leaning in close, his breath misted over the skin of her cheek as he confided to her, "You're the most fascinating woman I've ever met."

Surely it was just a line, though he seemed to be entirely sincere. Still, Maddy's belly did a slow roll at the words and then again when, instead of relinquishing his control and handing her the glass to sip, he dipped his index finger into the swirls of red and painted the liquid over her lips.

She inhaled sharply and her tongue slid out to catch the drops. Maddy watched Alex's eyes go dark as his stare followed the path of her tongue, and she could feel her skin turning red.

"That blush." *This is it*, she thought. He was going to kiss her again. She wanted to undress him ever so slowly and explore the contours of his body. It was going to happen.

Instead he turned to the first of the plates that crowded the island.

"What is that?" It looked and smelled good, but Maddy had never been an adventurous eater.

"Bison meat loaf." He filled a fork, then held it to her lips. She was ready to melt.

Alex Fraser is feeding me.

Even with her nervous stomach, she parted her lips to accept the bite. She chewed and swallowed—she was sure that it was delicious, but her senses were otherwise engaged.

"Good?"

"It's lovely." Maddy nodded her approval as the flavors burst over her tongue. Alex took a bite for himself, eating it off of the same fork. It was so intimate, and not at all what she'd expected from dinner with the business mogul—though she still wasn't sure what, exactly, that was.

"You didn't need to order so much, Alex." As Maddy spoke, Alex laid the fork down on the wooden counter and pulled a new plate close. With his fingers, he lifted what appeared to be some kind of shellfish, swirling it through a thick, rich broth before lifting the new offering to Maddy's lips.

"Open your mouth so you can try the mussels." He ignored what she'd said. She wanted to please him, so she didn't press, and again parted her lips. Something with an unfamiliar texture slid in. The taste was pleasant, but she didn't like the rubbery feeling and made a face before she could stop herself, freezing immediately after, knowing she'd just been rude.

Instead of being agitated, Alex threw his head back and laughed, shoving the plate away at the same time. "I don't much care for them either." Leaning toward her, he brushed the residual broth from Maddy's lips with his thumb. Before she could think it through, she nipped at it and he closed his eyes.

When he opened them again, they were dark and full of heat. "No more mussels. But you have to eat more." He placed his hands on Maddy's waist, squeezing briefly, and she shuddered.

"I'm not really hungry." Not for food, at any rate. There were so many emotions pummeling her that Maddy wasn't sure how much she'd actually be able to get down.

His expression stern, Alex continued to feed her, bites of tuna tartare, Brie en croute, crispy crab cakes, and deliciously spiced prawns. Between bites, he touched her casually here and there, a palm on her knee, a swipe over her mouth, lips whispering through her hair.

"Please." She couldn't do it. Not only was she unable to

swallow any more, she was on fire, consumed by heat from his light touches.

"Are you full?"

"I couldn't eat another bite." Maddy nodded vigorously to support her response, and he again laughed, in a wonderful soft sound that tickled inside her ear. His lips trailed lightly from her ear across her cheek and down to her neck. His fingers tugged lightly on the chain of the locket that she always wore, and she froze, suddenly panicked.

"Picture of a former lover?" The surface of his voice was amused, but it was swirled through with something that sounded like jealousy. His fingers toyed with the clasp of the locket.

"No!" Maddy snatched the locket from his fingers and leapt backward, off the stool. Her heart rate was up and her breath came in short pants. Her body was reacting now more from anxiety than desire.

Alex looked angry, not, she thought, because he so badly wanted to see the picture, but because she was keeping something from him.

"No. I don't show that to anyone." With her heart pounding in her ears, she stared back at him, clutching the locket tightly in suddenly sweaty fists—but she wasn't going to back down, not on this. This secret of hers was too precious, too fragile, to share with someone so new to her life.

The sensual haze that had wrapped them tightly together as they ate was broken. Maddy could see Alex drawing into himself, becoming once again the casino magnate, not the would-be lover.

"Well, even if you won't share with me, I have something that I need to share with you." His jaw was set, and if Maddy had to describe how he looked, she would have said apprehensive, or maybe resigned.

She couldn't imagine what he could show her that could elicit either sentiment from him. He had already discovered more about her than she'd let anyone else know, and he was still there.

"All right." What else was she going to say? He had been so sweet, had gone to so much trouble for her tonight. It had been a wonderful evening. She could hear him out, even if the dinner date had veered off of the sensual course that she had so anticipated.

"I know I've been hot and cold with you. It wasn't because I wanted to." Alex held out his hand; then, as if thinking better of it, he retracted it before Maddy could place her palm against his own. "There are things that . . . fulfill something in me, things that I very much want to do with you, but that I didn't feel right introducing to someone so sweet and innocent."

"I'm hardly an innocent." But she supposed she could see where Alex had gotten that idea. Maddy felt a rock settle in her gut, weighted with a hefty dose of irritation. Still, despite the ominous tone that now permeated the air, Alex was still gentleman enough to usher her ahead of him.

With the slightest of touches to her waist, he guided her down yet another hallway. At the very end was a closed door. Pulling a plastic key card from his pocket, he slid it into the slot beneath the handle.

Holy crap. He had a locked room in his home? What was on the other side? The bodies of every other woman who had been lured to the penthouse?

"You've shown me that you're plenty strong enough to make the decision for yourself, Maddy. And I'll do everything in my power to convince you to be with me, but I will also understand if you don't want any part of this." Maddy stepped backward, only to be met with the solid warmth of Alex's body. She prepared to flee, but the heavy metal door swung open, and the sight beyond it shocked her still.

What have I gotten myself into?

The room that Maddy was standing in was a study in black and gray. Directly in front of her was what appeared to be a swing, suspended from the ceiling. Beyond it, against the wall, was a giant wooden X and something that looked like gymnastics equipment. Shelves on the wall displayed a variety of instruments that, unless she was very much mistaken, were whips and canes.

Startled by the sight in front of her, Maddy looked to the left, where she saw a massive wooden post, a coil of leather at its base. Right, and there was another set of shelving holding bars, handcuffs, and other things whose purpose she couldn't even begin to guess.

The truth hit her like a freight train, and her knees buckled. What had she gotten herself into? Alex placed his hands at her waist, holding her up. She looked up at him, her feelings coalesced into a thick, unidentifiable miasma.

His face displayed no emotion—deliberately, she thought. "Do you have any questions?" This was business Alex, always stoic and in control.

Maddy looked around the room quickly, then squeezed her eyes shut. She wasn't repulsed—no, not at all. Confused, yes, and a bit disoriented, but underneath it all was a heat that was spreading out slowly from the apex of her thighs, suffusing her skin with its warmth.

"What is this place?" She had already guessed—she knew what he was about to say. But she still wanted to hear it from him.

"This is my dungeon." Alex still wasn't expressing any emotion toward her—or was he? There was the slightest flicker in his eyes when Maddy looked up at him that told her that what she thought of this place mattered to him.

She tore her stare away and sucked in a searing mouthful of air.

"I think I would like that drink now." Pulling out of his grasp, Maddy scurried out of the "dungeon" and back down the hall to the kitchen. She wasn't offended by the things that he'd shown her, but he'd thrown her for one hell of a loop, and she couldn't think straight.

Plus, the wine was in the kitchen, and she found herself desperately in need of a drink.

"Hell." Not bothering with the glass, Maddy lifted the bottle to her lips the second that her fingers clasped the smooth surface. She chugged, gulping once, twice, then wiped at her mouth with the back of her hand.

Alex entered the kitchen several moments later, after the wine had had a chance to fizz its way into her bloodstream. She appreciated the time he'd given her to compose herself, which she knew wasn't accidental.

"So?" Crossing the room toward her, Alex removed the bottle from Maddy's hand and tidily topped off the red liquid in his own glass. Every inch the gentleman, he seated himself on a bar stool and looked up at her, frank curiosity gleaming in his eyes.

"So." She remained standing—she was too antsy to sit. There were a million questions swirling through her head, and she plucked one randomly and spat it out of her mouth.

"What is the swing for?" Biding her time while waiting for his answer, she reached for his newly filled glass and sipped from it herself, using the action to hide her embarrassment. There was also a surge of something like desire running through her. From the smirk that crossed Alex's lips, she knew that she hadn't succeeded in hiding her interest.

"That is a sex swing." Taking the glass back, he drank, too, then reached out to trace a fingertip over Maddy's abdomen. She shivered at the touch. "A ceiling suspension swing, to be precise."

Right. Of course it was. "What is it for?"

Alex didn't bother trying to hide his smirk that time. "It is to support one partner during . . . let's call them unconventional . . . sexual positions."

"Oh." Maddy wasn't completely naive, but the lovers she'd had could have been counted on one hand.

She knew nothing of dungeons or sex swings.

"Why did you show it to me?" After taking one more sip from their shared glass, Maddy set it down on the polished wood of the island with a sharp *clack*, then twined her fingertips together and studied them intently. Alex trailed his fingers up from her belly, between her breasts, and under her chin, tilting her head until she was forced to look at him.

This was what she wanted—when he looked at her, when he touched her, she felt alive.

Now that he'd showed her the room, his touches—his attitude itself—had become exponentially more sexual. It was as if, now that he'd told her it was her decision to make, he was going to make damn sure that she decided in the manner he wanted.

"I am interested in you, Madeline. Very, very interested in you. But I am not ultimately interested in a vanilla relationship."

Maddy's stomach rolled and her mood soared before crashing. How was she supposed to take this news? What was he saying? She wasn't entirely sure what she wanted herself, but she knew from past experience that the idea of casual sex didn't sit well with her. Still, she wanted Alex and was tempted to take whatever she could get.

"So . . . you want to . . . whip me?" Maddy could feel herself blushing further, but it wasn't fully with embarrassment. A mental image of herself pressed against that massive wooden post in his dungeon, the flick of that coiled leather whip against her skin, did something to her insides, making her feel feverish all over.

She was surprised that she wanted that image to become a reality.

Alex smiled at her, but his eyes darkened with something that looked surprisingly like hunger, and she knew that he was thinking along the same lines as she was.

"It's more complex than that, Maddy. I am a Dominant. I want, very much want, for you to be my submissive. I want to use everything in that room with you, in every imaginable way." He paused and sipped, giving her a moment to process.

"For you, I'd be tempted to try something vanilla, but you need to know that ultimately I wouldn't be happy. I need . . . more . . . than the vanilla world offers."

"Vanilla?" Maddy's mouth went dry.

"I'm not interested in regular sex. No dominance, no submission. No bondage, no discipline." When Alex said the words, they sounded dark and delicious, even as they scared and titillated.

"As a Dominant, I might use punishment to train you in the proper behavior for a submissive, but the end goal is pleasure— a lot of pleasure—for both of us."

"You are so not punishing me." Her knee-jerk reaction was to reject the very idea. She didn't want that.

Did she?

Pleasure. Punishment. Maddy had never thought of the two together, but as Alex's words twined them irrevocably in her psyche, she found that she thrilled to them.

Punishment.

Her Catholic-school upbringing, long buried, started frantically clawing through the rubble in which it had been buried.

Good girls didn't want to be punished. Good girls weren't intrigued by secret, locked rooms that were filled with whips and chains.

"I understand that you'll need to consider it." Alex trailed his hand over her cheek, and as Maddy looked into his eyes, she knew that, no matter how strange this conversation was, she wanted to be with this man.

Wanting to touch him, to reassure herself that she wasn't dreaming, Maddy lifted her hand to where his fingers still rested on her cheek, twining their hands together.

"Right." Yes, she should probably think about this before jumping straight into his arms. This was a serious matter— whips. Pain. Punishment.

"We can talk. You can ask me anything, anything at all." His other hand reached up to her face, so that the warmth of his palms heated her cheeks. "Think about what you like about sex. Go from there."

"I don't like sex." Maddy physically recoiled as soon as she said the words, pulling back. *Shit. Shit.* Why had she said that? It was the truth—she'd never really seen what all the fuss was about—but added to it was this unfamiliar heat that Alex brought out in her, a heat that she very much wanted to explore.

She expected him to react to the strangeness of her statement—what kind of grown woman didn't like sex? Instead his features were painted in surprise, then heat.

Clasping her tightly around the waist, he tugged her forward until she straddled his lap. The bare skin of her legs was abraded by the denim of his jeans, and Maddy could feel his hardness against her heat.

"You haven't had sex with me."

CHAPTER SIX

lex continued their conversation as if unaware of Maddy's extreme arousal and nervousness. "Do you know why people embrace submission as a lifestyle, Maddy?"

She was standing beside a massive bed that was draped in steel gray sheets, in Alex Fraser's bedroom. He was standing behind her, the lean planes of his body a whisper away from her. He was stroking his hands lightly down her spine, in a touch as light as a feather, yet her world had narrowed in to focus on that ghostly sensation.

She shook her head; she couldn't speak. This was it, then. She was going to have sex with Alex. And if *he* couldn't make her like it, then there wasn't much hope.

She was pretty damn sure that she was going to like it.

"Because there is pleasure in being powerless. Being powerless is sensual, in that it allows you to explore your senses more fully than vanilla sex will ever allow you to." His finger dipped below the neckline of her shirt to trace her shoulders, then around to paint over her collarbone. "Take off your shirt."

"Now?" Maddy froze—what would he think of her naked? She had marks, pale scars from the car accident, that she didn't want his assessing eyes to see.

"Take off your shirt, Madeline." His voice became layered with steel, and she wondered what he would do if she refused.

Maddy's mind flashed back to the room that he called the dungeon and to the mysterious tools that she'd seen. She wasn't sure that she was ready to find out what he'd do if she refused.

What else was there to do, then? After all, she wanted this, wanted *him*.

She crossed her arms at her waist and took her cotton tee in damp fingers. One swift tug and her torso was bare.

"Ah, you're so beautiful." Maddy felt Alex's soft touch down her spine, exploring the bumps of her vertebrae. "That skin— cream and berries."

The striping of his fingers dipped just below the waistband of her shorts, just above the crease of her behind, before flying back up to the nape of her neck and beginning again. This time, when he reached the clasp of her bra, he deftly undid the hooks, and the garment fell to her wrists.

"Let it fall." Trembling like a blade of grass in the wind, she flicked her wrists and let the bra drop to the ground. His hands slid from her spine to trace her ribs, feathering over her belly.

"I am going to take off your shorts." His voice was matter-of-fact, and Maddy knew that, whether she was scared to be naked or not, her shorts were coming off. She held her breath as his fingers worked the button from its clasp, then tugged down the zipper. The metal sounded harsh in the hushed air of the room, followed by the soft shushing of khaki as it slid over her hips and down her legs.

Maddy was naked with Alex Fraser. *Holy hell.*

"Close your eyes."

She hesitated just a moment, and he took his hands off of her completely. She whimpered with want and need.

He clasped her tightly around her waist and brushed a kiss on the top of her head. "Good girl." Pushing slightly, Alex guided her the few short steps to his bed, then turned her around and pushed her back. The silky softness of his plush mattress hit the backs of her knees, and she sat, then lay down, guided all the while by his hands.

She could feel the mattress dip when Alex sat beside her.

She turned toward him, started to open her eyes, but a warning growl from deep in his throat had her squeezing them shut again.

"Do you want to explore one of your senses, Madeline?" Blindly, she nodded, her hips shifting restlessly. She was conscious that, with her front to him, he could see parts of her that she'd rather he not. Strangely, he didn't seem to mind her scars, or even to notice, and after a few minutes she relaxed a bit.

Something soft brushed over her cheek. She suspected it wasn't his finger. It felt even softer, lighter on her skin. It moved over her cheekbone, then over her lips. It flirted with the curve of her neck, then caressed the hollow between her breasts.

She cried out when the softness played over first one nipple, then the other.

"What is that?" Maddy's hips bucked, and her voice was a whimper.

"Shh." Even in a whisper, he managed to admonish her. "Do you like it?"

She sighed in affirmation. The softness trailed down her belly and swept between her thighs.

"Oh." The pressure was so soft, yet so insistent. She wanted . . . oh, she wanted more.

"Isn't it amazing that something as insubstantial as a feather can cause so much sensation?" His voice was thick, thick with desire, she thought. "Now imagine that intensified, magnified a hundredfold."

Maddy twisted her fingers in the sheets. She wasn't sure if she would even survive this.

"You taste so sweet." His tongue tasted along her jawline as his finger replaced the feather, tickling the soft skin between her thighs, and she gasped at the change in pressure.

Her eyes fluttered open, and the finger was withdrawn.

"Do that again, and I will turn you over my knee." Alex's

voice was slightly breathless, and Maddy's mouth fell open. She studied his face for a long moment before letting her eyes fall closed again.

He was serious. And she wanted nothing more in that moment than for his touch to return.

"Brat," he murmured as he stroked through her slit. "You like pushing boundaries. It will be fun to teach you to submit."

Maddy quivered under Alex's ministrations.

He stroked back and forth through her lower lips, and she shifted restlessly. Just when she thought that she couldn't handle it anymore, he slipped a finger inside of her and at the same time pressed against her clit with his thumb. She was so aroused from the teasing that the pressure made her shatter, her eyes flying open as stars danced in front of them.

"Ahh!" She felt as if she had lost control over her body—and reveled in the sensation. Maddy had never, never felt anything like it before. She was focused solely on the pleasure that was rocketing through her body. When the shudders subsided, she blinked slowly, taking in her surroundings as she came back to herself.

Alex had divested himself of his clothing and sheathed his erection in latex. Positioning himself between her legs as she lay on his bed, panting, he pushed her legs farther apart with rough hands and placed his cock at her entrance.

"Fuck, Maddy. I need to have you." He slammed into her in a hard thrust, bending to cover her mouth with his own at the same time. Maddy arched up to meet him—*this* was what she'd been begging for, this feeling of fullness. He was bigger than any man she'd been with before and filled her to the point of pain. It was good pain, stretching her, making her feel alive.

His mouth swallowed her moans. He kissed her over and over, exploring her mouth as he thrusted. There was nothing teasing or gentle about his touch any longer—he was possessing her, branding her with his touch.

"Maddy." She could feel his thighs tense, and she wrapped her legs around his waist with all of her strength. "Say my name."

"Alex." His pace quickened, and his hands found her breasts, pinching the tender tips and sending her flying again. "Alex!"

The feeling was shorter this time, but more intense, and her cries mingled with his own as he slammed home one final time and groaned.

She was shattered. Her mind was filled with him and only him. Next she was conscious of him withdrawing from between her legs, then of being picked up and moved so that her head lay pillowed on softness.

She had never felt more content.

Alex was more than a little bit stunned. It had been years since he'd had vanilla sex, and yet the orgasm he'd just had had been an explosion that started at the base of his spine and ricocheted throughout his entire body.

Maddy . . . what was it about this woman? He'd never been overly attracted to innocence, so he didn't think that was it. Besides, as her reaction in the kitchen, when he'd touched her locket, had shown him, she had secrets of her own, ones that she wasn't likely to share.

No, she wasn't as innocent as she appeared, nor as fragile. She was strong and giving, and everything about her appealed to him on a primordial level that urged him to claim her, to mark her.

Stroking fingers through her hair, he idly wondered what it would take to get her to sign his agreement. He didn't want to hurt her, as he was sure that he ultimately would in the end, but he'd burned through the reserves that had let him try to stay away from her.

He wanted to possess her, not as a thing, but as a Dominant did a submissive woman. He knew in his gut that Maddy's submission would be one of the most beautiful, gratifying things he'd ever experience.

"Little doe." Experimentally, Alex ran his hands over her naked thighs, her torso, and up to her breasts. It was never too soon to start the dance that was the relationship between a Dominant and his submissive.

Maddy sighed, arching into his touch. She stiffened when he ran his fingers between her breasts, then over the chain of her locket. Her body tensed in that moment.

He wasn't going to open it—she'd told him no, and he would honor that. But he didn't like having a part of her closed off, a part that he didn't have access to.

A submissive needed to be completely open, or her Dominant couldn't possibly provide her with what she needed.

For now, Alex just wanted to coax away one barrier—that was, he wanted Maddy to let him touch the locket, to trust that he wouldn't open it without her permission.

"Alex." The warning note in Maddy's tone softened as he continued to stroke his fingers over the chain, heating the metal with his skin but never making a move to open it. He felt the muscles of her body relax, bit by bit, as she began to understand that he wouldn't force her to discuss it.

"The locket . . ." It was Alex's turn to tense as her big blue eyes turned up to look right at him. A Dom—not to mention a successful tycoon—learned to read people very, very well, and he could see that Maddy wanted to tell him about the secret hidden inside the brass heart.

At the last moment, she froze, the shutters in her eyes sealing away her words.

"Get some rest." Though disappointed that she'd shied away, Alex was determined. Winning a woman's submission was so much sweeter than having it handed to him.

He was going to do whatever he had to, to get her to sign his Dominant/submissive contract and to start the exploration of his lifestyle with him.

But for now, it was pleasant enough to hold the sweet, fascinating woman in his arms as she drifted off.

He fell asleep as well, her body entwined with his and the scent of freesia in his nose.

CHAPTER SEVEN

Maddy wakened slowly, the muscles in her body as soft and supple as candle wax. She'd slept well, better than she had at any time in recent memory.

She opened her eyes gradually, and her stomach clenched in alarm when her sleep-fogged brain realized that she wasn't where she'd expected to be.

Her mind circled frantically, trying to piece together the events of the previous night.

Alex, waiting for her outside Dr. Gill's office.

Her drive to his casino, excitement buzzing through her along the way.

The sensual feast that he had waiting for her . . . the delicious wine . . .

His dungeon.

Maddy sat straight up as she remembered, in vivid detail, that strange room at the end of the locked hallway. Her heart began to race.

She didn't entirely know what she'd gotten herself into. Things between them had progressed much faster than she'd ever expected.

Warily, she glanced down at the man who was fast asleep beside her. Heat flushed her skin as she saw the intimate way his hand was curled over her thigh, as she looked down the length of him and remembered the feeling of him inside of her.

He was naked, and last night she had touched every bit of

his naked self. He had touched her. He had brought her outside of herself in the pleasure they found together.

It was so incredibly new for her.

Holding her breath, Maddy removed his hand from her thigh gently. He muttered a bit, then rolled onto his back, still fast asleep. It was so tempting to bend over, to wake him with lips pressed to the pulse just below his jaw.

But the part of her that was not at all happy to be out of comfortable surroundings trumped the one that was so drawn to this beautiful, enigmatic man, and so she slid out of bed as quietly as she could.

His breathing changed, and Maddy froze, but it was only for a moment, and then he settled back into a deep sleep.

Whatever his dreams held—and truthfully, though he had been inside of her, she had no idea what they were—they were clearly better than hers.

Swallowing against the hard lump that lodged itself in her throat, Maddy clutched a hand to her naked breasts and scanned the room for her clothing. She knew that it was silly to feel exposed when the only other person in the room was sound asleep, but she did regardless.

Her clothes were lying on the floor, right where she'd dropped them the night before. She could feel herself blushing as she stooped to pick up the shorts and simple T-shirt.

She'd let herself get carried away with Alex. And though the sensible thing to do would be to accept this for what it was—a night of surprisingly good sex—she already knew that she wanted to do it again. But she had to remember her job was waiting, her therapist was waiting, and so was her bucket list.

She needed some time, some space away from the all-consuming presence of Alex to gather herself together.

Maddy raked a hand through her sex-snarled hair and

turned to take one last look at him. God, but he was gorgeous. He almost hurt her eyes.

And even sound asleep, he radiated power. Dominance.

He scared the shit out of her, even as she wanted him desperately.

"Thank you." Maddy whispered the words to the slumbering man as she left his bedroom. She would call him later—she didn't think she'd be able to stay away—but right at that moment, she needed some space.

Steeling herself, Maddy turned to head down the hallway to the front entrance of the penthouse. No doubt it had some fancy security on it that she would have no idea how to get around, but she was sure that Declan or someone was around somewhere. She doubted that a man as rich as Alex cleaned his own toilets.

"Hmm." Her feet refused to move. She furrowed her brow as, instead of heading to the front door, she found herself walking to the closed door of the dungeon.

Her heart skipped a beat as she ran her fingers over the smooth metal handle. It was locked. She was sure it was locked. But she tried just the same—she couldn't seem to help herself.

The door opened. Maddy gasped as she all but fell into the room, only barely catching herself.

It looked different in the daylight. Less sensual, more . . . well, she didn't really have a word to describe what it looked like.

How did one describe something like this? Lost for words, she pushed the door shut behind her until only a sliver of light from the hallway showed through, then wandered across the floor aimlessly, trying to take in her surroundings without the distracting presence of Alex.

The shelf on the far side of the black-and-gray room seemed like a good place to start. Her steps were hesitant, even without anyone there to see her. But for heaven's sake, she was heading toward a shelf that held . . . obscure things. Devices of torture. It was just slightly surreal.

Her eyes flicked over the different . . . she didn't even know what to call them. Instruments? Maddy supposed that word would do as well as any other. Vibrators. Well, she knew what those were for, even if it had been years since she'd owned one. Something that looked kind of like a spatula, but with a long, flexible handle. A leather . . . Surely that wasn't a feather duster. In fact, she had a good idea what that one might be for, and it made her pulse skitter. Hastily, she moved on down the shelf, her eyes open and, though wary, still greedy for information.

There was an open black box that held a handful of silicone pieces shaped like elongated lightbulbs. There was a big pottery dish of things that looked like clothespins, but with sparkly stones hanging off one end. There was a leather strap with a silver ring holding a black rubber ball centered in the strip and a pair of heavy-looking silver globes the size of golf balls.

Handcuffs. She knew what those were for, too, though she'd never used them. An image of herself cuffed to the bed that she'd just scrambled out of made her blush.

Great coils of rope hung on the walls, all different lengths and widths. Their pale straw color broke up the deep gray color of the walls, much, Maddy imagined, as a whip would mark skin.

The image suffused her with heat. The whips hung next to the ropes, a full dozen of them.

Her eyes strayed to the big wooden X that stood in the center of the room. There were silver restraints at each tip of the X, and since she wasn't stupid, she knew what they were for.

"Shit." She couldn't ignore the interest that she was feeling. Maddy shook her head, squeezed her eyes tightly shut for a long moment, then moved quickly to the sideways cross.

The wood was dark and highly polished. Tentatively, she reached out and ran her fingers over it. It was smooth and cool.

She could imagine what it would feel like against her back, her arms, and her legs. Although she wanted to deny it, the daydream she was entertaining was . . . exciting. Arousing. As was the thought of one of those whips flicking against her skin, held in Alex's powerful grasp.

Maddy gasped out loud at the thought, then chastised herself just as quickly.

"If something like this excites you, Stone, then Dr. Gill has more work to do than she thinks." Maddy muttered the words, then, shoring up her resolve, decided that for the sake of her mental health, she needed to go.

She turned only to shriek when she found a large, masculine frame mere inches behind her. She slapped out with both hands, and the figure caught her wrists and held her tightly in place.

"Easy, Maddy." Alex slid his hands from Maddy's wrists up to her shoulders, and electricity followed in his wake. Though she was dressed, Maddy was still bedroom eyed, her hair tousled, and he could smell the musk of sleep clinging to her skin.

He had woken just in time to see her wavy ribbons of hair slip out the door of the bedroom. Guessing where she'd wind up, he'd taken his time pulling on a pair of printed navy pajama bottoms, the drawstring holding them up just below his hip bones.

The little doe looked mortified, and he thoroughly enjoyed the accompanying blush.

"I . . ." Maddy stuttered. He wasn't going to ask her to explain herself, though he couldn't quite suppress the knowing grin.

She was intrigued by this room, by the idea of BDSM—by him.

He wasn't alone in his desire.

"It's not wrong, what you're feeling." It pissed Alex off to see the hint of shame in Maddy's expression as she studied his face. Though mainstream society certainly said differently, the BDSM lifestyle wasn't anything to be ashamed of. Nor was it about a man needing to hit a woman or about a woman needing a man because she couldn't think for herself, or any of the dozens of other stereotypes that existed.

Some people simply had different needs, needs that couldn't be satisfied by bland sexual relations. It wasn't wrong; it was just different.

He knew from past experience, though, that he could tell her that until he ran out of breath, but ultimately it was something she would have to discover for herself.

Clearly wrestling with her conflicting shame and desire, Maddy groaned out loud and shut her eyes.

When she opened her eyes again, peeking up at him, Alex couldn't help but smile. "This is pretty heavy talk for first thing in the morning, Maddy." He removed his hands from her shoulders and took her hand.

Her face showed surprised. She tugged a bit, but he simply laced his fingers in hers and pulled her toward the door.

"Alex." When she said his name, so intimately, it felt like a caress on his skin. He paused, turning back to find her looking at him with an intent stare.

Tentatively, she rose up on her tiptoes until she could brace her hands against his chest.

Lifting her chin, she brushed a kiss over the line of his jaw. Heat began to coil in his gut as she moved her lush, moist lips up until they brushed over his.

"Fuck, Maddy." He closed his eyes and groaned as she tentatively explored his mouth, her tongue tracing the seam of his lips as she grew bolder.

She was a brave one. He had shown her his dungeon, and instead of running, she was chasing the thrill.

"Maddy, wait." It nearly killed him, but he reached up and caught her wrists in his hands. Allowing himself to savor one final brush of her mouth over his, he pulled back, bending down to press a kiss into her soft, warm hair, then pulled her out into the hall.

"There will be plenty of time to explore each other, Maddy. But right now you need some time to think."

As the door snicked shut behind them, she felt as though they'd left Neverland and arrived back in reality. Maddy blinked in the brighter light of the hallway.

Her eyes adjusted to the light, and she felt the desire of moments before replaced with irritation and uncertainty. "Did I do something wrong?"

Before she could even take another breath, Alex had her pressed against the wall, one hand caught in her hair, tugging her head back to expose her throat. He trailed a line of hot kisses over the skin, ones that left her weak in the knees. At the same time, he took her hand and, sliding it between their bodies, pressed her palm against the length of his erection.

"You've done everything just right, Maddy." When her hand squeezed involuntarily, he arched into the touch. "I'm trying to be a gentleman here."

"I'm sorry." Her voice was contrite. "I'm also sorry I went into your—room." She blurted out the apology before he could get mad at her, though she still wasn't about to call it a dungeon. It sounded absurd. Normal people didn't have dungeons in their homes.

Nothing about Alex was normal.

He eyed her with speculation, and with a hand placed at the small of her back, ushered her down the hallway.

"I left the door unlocked on purpose, Maddy. I hoped you'd be curious to go back and explore."

She inhaled deeply; she'd thought she was off the hook, and instead he'd gotten her right where he wanted her.

Alex Fraser was going to be a hard man to say no to—she doubted that he heard the word very often. But this was wrong on so many levels. A man like him didn't belong with a woman like her, for starters. Then there was the whole reality of her life, which, while slowly getting better, was still a tangle of strings where there had once been a tapestry.

Alex's lifestyle was only going to make that tangle tighter, not coax the strings back into their proper place.

"I've got to go, Alex." At the end of the hall, by the front entryway, Maddy turned to face him, though she didn't meet his eyes. He was wearing those glasses of his again, and he looked so sexy in them that it broke her concentration. He hadn't done anything to make her feel embarrassed, but still, this was the second time she'd all but thrown herself at him and he'd rejected her. "Thank you . . . um, thank you."

How did one say goodbye in this kind of relationship . . . or whatever this thing between them was? She almost felt as though she should hold out her hand and offer to shake.

She settled for stooping to grab her purse, which was tucked under the table in the entryway.

"I should spank you for trying to sneak out."

Maddy dropped the purse she'd just picked up and stood abruptly as the words shocked all sense right out of her. She looked straight into his eyes, and her mouth fell open.

"I beg your pardon?" She tried to put some frost into her words—he'd just told her he wanted to *spank* her—but she couldn't find the chill. No, instead his words made her think of his hand across her bare bottom, striking her until her flesh turned pink from his touch.

She wanted it. She craved it.

She was going insane.

"You heard me." Damn it, he *knew* what kind of pull he had over her. "I'm glad you went exploring, little one. I'm not glad that you tried to sneak away without an explanation or a good-bye. If you were my submissive, that kind of behavior would have me turning you over my knee."

Maddy tried to mask her face into indignation. She was fairly certain that she didn't succeed.

"That doesn't make me any more inclined to accept your offer, Alex." She didn't like being chastised like a child, but damn it, she still couldn't help the sensation that his words had wrought.

What was *wrong* with her?

"I think it does, Maddy." Like a predator sensing weakness, Alex stepped closer to her, until there was only a sliver of space between them. She swallowed hard, trying to keep her thoughts clear when all she could see, all she could smell, was him.

"I think you like the idea of being punished, very much. I think it excites you, just the same way that the thought of punishing you excites me. Why are you denying it, when it would bring so much delight to both of us?"

Maddy looked up at him, feeling her eyes go wide. His stare fastened on her lips, and he leaned down. She knew he was going to kiss her—she hoped he would—but when he touched her, she couldn't *think*.

"No." Maddy backed away from him rapidly, needing some air. She knew she'd never make it past the security system of his front door, so she backpedaled to the kitchen. It was a big mistake, because when she saw the enormous island in the middle of the room, all she could think of was the sensual feast of the night before, of Alex feeding her with such care. He followed, and she wondered if his words were a prelude, if he was actually going to do it.

"You can't. You won't." Maddy backed up until the small of her back hit the edge of the island. Her fingers scrabbled for purchase on the slick tile. "I'm a grown woman. You can't spank me!"

"I could." This time he gave her some space, staying just out of her reach. She found that she was a bit disappointed.

"But you won't." Maddy tried to make her words assertive. She fell flat.

To her surprise, he nodded in agreement. "But I won't." He echoed her words. "I won't, because you haven't signed my agreement yet. But I have hope."

Then, as if they had been discussing nothing more than the weather, he moved to a sleek-looking phone that was mounted on the wall. "I'm going to place my order for breakfast. What would you like?"

She blinked, thrown completely off balance, even more so than before.

"Alex, I'm not eating breakfast. I need to go." Now she was getting irritated. Being persistent was one thing, but . . .

He raised an eyebrow at her, then spoke into the receiver. He seemed to be calling either a housekeeper or one of the restaurants downstairs, someone who knew who he was, because he didn't identify himself, just asked for two of the usual.

"No matter how sexy you look in those damned pajama pants, you can't just completely ignore what I want, Alex!" Maddy bit her tongue when she realized what she'd said.

He grinned at her, at ease in his skin. "You think I'm sexy, huh?"

She stared down at the fingers that she'd twisted together,

her face turning red. "Obviously." Clearly she would never have let him do . . . well . . . everything, if she didn't think so. "And don't ignore what I said."

"I'm not ignoring you, Maddy. I will never ignore you." Placing the phone back in its mount, he looked at her, and she felt suddenly certain that she was the only thing on his mind right at that moment.

It was humbling.

It was terrifying.

"Then why do you keep doing what you want, no matter what I say?" Alex moved closer, and she thought, again, that he was about to kiss her. Instead he clasped her by her hips, lifting her until she was perched on the counter. He stood in front of her, and their eyes were nearly level as they looked at each other.

"Because I'm doing what you actually want, not what you think you want."

A strangled sound escaped Maddy's lips when his words sank in. What an arrogant ass. She opened her mouth to tell him so, but he ran a finger over her lips to quiet her and continued to speak.

"You're warring with yourself. That's not uncommon in submissives who aren't familiar with this kind of relationship."

Maddy's mouth fell open a little bit farther, and she glared at him. Submissive? Like hell she was submissive.

"Somehow, somewhere along the way, this kind of relationship came to be seen as taboo by the rest of the world. Twisted. Wrong."

She narrowed her eyes further and crossed her arms over her chest. He was describing her life, at least the way her life was before he came into it.

"But some of us just need a bit more than the vanilla world can offer. Nothing wrong with that, so I'm not surprised that you're confused about that." With one finger placed under her chin, he tilted her head up so that he could look her in the eyes. "But there's something more here, something you haven't told me. If you sign the agreement, you *will* tell me. You'll have to, or I can't help."

Maddy sputtered, furious, confused, and needy all wrapped into one giant bundle. How had he pegged her so well and yet gotten her so wrong?

"What agreement?" These were the only words that she could spit out. She shoved everything else away, to examine later.

Once she was alone.

"We'll talk about that after breakfast." He was as smooth and unruffled as ever. He was so . . . sure of himself.

She had no doubt that when he took charge, she wouldn't have to think about a thing, because he would be entirely in control. He would take care of her.

"How was last night for you?"

Oh, he just wouldn't give up. Maddy shifted uncomfortably at Alex's words. Last night was . . . well, it was a lot of things, things that she wasn't certain of.

Things that made her nervous.

Plus really, really amazing.

"Alex, I do need to go." She slid down from her perch on the counter, nervousness slicing through her veins like a thousand tiny knives. She'd never been so torn. Half of her, the part that she knew as well as she knew her own features, was shrieking at her to leave, to get as far away from this unfamiliar situation as she could possibly get.

The other half, which was nearly as loud, wanted her to sign whatever agreement he had, right then and there. Maddy couldn't deny that she wanted what he offered, craved the release that he'd already nudged her into grabbing hold of.

Alex studied her, his expression intent. He wasn't as inscrutable as she thought a man of his temperament would have been; rather, his emotions were displayed on his face, easy to read unless he was trying to hide them.

What she saw now was that he was as conflicted as she was herself. He wanted her to stay, but she didn't think he wanted to push her farther than she could go.

Maddy sighed inwardly. Even if he were to push, she wouldn't snap. She'd been through so much already.

Then she watched as a look of understanding passed over Alex's face. In the blink of an eye, he transformed from the compassionate man who was trying to understand her internal struggle to someone . . . strong. Someone in control.

"Maddy, I want you to eat some breakfast. You need to take care of yourself." His tone indicated to her that this wasn't a request. After a long moment in which she bristled at the demand, she relaxed in one big shudder, as if the tension that had been holding her taut for the last long months had suddenly snapped.

Yes. Yes, she liked this. Someone taking control of her scattered, wayward self, because heaven knew that she hadn't been doing such a good job of it herself.

"I—" She wanted to submit. She did, but it wasn't as easy as all that.

"All right, then," Alex muttered as if to himself, studying her as if he were committing something to memory. Then he crushed her against his chest and captured her lips with his.

Maddy was caught entirely off guard, and her worries were incinerated as he splayed one hand flat against her back, the other on her ass, pressing her into him until she felt like they might melt together. Her hands were trapped between their bodies, flat against the rock-solid expanse of his bare chest.

Bending his neck, he slanted his lips over hers, coaxing her lips into parting for the bold sweep of his tongue.

She couldn't remember what she'd been nervous about or

why she was upset. She couldn't think at all. She was consumed by heat, dominated by Alex, until all she could do was feel the pleasure he was introducing to her.

"That's better." His words were rough and vibrated along the line of her jaw when every last bit of defiance evaporated beneath his onslaught.

His hands moved to capture her waist, urging her closer. She could feel him grow hard beneath the press of their flesh, and the knowledge that she was arousing him was both surreal and exciting.

Tentatively, Maddy slid her hands from his chest and up, to stroke over his shoulders. The physical act took her straight back to the night before, when in the matter of a moment he had made her forget that she'd never much cared for sex.

"Good girl." His hands squeezed once, tightly, at her hips, then slid over her belly and between her legs. "Let it go. You don't have to hold on to control when I'm here. I've got you."

Maddy's knees buckled when he undid the button of her shorts and then the zipper with deft fingers. She was bare beneath, not having had a spare pair of clean panties with her when she'd left for the casino the night before.

"I won't let you fall." He slid a finger through her folds. Maddy was startled to find that she was already damp. Her hips moved involuntarily, pressing into his touch.

He made her forget.

"Alex." Her fingers scrabbled at the impossibly hard muscles of his shoulders. "Now. Please." If he didn't take her now, if he didn't fill that aching hole inside of her with his heat, then the panic would come back.

"Not yet." A dismayed cry slipped from between Maddy's lips, but it was swallowed in another scorching kiss. At the same time, Alex shoved her shorts down her hips. They fell to the floor as he tugged her shirt and her bra up over her head and off.

"Step out." He kicked her shorts away, then backed her up until the edge of the solid wooden table hit her just below the curve of her buttocks. She startled a little as the cool, glossy wood pressed against her feverish skin.

"Lie back." Maddy hesitated for a moment, self-conscious— he'd managed to get her entirely naked, while he was still fully clothed. She felt . . . vulnerable.

"Maddy." The look on his face told her that he expected her to do it. Again, she felt the slight anger at being told what to do, and again it was quickly followed by relief.

Is this what it would be like all the time? she wondered as, hesitantly, she settled herself back on the smooth expanse of the kitchen table. The corners of Alex's lips turned up with pleasure as she obeyed his command, and she found herself inexorably happy to have pleased him.

What was *wrong* with her? She tried to push herself back up onto her elbows.

She had issues, yes, and she had grief. But she'd gotten through it all, more or less, hadn't she? She was strong. And strong women didn't enjoy being bossed around.

"Alex, this isn't—" His pants were undone and he was spreading her thighs farther apart. He settled himself between her legs, then pulled a condom from the pocket of his pants, which were hanging loosely around his hips.

"Maddy, let yourself enjoy it." His voice was firm. With one hand, he stroked over the crease that divided her leg from her belly; with the other, he lifted the foil packet to his teeth and pulled until the wrapping ripped.

Oh God. It was going to happen again. Heat washed over her in a tremendous wave at the thought of being filled in the way that only he had ever filled her.

"Maddy, it's okay to let me be in control." Taking the base of his newly sheathed cock in his fingers, he settled the head of his erection against her entrance. Her hips rose, urging him to slide inside.

"Alex, oh yes."

His hands instead slid to her breasts, caressing her nipples, pulling at them, arousing and holding Maddy in place at the same time.

"I want to be in control. I need it. And if that lets you lose control for a while, with me, in a safe place, then there's nothing at all wrong with what we're doing."

Maddy frowned, trying to wrap her head around his words through the thick fog of lust that crowded her mind, when he pressed forward, easing into her bit by delicious bit.

"Ahh," she cried out, biting her lip. There was that same delicious stretching sensation, waking all the nerves in its path. There was also some discomfort, because he hadn't been gentle last night, not that she'd been complaining at the time.

"Shh." Alex stilled, letting her adjust. When she could feel the muscles that were clenching him so tightly relax, just the tiniest bit, he slid the rest of the way home, sheathing himself inside of her.

"It's not enough." Maddy reached up for him blindly, clinging to the final threads of control that she couldn't seem to let go of. "Alex, please, give me more."

He understood what she was asking. His expression became darker, more intense, and his fingers stopped their lazy caress to pinch, hard.

"Alex!" Maddy's voice was nearly a scream. In only a few minutes he'd brought a primal desire out of her very core. She was frantic, desperate for this strange ache to be assuaged.

"Hold on."

Her fingers searched for the edges of the island and clung tightly as he drew nearly all the way out of her heat. When he slammed back in, sheathing himself entirely in her tight passage, she shuddered.

It hurt, because he was too big and she was sore. But then he started to thrust in and out, hard and fast, and the pain was replaced with need so acute that it was almost an ache.

"Alex." For a woman who had never before enjoyed sex, this was insane. There hadn't been any foreplay, he was just a bit rough, and yet she felt like an animal. She wanted to lose herself in him.

Maddy watched through half-shuttered lids as he seated himself inside her again and again. She loved that it was her, her body, that was bringing him such pleasure. Yes, bringing him pleasure—and her, too. She could feel everything inside of her coiling tighter and tighter still.

Alex slid one hand from Maddy's hip and between her slick folds, right above the place where his cock was claiming her. He pinched her clit between his thumb and forefinger and rubbed back and forth.

She tried to close her legs against the onslaught of pleasure. It was too much. As she pressed her legs against his hips, he moved faster, and she settled for closing her eyes.

"Look at me." Maddy's eyes snapped back open at the command. She didn't even think of disobeying. "Look right at me. Now."

Her blue eyes met his.

"Come for me, Maddy." As if he had commanded it, the tight spiral of pleasure unfurled in a wild, potent burst.

Maddy cried out, her voice full of wonder even to her own ears.

Alex was the first man to ever make her come.

Once her wave had receded back to shore, once he had milked every last bit of pleasure out of the moment for her, Alex thrust one last time inside of her, and he groaned as her heat sheathed him to the hilt, urging him on to his own release.

They lay still for a moment, and Maddy could hear the sounds of their breath, mingled together in the quiet air of Alex's kitchen. As with last night, in this, the aftermath of what he had drawn out of her, her mind was clear. Her emotions were clean. It was a glorious sensation, and she clutched at it greedily, this brief moment of peace.

Alex leaned over Maddy, his cheek resting against her stomach. When, finally, he pulled away, slipped out of her to dispose of the condom, she sat up, the tile pulling uncomfortably at the skin of her back as she did.

As usual, Alex was the picture of self-possession as he moved to the sink and threw the used latex into the trash hidden beneath. Maddy was far more awkward, sliding off the island on shaky legs, then dressing herself in yesterday's clothing yet one more time.

Who was this woman who had taken over her body? She didn't do things like this.

"Here." Maddy looked up from fastening the zipper of her shorts. Alex was holding out both a tall glass of iced water and a sheath of papers.

"Thank you." She took the water gratefully; the encounter had left her throat dry and her mouth feeling like cotton.

The papers she accepted with a bit more wariness. "What is this?"

Alex smiled, that wicked smile that reminded her that he knew exactly how much she wanted him.

"Information for you."

Maddy's eyes widened and her breath hitched. Damn it, how did he know? How did he know that, despite all of the protests that sounded so valid to her own ears, she was truly intrigued by what he was offering her?

Her wonder was threaded through with irritation. "What makes you assume that, after all the times I've told you that I can't do this, I will anyway?"

Alex raised an eyebrow. Damn it, but those glasses perched on the end of his nose were hot.

"Part of a Dominant's job is to know what his sub needs."

Maddy groaned with frustration. "Alex, I'm not your sub. I don't even know what that means." She needed to get out of there. When she was around him, he encompassed her entire being. She wasn't rational. "And since I've told you so many times that this isn't what I want, I think you must just be hearing what *you* want to hear."

Alex's expression grew more serious, and grasping her arm with one hand, he pulled her to him, quick and hard.

"You're the one who isn't listening, Maddy." She sucked in a startled breath when he slipped his hand beneath the waistband of the shorts that she'd just refastened. His fingers trailed down the plane of her stomach, then slid into the folds that were still damp. "I didn't say this was what you wanted. I said it was what you needed. And as for how I know, this is how."

He pulled his hand from between her legs and lifted his fingers between their faces. Maddy could see them shining with wetness, and she squirmed with embarrassment.

"You want me. I want you. We each have something that the other needs. It doesn't have to be any more complicated than that." Her mouth fell open with shock when he ran his tongue lightly over the fingers that had just been inside her. He smirked at her shocked expression.

She felt herself scowl despite her intense attraction to him. "I haven't signed that . . . that agreement thing you talked about yet. And I might not." She expected to see disappointment on his face.

Instead he grinned. "I can hope. In the meantime, I find I have a taste for vanilla."

Maddy was sure the resultant thump of her heart was audible. Then he continued, and that same heart sank all the way to her toes with nerves and anticipation.

"Unless you glower at me like that again. Then you're in for a decidedly nonvanilla spanking. I'm looking forward to it."

Maddy stared at him for a full ten seconds, trying to wrap her head around what he had just said. When he again smirked, she decided to preserve what was left of her dignity.

She left.

CHAPTER EIGHT

t wasn't until she closed the door of her apartment behind her and sagged back against it with relief that Maddy found herself able to draw in a full breath.

What had she gotten herself into?

The sheath of papers that Alex had foisted on her was clutched tightly in her right hand. Though she was tempted to start reading right away, she instead laid them down on her kitchen table, smoothing out the crinkles made by her damp palm.

His scent clung to her clothes, her skin. It was distracting her.

Her shower was brief and hot. She had expected it to wash away the sensation of his hands on her body, of his lips on her own, to help her get her bearings. It did erase his scent, leaving her smelling of her own lavender soap and rosemary shampoo, but the ghost of his touch lingered.

It was as if he had branded her . . . had already begun to possess her. She wasn't entirely comfortable with the idea, and yet, as she combed her wet hair into a slick ponytail and pulled on stretchy yoga shorts and a loose tank top, she found her thoughts stayed stuck on the image of him thrusting inside of her again and again.

Circling around the stack of papers that were screaming at her to be read, Maddy brewed a pot of coffee and put a slice of bread in the toaster. She had left before Alex could force-feed her, and though she wrinkled her nose at the thought, she knew that he had been right.

She was starving. She'd had a lot more exercise than usual over the last twenty-four hours.

Her phone beeped with an incoming text. Maddy picked it up, smiled when she saw that it was from Alex.

> READING ANYTHING INTERESTING?

> WELL . . . I'M NOT SAYING NO. YET.

> I WILL SEND DECLAN FOR YOU TOMORROW NIGHT
> AT 7:00 P.M.

Maddy knew that she should have expected it, but she was still speechless. Give the man an inch and all that. She waited for the irritation to hit her, but as she chewed on her lower lip, she found that, actually, she liked his confidence.

The phone rang, vibrating against Maddy's palm and startling her from her thoughts. She stared at it for a moment, then flipped it over to see the call display. Her pulse was fast, and her breath came rapid and shallow.

Maybe it was Alex.

When she saw the name displayed on the screen of the cell, though, her heart sank and her stomach clenched.

> HUDSON, NATHAN.

"Phone. Right. Answer the phone, Maddy." Her sense of guilt was so strong that she couldn't do anything else, even though she knew that the rest of her day was now going to be agony.

Well, she deserved it.

"Hi, Nate."

"Maddy!" Though the voice on the other end of the line was friendly and familiar, every muscle in her body felt stretched taut. "It's been too long."

"It has been a long time." For Maddy it was never too long.

Nathan didn't blame her, never would if she knew him, but that didn't matter when she blamed herself.

"So how's Paradise?"

She heard Nathan swallow. She could picture him, leaning against the counter in the house they had all shared, his battered green mug full of scalding black coffee.

Except he wasn't at that house. None of them—Nathan, Erin, Maddy—lived there anymore.

"Oh, you know. Another day in Paradise. What else would it be?" Maddy managed a dry laugh. She had chosen Paradise, Nevada, to run to because she had been wryly amused by the irony of the city's name.

"Still waitressing?" Nathan's tone was light, but she knew that he disapproved of some of the choices she'd made, even though he would never tell her so.

"You know I am." She didn't want to talk about herself. "How's the gallery going?"

The diversion worked. Sounding excited, her sister's former fiancé told Maddy all about the details of the business that he had started a few years earlier, when they had all shared a house. He was a woodworker, made incredible pieces of art from wood, and had started the gallery to showcase his own work, though it had expanded from there.

Inevitably, of course, he circled back to her. The man was amiable, even sweet, but under the teddy bear demeanor was a steel resolve.

"Maddy, how long are you going to lock yourself away in exile?"

Maddy's jaw snapped closed so abruptly that her teeth bit into her tongue. The warm, bitter taste of blood filled her mouth. "I'm not in exile, Nathan." Though he'd made a habit of checking in on her since she'd moved away, he'd never come right out and asked her anything that pointed before.

"What else would you call it?"

Maddy scowled even as her fingers found the locket that she never took off. She stroked the polished metal, looking for comfort and finding none.

"I'm . . . I just . . . I needed a change, okay?" Her words were defensive. Of all people, Nathan was the one she owed explanations, apologies, recriminations.

But when she'd offered all of that time and time again, what else was there to give?

"A change." She'd poked the sleeping bear. Irritation colored the voice of the man she'd considered her brother-in-law, though her sister and he never had a chance to marry. "Right. Leaving your family, abandoning your career . . . You were just looking for a change. Not running away at all."

"I was an optician, Nathan." Maddy cringed as she said it. "There are lots of us around. And I like what I'm doing. There's nothing wrong with it."

She was defensive, but damn it, he was starting to make her mad, which was exactly the opposite of what she wanted. Why couldn't *he* just be mad at *her*? If he could just be mad at her, furious even, if they could have one big knockdown, drag-out fight where he told her that he blamed her as much as she blamed herself for her sister's death. And then maybe she could begin to move on.

But instead Nathan Hudson was nothing but kind, nothing but loving and forgiving.

"You serve bacon and eggs to truckers, Maddy." Nathan's voice was flat. "And there's nothing wrong with that, except that it's not what you actually want to do. But if you want to hide away out in the desert, away from your family, denying yourself the right to live a full life, then I guess it's your business."

"Damn straight it's my business." The feelings that swam rapidly to the surface were mottled, mixed, but manifested in anger. "And I can't run away from my family when none of them are left!"

Silence was thick as soup. Maddy realized what she'd said and hastily backtracked.

"Nathan . . . I didn't . . . I mean . . ." Oh, what a fuckup she was. She'd just said the worst thing she possibly could have to the one person who *was*, for all intents and purposes, all the family that she had left.

"Yeah, well, I guess that would be what they call a Freudian slip." Gone was the teddy bear; in his place was a man with all the bitterness that Maddy had thought she wanted to hear.

She'd been wrong.

"Erin was the one who died in that car accident, Maddy, but for all the effort you're putting into life, it might as well have been you."

It took her nearly a full day to work up the nerve to do what she knew she needed to.

I CAN'T DO IT. I'M SORRY.

Biting down on her lip, Maddy hesitated before hitting send on the message to Alex. When she finally did, she felt as though she had been punched in the gut.

THAT'S IT? EXPLAIN, PLEASE.

Feeling sick, Maddy scrolled to her contact list and very deliberately deleted Alex from it, then dropped the phone in her small locker. The staff room in the back of the diner was freezing, or maybe it was just her, so she pulled the black cardigan that she kept at work over her shoulders before heading out to start her shift.

"Hey, Maddy." Susannah looked eager to be going. "It's been slow. I bet you'll have a quiet night."

Damn it. Maddy wanted to be run off her feet. She wanted to be distracted.

Instead she found herself rolling flatware into napkins, berating herself for pursuing anything with Alex, for the accident, for life in general.

"Get a grip!" she chided herself as she dropped yet another set of flatware. It clattered to the floor, and she glared at it.

She couldn't help it. She was so damn mad . . . mad at everything.

She had spent the previous afternoon and evening in a state of numbness that was unfortunately all too familiar to her. Talking to Nathan had that effect on her.

No matter what he said, what he did, she couldn't face the thought of being around him. The phone calls were bad enough.

The car wreck that had killed her sister had been unavoidable, so said the emergency responders. Unavoidable, however, didn't mean no fault, and Maddy had been driving.

More than that, she had walked away with a few cuts and bruises.

Erin hadn't walked away at all.

Maddy had learned to simply hide the guilt from most people, even from Dr. Gill, whose primary job was just to help her function from day to day. But she held her guilt tightly to her, knowing that she deserved every agonizing minute of it.

That was why she'd reneged on her date with Alex. She might have been drawn to the punishment aspect of what he offered her, but she didn't deserve to find satisfaction even in that.

With a shaky sigh, Maddy loaded a rubber bin with the rolls of cutlery. She knew that Alex, the man used to getting everything he wanted, was not going to be impressed with her. In fact, it was a good thing that she'd left her cell phone in her locker, because she imagined that he was texting and calling, demanding an explanation.

He made her so weak in the knees, she wasn't sure that she could ignore him for very long. More than that, she thought— no, she *knew*—that she wasn't going to be able to stay strong in the face of his arguments.

"He wouldn't understand," Maddy mumbled as she reminded herself of why she was cutting him off. He couldn't possibly understand the demons that she held inside of her, and what was more, she had no desire to share them. They were her burden, no one else's.

"Are you answering yourself, too? If you are, we're in trouble."

Maddy felt the warmth of a large hand on her shoulder and looked up to find Joe standing next to her, his eyes crinkled with concern.

She laughed weakly, turning away so that he wouldn't see the despair that she knew was painted over her features. "Not out loud, I'm not, so that's something." She hefted the tub of silverware to the back counter, where it was kept once it had been filled.

When she turned back, she saw something that she didn't quite recognize in Joe's eyes.

"That rich guy you've been seeing... he hasn't done anything to you, has he?" Joe glared, looking like he wanted nothing more than to punch Alex in the jaw.

"God, no." Maddy barked out a laugh. Probably not wise to punch a man who owned an entire roomful of instruments of possible pleasure, possible torture. "No, he... we're not... hmm."

There wasn't any way to phrase it without making Joe angry and indignant on her behalf. What could she say, after all? *No, he hasn't done anything to me, except make me realize how much I do like sex—sex with him, anyway. And after he made me come more times in one evening than I have in years, he showed me his dungeon and told me that he wants me to be his love slave.*

Maddy's boss was a mild-mannered kind of guy most of the time, but she was pretty sure that he wouldn't care to hear any of that. No, he wouldn't like that at all.

"You're not seeing him?" Joe's voice grew warmer, and he took a step toward her. Uh-oh. Warily, she eyed the hand that reached out to touch her shoulder. She thought he meant it to be a comforting touch, but had her confession changed things a bit in his mind?

Though she wasn't usually the kind of woman men were interested in, Maddy would have to have been blind to miss the signals that were suddenly emanating from her boss's body.

For a long moment, she wished, wished hard, that she could have been interested in Joe. It would have been so much simpler. Joe was so blessedly normal. With him, maybe, she could learn to live with what she felt about herself.

Then Alex's face swam before her eyes, and she knew that it wasn't even a little bit possible.

"Joe . . . I'm not really seeing anyone right now. Deliberately," Maddy added as the interest in Joe's green eyes intensified.

"I see." The hand on her shoulder squeezed after a long hesitation, and then he let go. "Well. I'm going to head back to the kitchen."

She thought he was a bit embarrassed about the blatant interest that he'd just showed in her, and she forced her lips to curve up into a reassuring smile. "Okay. It's so slow. It's going to be a long night, so come out and chat when you can."

The relief on his face was obvious. They would both just forget that that moment had ever happened. And maybe some pleasant company from a man whom she genuinely liked, one who didn't confuse her with every breath that he took, would help her sort through so many jumbled feelings that she didn't know how much longer she could hold them in.

"Tell them they can have a burger from the grill before I clean it, if they want, but everything else is put away!" Joe shouted this at Maddy from the kitchen, where he was closing up for the night, right after the bell over the glass door at the front of the diner jingled, announcing the entry of a new customer, five minutes to closing.

Frustration washed over her. She hated it when people did this. Their hours were clearly marked outside the diner—in neon, no less. Just because their doors were unlocked at five to midnight didn't mean that it was a great time to come on in and order a meal.

The customer was *not* always right, but Maddy pasted a smile on her face anyway, turning toward the noise.

"Alex." Surreptitiously, she pinched herself. Ouch. Yes, she was awake, and Alex Fraser, the billionaire who would not be deterred, was in the tiny diner where she worked, yet again.

"Madeline." His voice was frosty, and goose bumps skittered along her skin. He wasn't happy with her, understandably so. But . . . why was he here, then?

The word *discipline* flashed through her mind, and heat pooled low in her belly. As if he could sense it, the corners of Alex's lips lifted in the palest ghost of a smile.

"What are you doing here?" Nervously, Maddy ran a hand over her hair. It had gone frizzy from the heat of the kitchen. She was suddenly painfully aware that she must reek of French fry grease and that she'd spilled cola down the front of her apron.

Alex studied her so intently that she felt naked, which didn't help the clenching sensation between her legs.

"I've told you. I'm going to give you what you need. I'm only starting to learn what that is, but I do know that exploring yourself sexually is the key to relaxing you enough for me to find out."

"I don't see how you can know what I need when I don't even know myself!" Maddy's eyes widened as she realized what she'd said. Smiling as if she had pleased him greatly, Alex stepped forward, and the scent of his expensive cologne teased her nostrils and made her want to nibble on his earlobe.

"Well, there it is in a nutshell, Maddy. You need me because I will know what you need even when you don't."

She opened her mouth, then closed it again without speaking. What would she have said?

It would have been pointless to deny that Alex saw everything about her with uncanny clarity.

"Maddy?" She groaned out loud as Joe called out from the kitchen. "Everything all right?" Before she could reply, he was walking out from behind the counter.

When he saw Alex standing just inside the door to the diner, he came to stand directly behind her, planted his feet, crossed his arms over his chest, and scowled.

"What is he doing here?" Joe didn't hide behind even the pretense of friendliness. The belligerence in his stance told Maddy that he couldn't have cared less about being polite. He placed a possessive hand on her shoulder.

Maddy wanted to shrug it off, but she didn't want to make light of the fact that he was trying to protect her. "Joe!" She felt her cheeks flush at his overt rudeness. Why was he being so rude? He was her boss. He was a friend.

She thought of their conversation earlier in the evening.

Oh man.

Maddy looked at Alex, trying to gauge his reaction. On the surface, he seemed amused, but his jaw was clenched. He didn't like seeing Joe's hand on her.

"I would like to speak with you, Maddy. Alone. It's why I've come here." Alex raised his eyebrows contemptuously at Joe. This was only the second time the pair had ever met, but clearly it was hate at first sight.

"She's not done work yet."

Irritated, Maddy finally did shrug Joe's hand away and turned to frown at him. "Joe, I'm fine."

He looked as though she had struck him.

A wash of guilt flowed over her, but it quickly evaporated in the face of her irritation. There was nothing between them but friendship. There never had been. If he wanted that to change, there were better ways than by entering into a pissing contest in front of her.

"I thought you said you weren't seeing him."

Though it didn't seem possible, Maddy flushed even hotter, sneaking a glance at Alex on her way to looking at the floor. His face was expressionless. Somehow, not knowing what he was thinking made the situation worse.

"Joe, I've done everything up front except for the cash-out. May I go?" Maddy looked him straight in the eye as she spoke in a quiet voice.

His face registered disbelief. "Do what you want, Maddy," Joe finally answered after a long pause.

She could tell that he was disgusted, and it pissed her off. None of this was any of his business. She opened her mouth to tell him so, but she didn't want to create more fuss in front of Alex. "Thank you."

Trying not to let her shock show that he was here again, wearing a suit that surely cost him thousands of dollars, standing in the small greasy-spoon diner, Maddy tried to ignore the kick start that just looking at him gave her. "Let me just go grab my bag."

He nodded, shoving his hands deep into the pockets of his

trouser pants. "I'll wait right here." He scowled at Joe, who glared right back. The tension was so thick in the room that, despite the discomfort, she wanted to roll her eyes to the heavens.

Only so much testosterone could fit in one room, and the diner appeared to have reached its limit.

"Maybe you should wait in the car." She threw this over her shoulder as she scurried to the staff room, untying her apron as she went. She didn't trust the two of them alone together—she was afraid that if she took more than a few minutes to gather her belongings, they would go at each other like wolves fighting for dominance of the pack.

Hastily, Maddy pulled her purse and cell phone from her locker. Taking a moment to quickly check her messages, she was surprised to see that Alex hadn't texted her at all. From what she knew about him, that seemed strange, but she didn't have time to ponder it now. She hurried back to the dining room, where Joe was wiping down a table that she'd already cleaned. He was polishing the Formica with such vigor that Maddy wouldn't have been surprised to see a hole in the flat surface come morning.

Alex was standing exactly where she'd left him, watching Joe with just the slightest hint of distrust on his face.

" 'Night, Joe." Maddy offered a tight smile to her boss, even though she wasn't sure he deserved one, after his behavior. He nodded once, curtly, then returned to his table.

The smile slipped off her face. Fine. If he wanted to be like that, she would just leave him to it. Maddy looked at Alex quickly before pushing against the glass door of the diner, the bells tinkling merrily over her head.

Although there was no need for explanation, Alex pointed to the sleek vehicle, saying, "This is my car." Maddy didn't know anyone else who would park a sleek black Porsche Turbo there. "Where would you like to go?"

She eyed him warily. He seemed sincere. "I get to choose?" She'd thought he would have planned out the evening already.

He smiled faintly, though now that they were away from Joe and the macho act had been dropped, Maddy could see that he looked tired. "This time. So. The casino or your apartment?"

"My apartment." She didn't even have to consider. Her apartment was familiar. She was stronger there. Besides, he'd already seen that it was less than fabulous—there were no secrets.

"All right." Rounding the small car, he opened the passenger-side door, and after a belated moment, Maddy realized that he was holding it open for her.

"I need to drive. I'll take my own car." Alex scowled, but Maddy returned the expression. She wasn't budging.

"What is it with you and driving?"

"It's safer."

This was true, but Alex's face darkened. "You can trust me."

Though she didn't know why, Maddy somehow believed that she could. She hadn't known him long, but she'd always believed that the ticking of a clock wasn't a good measure of how well you could know someone.

Guilt was a little needle, pricking into the same soft skin over and over. "I think I can. But . . . I need to drive."

Before he could argue further, she unlocked the door to her own car, which was parked next to his phallic symbol on wheels. She grimaced when the hinges of her driver's door squeaked.

She turned her head to look at him before she turned over the ignition. Alex was still standing by his car, his arms crossed over his chest. But mixed in with his irritation was a hint of perplexity.

Maddy was pretty sure he wasn't used to anyone disagreeing with him.

Before she could overthink the worry that niggled at her for upsetting him, she shifted her car into drive and pulled out of the small gravel lot. The chill that she'd had since Nathan's phone call eased in the unexpectedly—even for Nevada—warm evening. As she drove the familiar route from the diner to her apartment, her mind wandered.

Joe. Before today, she never would have guessed that he had feelings of any sort for her. In fact, if he had let her know before she had ever met Alex, she might have reciprocated his interest—after a fashion, at least.

With Alex following her from two cars back, it was hard for Maddy to imagine him out of the picture. And that brought up her real dilemma.

He was a very persistent man and, truth was, he was wearing her down. She couldn't keep protesting when what he was offering was what her very soul craved. If only she could discuss her one final hang-up.

He had offered her punishment. For some reason, and Maddy assumed it had to do with her guilt over Erin's death, she thrilled to this idea. This translated into sexual need, though she couldn't fool herself into thinking that the punishment was all that was drawing her to Alex.

She had been plenty attracted to him before she'd seen his dungeon.

The flip side of the coin was . . . did she allow herself to accept this punishment, when it brought her pleasure at the same time?

In her gut, she felt the need to do penance. Sex with Alex Fraser did not fit into even the loosest of definitions of the word. So if she pursued a relationship with Alex, she would have to admit to herself that she was doing it for herself, seeking what she wanted, for a change.

Maddy's dingy, one-floor apartment building came into view. Time was up. She could already sense Alex's presence, invading her space, taking her attention as she parked and pressed damp palms to her jeans.

This was it. Go for it or not.

She had no idea what she was going to do.

The dry heat stole her breath as she closed the driver's door behind her. She watched Alex cross the lot toward her.

He was dressed entirely in black, his suit fitting him so well that it had to have been made especially for him. The black of his hair seemed to swallow the shine of the moonlight, and when he drew closer, his eyes were as blue as the center of a flame and burned just as hot as he looked at her.

"Alex." Maddy twisted the hem of her T-shirt in suddenly nervous fingers. "I—"

The words she was about to say were cut off by his lips. Without warning, he crushed her to him. His movements were precise, strong, and graceful, as one hand slid behind her left knee and drew her leg up so that it was wrapped around his waist.

She gasped into his mouth as the soft center of her heat pressed into his pelvis. He was hard, and it still astounded her that his arousal was because of her.

Maddy was out of breath when he finally pulled back. She eyed him warily as he cocked an eyebrow down at her.

"What are you doing here, Alex?" She was nervous, but the feeling was only superficial. Once again, being around him eased the tight snarl of tension that had been her ever-present companion for so long.

"I thought I'd show you what you were missing."

Maddy expected cockiness to follow his words, but instead she saw that he was being serious. He was aroused, but she could see from the look on his face that it wasn't a game. The solid ridge of his cock rubbed through the thick denim of her jeans, and liquid heat surged to her center.

"I can't get you out of my head."

"That's not fair." Damn it, she couldn't *think* when he was touching her.

His expression unreadable, Alex released Maddy's leg and she slid down his body, feeling every ridge of his muscles along the way.

"I'll use everything I've got if it means that I can have you."

Her insides churned. *If he can have me.* He was talking only about sex. She had known it all along, but hearing it in so many words tasted like vinegar.

If she let herself, she could have feelings for him. The last thing she could handle was getting close to someone again.

So perhaps it was best that she was just a conquest.

She bit her lip as she looked up at him, not sure of what to say.

"I'm tempted to punish you right now."

Maddy's trepidation melted quickly into lust tempered with anger. "For what? Not signing your little document yet?"

The look on his face made her blanch with fear . . . not fear that he would actually harm her, no, but she knew he would do *something*, and her mind couldn't even begin to process the possibilities of what that could encompass.

"Don't push me, Maddy." The set of his lips grew even more firm.

"Or what?" Her reserve flew out the window. She was so incredibly frustrated with her life, and the safeness that she felt around Alex made him the perfect target. "What will you do? Spank me? Lock me in your dungeon? Use your ropes and whips?"

His hands were under her ass, lifting, before she'd finished speaking. She clung to his shoulders for support, startled as he lifted her right off the ground. One hand slid up the hem of her T-shirt. Pulling the wire of her bra down until her breast plumped out over the top of it, he began to stroke his fingers over her nipple, which bunched up tightly beneath his touch.

"All of the above, Maddy, and more. I will do whatever I want to, for no reason other than the fact that it pleases me." His lips were a whisper from hers, but though she closed her eyes in anticipation of a kiss, none came.

She moaned softly and tilted her head back. His lips trailed down to the hollow of her throat, where he pressed a kiss against the soft skin that lay in the crevice of her collarbone.

"Don't pretend anymore, Maddy." Bracing her against the door of her car, Alex tangled his fingers in the length of her ponytail and tugged gently. "Be honest with yourself. I know you want this. I can see it in every inch of you. I know what I've proposed is scary. But I'll take care of you, take care of every single one of your needs. That's the whole point of your ceding control to me."

She trembled as he continued to work the fingers of his one hand over the achingly tight bud of her nipple. Everything that he said was true. She wanted this. She wanted him.

The idea of giving up control to him appealed to her on every possible level.

"Alex, I . . ." Maddy's voice trailed off. The reason that she was shying away was likely not one that he'd think of.

"Just one night, Maddy." His voice was husky as he stroked his fingers through the length of her ponytail. "Just let me show you what I can give you."

"We've already had one night." His fingers continued to strum her nipple, and she quivered. She wanted him inside of her, now. It was all that she could think about.

"That was vanilla sex, Maddy. And while I admit that vanilla sex with you has given me a taste for it, I want to show you more. I want to take you farther." She arched into his hand. They were in the parking lot of her apartment building, where anyone could see them, but she just didn't care.

"Okay."

Alex's body went rigid against Maddy's as she agreed. He exhaled, long and deep. "You won't regret it."

Maddy buried her face into his neck. She was too embarrassed to look him in the eye.

"Maddy." The tone of Alex's voice changed in an instant. The stern way he pronounced her name had her jerking her head up to look at him full on. There—there. He'd wrapped dominance around himself like a cloak.

"Maddy, you will hold your head up about your decision. You will not be ashamed of it." Holy hell. He wasn't kidding. Maddy wondered what he would do if she dared to disobey . . .

That question encompassed entirely too much. Instantly, she was struck with a surge of nerves. Pleasant little sizzles of sensation, they begin to tap-dance in her belly.

"All right." Uh-oh. There was that frown again. What had she done? Maddy eyed him warily, and his lips curled up in the start of a sensual smile.

"The correct response is 'Yes, Sir.'"

He read her thoughts on her face. He was not pleased.

"Maddy, I know you're new to this. But you have to trust me. You feel a need to please me, and in turn, I will give you what you need. But you have to play by the rules."

Maddy considered her options. There weren't any. If she wanted to continue—and oh, she did—then she had to do as he said.

"Yes . . . Sir." She placed a sarcastic emphasis on the title, reflecting that at least he hadn't asked her to call him Master of the Universe, or something like that.

She squeaked when, without warning, he flipped her over his shoulder and began to walk toward the building. She squirmed, but one of his arms was wrapped around her knees and his other hand was splayed firmly over her ass. She was upside down, her eyes level with the exquisite view of his sculpted ass.

"What the hell are you doing?" The hand splayed on her ass pulled back, then came down on the globes of flesh with a large crack. Maddy jolted, shocked. "Alex!"

Alex didn't respond. Maddy fumed silently as he carried her right up to her front door. There, he slid her down his body—deliberately, she knew—so that she could feel how very aroused he was.

"Your keys, Maddy." The metal ring was fisted tightly in her hand. Maddy clenched her jaw, suddenly second-guessing her decision to go further with this . . . with him.

"You *spanked* me. In public!" If she were honest, she would have had to admit that, while definitely mortified, she was also incredibly aroused.

Alex placed a finger under her chin and tilted her face up so that she had to look right at him. With his free hand, he nipped the keys from her fingers and, taking his eyes off of her for only a second, unlocked the door to her apartment.

"The rules, Maddy. Play by the rules." He looked at her steadily, and Maddy swallowed hard. "Do you trust me?"

She did. There was no rational basis for it, but she did.

"All right." A smile of satisfaction covered Alex's face before he again morphed into that other persona. Maddy gulped, a mouse facing a lion, as he ran a finger over her collarbone and down to the hollow between her breasts.

"You don't get to mouth off to your Dom. If you do, it will result in a punishment, such as a spanking. The spanking will be administered whenever and wherever I see fit, since it is to please me and me alone. Do you understand?"

Maddy opened her mouth to remind him that he wasn't her Dom yet. He arched an eyebrow before she spoke, and she swallowed back the words hastily.

"Okay." She was trying, she was, but he was waiting for something else. Belatedly she added, "Yes . . . Sir."

She thought she'd managed to keep any hint of sarcasm out of her voice, but only marginally. Still, he finally nodded, then placed his fingers on the small of her back and urged her inside.

Immediately, she noticed the apartment was hot—Maddy tried not to run the air-conditioning too often, to save on the bill. She began to perspire, her shirt sticking to her back and stomach. Alex, damn him, looked as cool and collected as always, even though he was the one who was wearing a button-down shirt, suit, and tie.

"Is your air-conditioning broken?" He frowned slightly, then loosened the knot on his tie. *Ha*, Maddy thought. *He's warm, too.* It was a hint that he was human.

"No, it works." She wasn't about to tell him why she kept it off. He nodded, then looked around the small room. When he saw the wall register, he headed toward it.

"Don't!" Maddy's voice was sharper than she'd intended.

Alex turned and raised an eyebrow at her. "Maddy, it's steaming in here, and I intend to have you even hotter in a few minutes." His words alone had exactly that effect. "If it's the bill you're worried about, I'll take care of it."

"You will not."

He glowered, and Maddy scowled right back. She didn't care about playing by his rules right at that moment. He would not pay her bills. She was not a whore.

"It's part of my responsibility as a Dom." He looked like he was ready to ignore her and turn the air-conditioning on anyway. Maddy schooled her face into a mask of severity, as much as she was able to. "I'm supposed to take care of your needs."

"We haven't discussed things in much detail yet, Alex. Aren't we supposed to discuss . . . what are they called? Hard and soft limits? You paying my bills is a hard limit." Crossing her arms over her chest, she tapped her foot. "Besides, tonight is just a trial run, remember? You're not my Dom yet. *If* we continue with this, then we can discuss your desire to . . . to take care of my needs."

He looked so sexy, all angry and with his tie half loosened. Right now there was only one need that Maddy wanted him to take care of, and it wasn't her electricity bill.

Leaving the thermostat, he began to move toward her. His expression was ominous. Maddy retreated a step, not sure what he had in mind.

"Until I sign it, I get some say. This isn't about playing by the rules, Alex. This is about my dignity. And you're not paying for anything yet, so for now, the AC stays off."

It was the word *dignity* that got his attention. She could see his quick contemplation, his infinitesimal hesitation, and then he was moving toward her again.

"Very well." Loosening his tie the rest of the way, he tugged it over his head and sent it flying. "We'll save the shower for after, then."

"After?" His fingers were undoing the buttons on his shirt, and the hard flesh that was revealed nearly rendered Maddy mute.

He grinned, the expression wicked, and finished opening his shirt. It hung loose and open, revealing a taut stomach, ridges of muscle, and the sexy jut of his hip bones.

She tried hard not to drool.

"Yes, Maddy. After." Tucking a finger into the neckline of her shirt, he pulled her against his firm chest. Bending to brush his lips over her ear, he whispered something that made her heart stutter.

"We're about to get very sweaty."

. . .

Alex threw his shirt to the floor as soon as they were through the bedroom door. Slowly, he placed Maddy on the ground, again sliding her down his body ever so slowly, something he loved to do because it let him feel every bit of her body against his skin.

Releasing her with a last gentle play of his fingers on her skin, he seated himself on the edge of her bed, leaning his weight back on his hands, and instructed her to undress.

A visible tremble passed through her. Did she still feel exposed under his gaze? He wanted her to feel more comfortable around him.

But if she didn't strip, he would take care of the job for her. And to that end . . . she wanted to please him. Watching her undress would clearly do this.

Inhaling deeply against him, Maddy fisted her slender fingers in the hem of her T-shirt, then pulled it over her head. Alex watched intently as she tossed the worn cotton to the floor, enjoying the way she moved.

"Very nice." Unzipping the fly of his dress trousers, he pulled the elastic of his black boxer briefs down for his erect cock to spring free. Continuing to watch her, he fisted his erection in his hand and stroked up and down.

Maddy gasped. He had touched himself deliberately—if she had any doubts at all about how strong his desire for her was, he wanted her to see the rigid length of his erect penis and to know the strength of his arousal.

Maddy lowered her lids, the fringe of her lashes casting shadows on her cheeks. Fuck, but she was beautiful and so sweet. She pulled at him.

He wanted to be inside of her.

"Undress." Hastily, she shimmied her jeans down to the floor. She hesitated momentarily with the clasp of her bra, but one glance at Alex's face seemed to urge her forward. The simple bra fell to the floor with the rest.

Under his stare, Maddy hooked her fingers in the elastic at the sides of her bikini panties. Alex shook his head, and she froze.

"Come here." With his free hand, he beckoned her forward. He wanted to touch her.

He knew that she would expect his hands to move to the usual places. Wanting to throw her off balance, he bent his head and pressed a damp, openmouthed kiss to the swell of her belly.

He heard a soft sigh of pleasure.

Relinquishing his grip on his cock, Alex reached for Maddy's hips. He pulled her panties down until they, too, fell to the floor.

"Step out." She did, swallowing thickly. "Hold still."

Maddy froze in place as he looked her over, top to toes. He wanted to lick every last bit of that gorgeous, creamy skin, and took his time looking his fill.

She reached out with eager fingers for his erection, her expression surprised when he caught her hands before they could grasp him.

"Did I do something wrong?" Maddy sounded suddenly unsure.

Clasping her wrists in one hand, Alex reached across the bed for the leather toy bag that he'd brought in from the car. He squeezed her wrists firmly as she asked.

"You will never have to wonder that with me, Maddy." He needed her to know that. It was the responsibility of a Dom to tell his submissive exactly what he wanted and expected, so that they didn't have to decide on their own. Pressing a quick kiss to her knuckles, he opened the zipper of his leather bag with his free hand. "You don't have to question things. I will tell you if I don't like something. I promise."

"O-okay," Maddy stuttered, watching through nervous eyes as he pulled a long, silky scarf from his bag. Her body jerked beneath his fingers when he looped it around her wrists and tied a firm knot.

"We're going to take it easy tonight, Maddy. Okay?" He slid a finger between the scarf and her skin, testing to make sure that it wasn't too tight. "Right now we're going to choose a safe word. If at any point you want me to stop, you'll use this word. Are we agreed?"

Her wrists secured, he pulled his bag into his lap and looked up at Maddy. He loved the way she looked, so wanton, standing there in front of him, naked and bound.

Maddy pulled against the restraint. He let her test. It wasn't that tight. If she wanted to, she could probably free herself from it. It was more symbolic than anything.

It represented the fact that she was ceding control to Alex. She wouldn't get control back until they were done, or she used the safe word.

Before his eyes, he saw calm begin to wash over her. No decisions. She didn't have to do anything except what he told her to.

"Safe word, Maddy. What's your safe word going to be?" She blinked as he asked. But he needed her to repeat it, needed to remind her that she had one. If she used it, everything stopped.

"Um, I'm not sure. Isn't there, like, a generic word? One that everyone uses?"

From his bag, Alex pulled out a set of elastic cords that resembled a pair of incredibly skimpy underwear but that had a much more pleasurable purpose. Wrapping them around her hips, her legs, he clipped the garment closed in the front.

"Red is a fairly common one, and I'll consider it a safe word if you use it."

Maddy gasped when Alex parted the folds of her labia, then settled the small, hard part of the garment directly over her clit.

He adjusted the way the elastic cords sat so that the small thing stayed where he put it.

"However, I would like you to choose your own unique word." Alex showed Maddy a small black remote. Pressing a button on it, he grinned up at her, then pressed it again.

After a second's delay, a quick burst of vibration worked through the small object. Maddy cried out, her knees buckling as she leaned forward to grab for Alex's shoulders.

Her hands were bound, and she would have fallen had he not caught her. Letting her think on that, he stroked one hand over her forearm as she regained her senses, glaring down at him.

"No glaring," he reminded her, pulling yet something else from his bag, though he didn't let Maddy see it yet. "Now. Safe word. Choose one, and we can have some more fun with this."

One more quick blast of sensation, and she pulled at her bonds. Her head fell back, the ends of her ponytail caressing the skin of her shoulders beautifully.

"Maddy!" She shook her head, her entire body braced for the next tease. "Now."

"Blackjack!"

He rewarded her with another, slightly longer vibration from the powerful vibrator between her legs.

She sagged against Alex when he again turned it off, her arms pressing against his chest, and he chuckled into her neck. "What is this thing?"

"Come here." She let her weight fall onto the arms that were pressed against his chest. He coaxed her into his lap so that her legs straddled his, open wide, and her center was slick against the heated tip of his erection.

"This is called a butterfly." He ran a finger over the device between her legs. "This little remote gives me full control over your pleasure. You will feel only what I want you to feel, come only when I say so."

Maddy looked into his eyes, and he saw that she was both terrified and entranced.

"Still with me?" She nodded, and she seemed eager. Alex then slipped one finger past the small vibrator and into her.

"Oh!" Maddy gasped, and her inner muscles pulled at his finger. He murmured his approval and slid his finger out.

Fuck, but she felt good. So hot and tight and wet.

She groaned with disappointment, and he laughed softly.

"You're so wet for me already, Maddy. It pleases me." His free hand came out of his leather bag of tricks, and in it was a long, slender wand.

A small sound of protest escaped her lips, and Alex couldn't help but smile. He knew how she felt. He wanted to be inside of her as much as she wanted him to be.

But he intended to drive her a little bit crazy first.

"Open for me." He didn't give her a choice as the slender wand replaced his finger. Slowly, he sheathed the slim length inside of her until the base was the only thing outside of her heat.

She shifted uncomfortably. He knew it was a bit longer than would be comfortable and was unyielding, unlike the flesh of an erection.

It would push her senses, giving her a knife edge of pain with the pleasure.

Alex placed the butterfly back over her clit and turned it on. The tiny vibrator hit both that small, supersensitive area of her flesh, as well as the base of the wand inside of her, forcing it to move in just the tiniest way.

"Oh my God." She tried to close her legs in defense, but his hard thighs were between them, unyielding, holding her wide open for him. "Alex, no. That's too much."

"Give it a moment." Her hips rocked restlessly against him, her body trying to adjust, to find comfort. He saw the moment her body gave way, the discomfort relaxing into pleasure.

She closed her eyes, holding her breath for one long moment. When she exhaled and again looked around, Alex gazed
at her with deep satisfaction.

"Good girl." He sensed her wariness when he opened his
toy bag yet again.

"What are you doing?"

Stilling, he fixed her with a stern stare. "Little subs do not
get to question their Doms." Drawing out a small bottle of a vis-
cous liquid tinted the palest green, he reached around to smack
her once, on the ass. It was a reminder to be polite.

He loved the heat that rushed to her skin under his hand.

Maddy quieted, though her hips still shifted restlessly
against him, making his cock jerk with tension. He couldn't indulge himself, not yet. Right now he wanted to give her just
enough to keep her needy and aching, but not enough to send
her over the edge.

What he had in the bottle would give her the extra edge she
needed.

Pulling up the part of the lid that kept the oil from spilling,
he squirted a small amount onto the fingers of one hand. The
scent of the mint oil always made him think of candy canes and
iced tea in the summer. On his lap, she inhaled the refreshing
smell, too, drawing the aroma into her lungs.

"This will be a little bit cold." Slipping his fingers beneath
the butterfly, Alex found her clit and began to rub.

"Oh. Yes." Maddy arched into the touch as he played his fingers over her clit. He loved how responsive she was. Taking the
hard nub of her clit between both his forefinger and thumb, he
rolled the tissue, working her until she was groaning and writh-
ing against him. The oil allowed him to slide in all the right
ways, and he took full advantage.

"You're so responsive. It's beautiful."

She cursed when he retreated, then tensed.

Instead of smacking her bottom again, Alex chuckled and turned on the butterfly. Maddy's soft moans turned to louder cries as it pressed against the wand inside of her.

From the oil on the skin of his fingers, he could judge the time it took for cool air to hit her clit. The sensation went from pleasantly cool to hot ice, and he drank in her strangled cry as her clit set on fire.

"No, please. Too much." The purpose of the mint oil was to make the sweet burn of frost play over her clit, worked anew with each rolling vibration from the butterfly. He knew it was working from the way she rocked against him.

"Please." Maddy leaned forward and buried her face in Alex's bare chest. He found the gesture unexpectedly sweet.

"Please what, Maddy?" Replacing the bottle in his bag, he pulled out yet another, one that was nearly identical, except that its contents were the amber of whiskey.

Her eyes widened as she looked at it, and he let a wicked grin cross his lips. She would be desperate to come by now, but he wasn't quite done torturing her yet.

"You're so beautiful when you're aroused." Pressing kisses over each of her flushed cheeks, Alex squirted oil onto the hand that didn't contain traces of mint oil. This time it smelled of spicy candy, of warm tea.

"Cinnamon." Maddy's voice was breathy with anticipation. She seemed to anticipate what he was about to do, because she arched her back, offering her gorgeous breasts to him.

"Lean back." With one hand splayed over her back to support her, he urged her to arch her spine. Her bound hands framed her breasts, pushing them up and out like an offering.

"Look at me." Her eyes were wide in the dim light. A cloud had passed over the moon leaving them in darkness. Shadows played over the sweet curves of her face.

God, but she was lovely.

"So sweet." The hand with the cinnamon oil stroked over her collarbone, then down between her breasts as he painted liquid fire over her skin.

When his fingers reached her left nipple and painted the oil over the top of it, he watched as her busy mind finally stopped thinking, stopped analyzing, and just *felt*.

She murmured as he finished with one breast and moved to the other. She shifted restlessly, telling him that she was absorbing the sensations.

Then he blew a cool breath over the heated tips of her breasts. She jolted and cried out.

"What's your safe word, Maddy?"

Her eyes flew open, and she blinked like a newly roused owl. "Maddy."

"Blackjack!" Her brow furrowed. "Why?"

"Don't question your Dom." One more smack on her buttocks. The crack of his hand against Maddy's naked flesh cut the heavy silence in the room like a clap of thunder, and at the same time he turned up the intensity of the vibrator.

"Ahh! Ahh, ahh, ahh!" She clenched her legs on either side of his thighs, which served only to drive the wand inside of her in farther. She shook her head wildly.

Alex caught her chin in his hand and, dipping his head, took her lips in a steamy, possessive kiss that was hotter than the burn of the cinnamon.

"Come for me, Maddy." He pulled away from the kiss just long enough to whisper this against her lips and to turn up the intensity of the vibrator.

Throwing her head back with abandon, she closed her eyes and pressed into him, blind to everything but Alex and her release. Shudders continued to rock her as the release worked through her. When the tremors subsided, she fell against him, in her own little world.

A stream of tears had cascaded down her cheeks when she came.

"I'm sorry. I don't—I mean, I liked . . ." Maddy buried her face in Alex's chest.

She seemed embarrassed, but he was proud of her for letting go.

"Tears are completely normal after an intense scene." Wrecked, she clung to him, limp as a rag doll, as he unfastened the butterfly and, with the quick insertion of two fingers inside of her heat, removed the slender wand.

"How do you feel?" Alex pressed his forehead to hers, and the raw need in those ocean blue eyes of hers made his heart stutter.

This woman was under his skin. He wanted her, needed her now.

"Good. I feel good, I think." Maddy shifted on his lap, her legs still open wide.

She *was* good, but at the same time, she didn't feel quite complete.

Though he'd given her intense pleasure, she still craved the intimacy of being possessed by his body.

"Good girl."

A rush of giddiness washed through Maddy at his praise.

"This was for your pleasure, to show you what I can do to you." As he spoke, Alex worked a hand into his pants pocket and came out with the foil wrapper of a condom. Tearing it with his teeth, he rolled it down his impossibly hard length, then grasped the silk that still bound Maddy's wrists.

"This time it will be for both of us. I want you so badly, I can't hold back anymore." Tilting his hips up, he slid the head of his cock through her lower lips, then pressed against her tight opening.

"Yes." She'd thought she was too tired for more, but her pulse again quickened as he seated himself quickly in her impossible wetness. Together they groaned aloud, reveling in the unique fit of their bodies together.

He was so big that he stretched her to the point of pain, a sensation that Maddy found made her wild with need. In return, she could feel her tightness pulsing around his turgid erection, pulling at his flesh, urging him to move.

They fit like they were made for each other, like their bodies had been designed for nothing but to give each other pleasure.

"More." Maddy had opened her mouth merely to sigh, and instead found herself looking straight into Alex's eyes. This, all of this—this was exactly what she wanted. The pleasure with the edge of pain, the incessant onslaught of sensation, the feel of Alex, his smell, his kiss.

She felt alive in a way that she hadn't since before the accident.

It felt amazing.

Growling, he placed one hand on her hip to hold her still, his touch firm enough to tell her that he and he alone would set the pace.

Bending, she nipped at his neck and rubbed up against him shamelessly.

Their eyes met, and sensation took over.

Alex thrust his pelvis upward, slamming into Maddy hard enough that she knew her inner thighs would have bruises come morning. She met every rock of his hips with a downward thrust, ensuring that he pushed inside her as far as he could, loving the way her body gave way to make room for his impossible length.

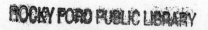

His one hand held tight to the bondages that held her wrists, a reminder that he was the one in charge of her pleasure. His other hand skimmed over her nipples, her clit, the skin of her back and bottom, awakening her nerve endings and occasionally urging her into his thrusts even more deeply.

His low, heartrending groan told Maddy that he was getting close to release. She could feel the tension coiling tightly inside of her as well, for an impossible second time. The tops of his thighs smacked against the bottoms of hers as he began to move faster and faster, his fingers touching her wherever they could, finally fisting in the length of her ponytail and pulling.

Both of his hands splayed over her ass as he shouted and pushed inside of Maddy one final time. She could feel the spasms of his orgasm as he came, tightly sheathed in her heat.

"Sorry. You should come first. You make me lose control." He rocked up gently with his hips, even as he continued to ride the wave of his own pleasure. The coarseness of his pubic hair rubbed against the wickedly sensitive nub of Maddy's clit, and pure sensation washed over her for a second time.

They clung to each other for a long moment as the shudders subsided. Then Alex turned her head with fingers pressed gently to her cheek, turning her until she faced him.

"Mine." There was no arrogance in his tone; it was a statement of fact.

Maddy was so wrecked that she couldn't argue. She nodded in response and murmured in agreement to him. Laying her head on his shoulder, she drifted to sleep, Alex still deep inside of her.

CHAPTER NINE

When Maddy awoke the next morning, the bed beside her was empty. For a moment her stomach clenched, thinking that Alex had left without saying goodbye. However, her apartment was so small that once she was fully awake, she could hear the sounds of someone moving around in the next room, and she relaxed when she realized that he was still there.

Easy, Maddy. This was just sex. Still, she couldn't help the ridiculous grin that threatened to split her face in two as she remembered what she'd done the night before.

She wanted more. She wanted to sign his agreement and grab hold of the way he made her feel.

It would probably be smart to read it first, though. Still, she grinned as she gingerly threw back the covers and slid off the mattress, wincing as her feet touched the floor. Though thorough, Alex was never gentle, treating her as though he expected her to be strong, and last night had been no exception. Her body felt bruised in several sensitive areas, but the lingering soreness brought a hint of a smile to her face as the naughty memories rioted around in her head.

The day she'd gone to the casino to play that game of blackjack, Maddy never would have guessed that she'd be brave enough to do something like this—to have a fling with a man like Alex Fraser. It was with not a little bit of pride that she smirked as she hastily used the toilet, ran a comb through her sex- and sleep-snarled hair, and brushed her teeth. She thought about getting dressed, but she knew that Alex would give her one of those looks of his and want to know why she felt the need to perfect herself for him.

In the end, she shrugged and tugged at the hem of the oversized T-shirt that she usually slept in. She'd loved falling asleep skin to skin with Alex, but had awoken in the middle of the night with icy fingers and toes.

"Good morning." Alex was standing at her kitchen sink, looking out the small, dingy window. He turned when she entered the room, and Maddy was taken aback by the scowl that he displayed over the edge of the coffee mug.

"You have no groceries. How do you live like this?"

She wasn't sure that required a real response and chose to keep quiet for the moment. So, cautiously, she edged into the room. She wasn't very experienced with morning afters, and she had no idea how to act.

"Well, it's just me here. I eat at the diner a lot. Joe likes to feed me." She realized she had tiptoed into troubled waters as soon as Alex's glower darkened, and she clamped her mouth shut. Clearly, the two men were at an impasse, one that would be easier to navigate if they were simply kept apart.

"I don't like the way he looks at you." Placing his coffee on the counter, Alex crossed the tiny room to where Maddy stood and caught her face in his hands.

"He doesn't like the way you look at me, either." Something dangerous flashed through Alex's eyes, and a renewed attack of nerves seized her. She wondered if she'd gone too far, but he let it go, releasing her to open the refrigerator, remove an egg carton, a brown bag of what she knew must be shriveled mushrooms, and a partially used stick of butter.

"We'll make use of this, but, Maddy, if this relationship is to go any further, you need to take better care of yourself. That involves grocery shopping—healthy groceries."

It was strange to have someone looking out for her, and although she liked his concern, she wasn't sure she cared for his order.

Still . . . after last night, she knew what he was going to do.

"You're drinking out of a Buffy mug, you know." It was the one she usually used, and it said WWBD—WHAT WOULD BUFFY DO? in large block letters.

Maddy couldn't hold back a slight chuckle as she pulled a second mug from the cupboard and poured herself some coffee. Alex turned the Buffy mug in his hands, looking puzzled. She wondered if billionaires did mundane things like watch television, though in her world, she couldn't even imagine someone who didn't know about one of her favorite shows of all time.

"Keep calm. Call Giles."

Maddy blinked, not sure she'd heard right as Alex stared at her solemnly before taking another sip. He couldn't quite hide a grin, and Maddy burst out in delighted laughter as she realized that he'd answered the cup's query—he'd made a joke.

Strangely, it was the fact that he was familiar with something like a Joss Whedon show that pushed her the final step. Enjoying Alex might be a brand-new item on her list, but the opportunity was there, and she wanted to take it.

The words on the silly mug chanted in her head.

What would Buffy do?

Buffy would take the vampire—or the billionaire—by the horns and forge ahead.

"Maddy?" he prompted her as he scooped the eggs he'd made onto a plate, grabbed a fork, and carried the plate to the table. She was puzzled until he pulled her out of her chair, settled himself into it, then pulled her back down onto his lap. "What's wrong?" He turned Maddy's head so that she had to look at him.

She squirmed and could feel that her movements had an interesting effect on certain parts of his anatomy. "I can't think when you touch me, and I want a clear head while I ask you something."

She wanted to please him. Maybe it wouldn't be so hard.

Some things, though . . . some things she'd found online were a definite no-go, and that was what she needed to discuss, what she needed a clear head to negotiate with him.

"Very well." After a long moment, Alex removed the steel band of his arm from around Maddy's waist, letting her up. She didn't make it more than a step before he clasped those long fingers of his around her wrist. Hooking his ankle behind the leg of the second chair at the small table, he drew it close to his own. "Sit. I still want you close to me."

He wanted her close so that he could feed her, she realized a moment later when he moved a forkful of egg to her mouth. Obediently, she opened. Actually, she didn't know how obedient she was being, because she was hungry and eating was something she wanted to do for herself.

"How much do I have to do what you say?" Maddy narrowed her eyes as she chewed the next bite that Alex fed her. Strange, but this was the third meal that they'd shared in this manner, and it was starting to feel almost normal, accepting bits of sustenance from his hand.

"Do you mean, will my dominance over you extend beyond the bedroom?"

Maddy nodded warily as thoughtfulness crossed his face. Though she liked the idea of having many of her decisions made for her, she also knew that she didn't want to be under his total control. Panic surged through her at the thought, and her muscles tensed, something that Alex noticed.

"Easy." Another bite of egg was delivered to Maddy's mouth. "Well, there's not a hard-and-fast rule for that, Maddy. It's something we'll have to work out on our own. I will say that

I've never much cared for the idea of a full-time slave. I will enjoy making decisions for you in the bedroom, absolutely, and in some instances when we're outside of it, too. But I need a break once in a while."

"What do you mean?" She still couldn't believe that she was actually having this discussion.

"Making all of the decisions for another person can be exhausting. I don't like to do it one hundred percent of the time." Relief washed over her. "So how about we start with your submission in the bedroom, where it already seems to be working, and we'll figure out the rest as we go? Does that sound acceptable to you?"

Maddy contemplated, eyes fixed on her twisting fingers. She couldn't believe the words that were tumbling to her lips were coming from her mouth.

"I think . . . I think I'd like . . ." *What would Buffy do, remember? Come on, Maddy, spit it out.* "I think I'd rather start with more control than less and rein it in if it's not working."

Alex looked surprised, but the surprise quickly melted into pleasure and heat. She was relieved that he wasn't appalled or disgusted by her request.

The thought of relinquishing control over so many things that made her feel *out* of control every day . . . it was appealing on a very basic level. All she had to think about was pleasing him.

"You're already pleasing me," Alex murmured as if he had read Maddy's thoughts. "As for time, I thought that we'd figure that out as we go as well. With my work, we'll have to, since I don't keep a very regular schedule, and there will be weekends . . . there will be times when I'm not available."

Maddy frowned. There it was again, that secret that she'd picked up on. She *knew* it was none of her business, but the thought just popped into her mind, of how many other women would die to be in her place right now. They might even have agreed to all of his demands without protest, something she knew she wouldn't and couldn't do.

She tried to shake off the insecurity. She had enough to worry about right now without throwing in imaginary girlfriends for her . . . her lover.

That said . . . "Are we . . . I mean . . ." Alex raised his eyebrows, encouraging Maddy to finish. It was hard for her to spit out, but it was also one of the most important things that she had to say. "I don't . . . I'm not comfortable with multiple partners." She could feel the blush of scarlet rioting over her cheeks. "I mean . . . I know this isn't a typical relationship. But I can't be with you in that way unless . . ."

Alex leaned forward until his lips whispered over hers. They were warm and made her want to nip at them possessively. "I don't believe in sleeping around."

Unable to resist, Maddy leaned forward until they were actually kissing, his lips slanting over her own. He sampled her lips until she was out of breath, and her head spun as she sat back in her chair.

"Good." Their eyes met, and the words questioning what, exactly, this relationship was were on the tip of Maddy's tongue, but she forcibly swallowed them back.

"That said, some BDSM relationships involve sharing with other partners—voyeurism, swinging, ménage. I'm not interested in any of that for the long term, but if it intrigues you and will help open you up to your sexuality, then I'm open to it."

"I'm not intrigued!" Maddy blurted hastily, and Alex cast her a *Methinks the lady doth protest too much* look.

And damn it, but he was right, as per usual. She didn't know if she could ever actually follow through, but after the shock faded, she couldn't get rid of the image of the hands of more than one man on her, of someone watching as Alex thrust deep inside of her.

"If it's something I think you need, then I'll arrange it, and we will do it." His voice was matter-of-fact.

"Unless I use my safe word."

Suddenly intense, Alex leaned forward and clasped both of her hands in his, those glacial pale eyes fixed on her own.

"Understand now, Maddy. You may use your safe word at any time, and I will stop. We'll talk about what you're experiencing. But if you decide to end whatever it is we're doing, then that's it. Forever."

Maddy hissed in a breath; there went her safety net. "Why?" Her voice was soft. She felt incredibly vulnerable.

"Submission is about trust. You need to trust that I'm going to take care of you, that I'm going to push you to get you what you need, but that I won't take you farther than you can handle. A safe word tossed out all the time negates the trust, so I don't allow it."

Holy hell. She didn't know if she could do this. She trusted him not to hurt her physically, and she trusted him to take care of her. But to trust him so entirely that she couldn't pull away when she needed to, when those emotions from her past came rolling through like a fog . . .

Maddy wasn't sure that she could do that. She wanted to, but she truly didn't know if she could.

She could feel Alex's eyes, evaluating her, assessing her in that way he had. She could see the need that simmered just below the surface for him, but he was holding it in check . . . for the moment.

"Before you sign, Maddy, understand this. Once you give control to me, I will immerse you. There isn't a halfway point."

Maddy swallowed against the sudden thickness in her throat. She wanted to. Everything in her wanted to.

"What are you thinking, Maddy?"

She knew that this was ultimately about sex for him, but

when he looked at her like that, she felt as if she were the only woman in his world. She tried to look away, but he turned her back with one long finger pressed against her cheek.

"Maddy." His voice was stern.

Maddy bit her lower lip, knowing that he wasn't going to like what she was about to say. "I want to. I really want to. But . . . I'd like to talk this over with Dr. Gill before I jump in."

Though he controlled it well, the slight flare of Alex's nostrils and the dilation of his pupils, visible at this close range, alerted Maddy to the fact that, as she had guessed, he was not at all impressed.

"I would really rather you didn't discuss it with the shrink."

Even though she'd been expecting it, his words were a slap in the face. Maddy could feel irritation begin to simmer, an acidic burn in the pit of her stomach. "Her name is Dr. Gill. She is a *psychologist*." She didn't think the word *shrink* alone was all that derogatory, but the tone in Alex's voice certainly was. "And she's helped me a lot."

Alex opened his mouth to say something else about Dr. Gill that she wouldn't like, she was sure, but surprisingly, he choked it back before narrowing his eyes, his expression deadly serious.

"Fine. If you feel it is something that you need, I won't say any more about it. But I would prefer that you not discuss me with the *psychologist*."

Now Maddy was angry.

"What is your hang-up with therapists, Alex? She's not some New Age quack. She's got a doctorate. She's smart. And without her suggestion that I make my list, I would never have met you!" Maddy bit her tongue as soon as she was done speaking. She wasn't sure that she wanted Alex to know what a huge role he had played in her life in the brief time they'd known each other.

They glared at each other where they sat, nearly nose to

nose at the tiny card table that sat in her kitchen. She wasn't happy about his high-handed attitude.

There weren't many things that would entice Maddy to go head-to-head with Alex Fraser, who, truth be told, looked a little bit frightening at the moment. But though she knew what her answer ultimately would be, she just wanted a little reassurance that she wasn't crazy before agreeing to be bound and disciplined.

"Alex, I just want to talk to someone a little more . . . objective. If you can try to understand that, then . . . I promise I will at least try." Thinking of the night before, when Alex had bound her hands behind her back, had used cinnamon and mint oils and vibrators, Maddy shuddered lightly with pleasure.

It wouldn't be that hard for her to try; she knew that. She wanted to know that she wasn't crazy.

"I know you'll try, because you want this as much as I do." Something in Alex's eyes softened, just a tiny bit, though his lips were still pressed tightly together. "A few years ago I . . . I had a really bad experience with a therapist."

Maddy waited for him to relax a bit now that he'd told her this. He didn't. Instead, he changed the subject by placing the fork on the table and lifting her over his shoulder the same way he had the night before.

She yelped as her sleep shirt rode up and cool air hit her bottom.

"Time for you to get showered and dressed, babe." He carried her bodily to the tiny bathroom and crowded in with her. He made himself busy, starting the water, adjusting the temperature, and stripping her out of her T-shirt. Her skin flushed as his eyes raked over her naked frame. Maddy could see the front of his pants beginning to tent with his erection, and she reached for him with eager fingers.

"Nope." She frowned as he coaxed her beneath the stinging

spray, then closed the plastic curtain with a snap. She pulled it back to share her scowl, which he regarded calmly.

"Get going, babe." Reaching an arm beneath the water, he smacked her lightly on the butt, just hard enough to make her jump. "You've got twenty minutes to be at the front door, ready to go."

"Where are we going?" A frisson of nerves shot through Maddy's veins as she reached for her soap. The lavender and tea tree scent calmed her a bit, as always, but not nearly enough.

"You'll see. Wear long sleeves." She felt a whoosh of cold air as he opened the bathroom door, letting steam escape. She scraped the exfoliating bar over the fresh goose bumps as if trying to scrub them off while her teeth chattered. "Seventeen minutes, Maddy."

Excitement surged, mixing with the nerves that had already collected in her belly.

She may not have thought that she was ready for something new, but around Alex there certainly wasn't much time to think.

"Alex, what are we doing? I really want to know." The farther away from Maddy's house that they drove, the more nervous she became. By the time Alex pulled off onto a small gravel road, her palms were sweating.

She rubbed them on the front of her jeans as he parked his Turbo beside a small car hauler. Declan was there, sitting astride something that looked like a smart car on which someone had removed the doors and injected the tires with steroids. He rode the contraption down off the car hauler, waving when he saw them.

"What the hell is that?" Maddy's nerves ramped up to anxiety. It was obvious now what Alex had planned.

It had been hard enough for her to get back behind the

wheel of a normal car after the accident. She still had an illogi-
cal fear of other motorized vehicles, which, according to her
hammering pulse, included that death trap.

"That's my quad." Alex grinned, a boy showing off his shiny
toy, until he turned and saw Maddy's face, which she could feel
was paper white, the blood having drained right out of it.

"Maddy, what's wrong?" In a flash, he parked the car and
was out and around to her door. Leaning in, he undid her seat
belt and urged her to bend over, her head between her knees.

"I—I—" She couldn't breathe. Damn it, she hated losing
control to a panic attack. Focusing on the breathing techniques
that Dr. Gill had taught her, she tried to calm herself down, the
doctor's words echoing in her head.

*You can't stop a panic attack once it's started—you can only
ride it out. Don't fight it, and it will be over all the sooner.*

Sure enough, as Maddy willed her body to relax, the suffocating waves began to splash smaller and smaller, until she
could finally draw in one deep, shuddering breath, looking up
at Alex as she did.

"What the fuck was that?" His face was bone white. He captured her face in his hands, combing his fingers through the
strands of her ponytail that had come loose. "What scared
you?"

Maddy shook her head irritably, dislodging his hands from
her skin. She wasn't telling him about her past, her problems, no
matter how safe, how warm he could make her feel.

His face closed off as she shrugged away his touch. Maddy
was furious with herself.

Screw this. Scrambling out of the car, she gestured to the
death trap with a jerky nod.

"So what do we do with this?" Turning away from Alex, she
marched across the gravel to the small vehicle, her sneakers
crunching over the rocks. Declan's face flickered with surprise

as she clambered up on the back of the thing, and then he smoothed the expression away.

"Miss Stone." He nodded, then looked behind her, to where Maddy could sense Alex's all-consuming presence.

"Maddy, get down." Alex the Dominant was out in full force, but she simply narrowed her eyes. She wasn't going to let herself ruin this. "You're terrified. We're not going quadding."

"Yes, we are." Maddy had sunk her teeth into it now, and she wasn't going to let go. Maybe some flood therapy was exactly what she needed.

Bending, she picked up one of the two helmets that were stowed away at her feet. She placed one on her head and buckled the strap under her chin, then extended a hand holding the second helmet to Alex.

"Please." She was so scared, she could feel the pervasive chill in the marrow of her bones. At the same time, she *needed* this.

Alex scowled, then exchanged a grim look with Declan, who shrugged noncommittally at his boss. Though they hadn't spoken, Maddy got the impression that the two men had just had an entire conversation.

His tightly clenched lips did nothing to distract from his gorgeousness as Alex took the helmet from Maddy, placed it on his own head, and climbed aboard the quad. "We're going to discuss this later."

She ignored his ominous words, focusing on the wind blowing through the tips of his raven hair, which was sticking out of his helmet. She grabbed his waist in a death grip as he turned a key in the ignition.

The thing rolled to life, and terror brought nausea to coat her throat. The quad began to move, slowly, no more than about two miles an hour, but she still let loose with a small scream.

With great control, Alex stopped the quad. Turning halfway, he met her eyes, his expression serious. "I will always keep you safe, Maddy." She could barely hear him through the thick material of the helmet. "Just remember that you can trust me."

"You'll keep me safe as long as I sign the contract?" She was surprised that she had the presence of mind to joke.

He reached back with a gloved hand and squeezed her knee. The touch spread heat, not the incendiary kind that could set her on fire, but more the steady glow of a hearth fire.

"This has nothing to do with the contract."

Maddy's mouth fell open slightly as his words sank in. It was while she was stupefied that he again started up the quad, moving forward off the gravel and onto the desert sand, the pace glacial—which she knew was for her benefit.

Maddy squeezed his hips with her thighs, wrapped her arms around him like a boa constrictor, and chanted his words over and over in her head.

Trust him. Trust him. Trust him.

The vehicle rocked a bit on the sand, and Maddy could feel the suspension of the ATV bouncing her in her seat. She swallowed back the fear that kept trying to rise and continued clutching Alex tightly, her muscles stiff with tension.

Trust him.

Minutes passed by as she chanted. Gradually, she became aware of the fact that Alex had picked up speed, probably not nearly fast enough for his liking, but enough to make her gasp. Still . . .

They'd been riding for . . . well, it had to be a good fifteen or twenty minutes now. He was still alive. She was alive.

Cautiously, she removed her face from where she'd buried it in the back of his leather jacket. The chilly wind stole her breath as she peered out from the safety of her little cocoon.

Though nerves again rioted through her as she did, due to

the need to try to orient herself on the ever-moving landscape, Maddy felt her breath catching for an entirely different reason.

The vista was breathtaking.

All around them, as far as the eye could see, was sand. Brown sand, golden sand, shimmering sand, great waves of it stretching so far that it would have been easy to believe that that was all there was in the world. Above the earth-toned rainbow was a brilliant blue sky broken only occasionally by a cream or dove gray cloud.

The view, combined with a hit of adrenaline from the motion of the quad, was like a drug. A cautious smile broke out over her lips.

Maddy felt some of Alex's tension ease when she stopped clutching him like a lifeline, though she still couldn't swallow the shrieks that escaped her lips every time they flew over a dune.

Okay, she kind of got it. She was still on the far side of scared, but the fear was tinted with exhilaration.

They rode for another twenty minutes. She relaxed a little bit more every step of the way. If she had been driving the quad herself, she suspected that all of her fear would have come back in a great rush. But trusting her safety to Alex . . . Somehow, since she inexplicably trusted him, it eased the burden.

Maddy's cheeks were flushed with windburn when Alex finally maneuvered the quad back to the gravel pad where the truck hauler waited. She was astonished by the trickle of disappointment that the ride was over.

Squinting, she saw that Declan was in the Turbo, the seat tilted back. He appeared to be napping.

Alex pulled off his helmet, his gloves, his leather jacket, stowing them away again at her feet. He slid off the quad gracefully, then reached back up for her.

His sure fingers unfastened the clip that held her helmet on, and then he removed the helmet itself.

He gave her one of those looks again, the one that told her he could see things in her that she didn't even know about herself.

"How was that for you?" It seemed strange to hear his voice after nothing but the roar of the wind for nearly an hour.

Maddy allowed Alex to wrap her in his arms and pull her down from the quad. She dusted her hands off on the thighs of her jeans, buying a moment, before looking up into his eyes.

"Good," she whispered, licking her tongue over her lips. "It was good."

They stood still, looking into each other's eyes for what had to be a full minute. As if they were of one mind, they lunged at each other, lips mashing together, hands groping, hips grinding.

Without pulling his lips away from hers, Alex cupped his hands under her ass, lifted her so that her legs wrapped around his waist. Her center pressed against the length of his erection, driving her wild as he carried her up the ramp and into the back of the car carrier.

"Alex!" Maddy tried to keep her voice to a whisper as Alex pressed her back against the metal wall inside the truck. Holding her in place with his hips, he lifted his T-shirt over his head with one quick movement, leaving the rippled muscles of his rock-solid chest open for Maddy's fingers to eagerly explore.

"Hold still, damn it." Maddy couldn't quite hold back a giggle when her finger traced the mouthwatering planes of his hip bones, and he froze. "I can't focus when you touch me like that."

"Now you know how I feel around you all the time!" Maddy could hear the breathlessness in her voice. "And why do you need to focus?"

"Because of these." Loosening his hold, Alex let her slip down the length of his body. Lifting her shirt so that her bra was exposed, he turned her quickly, catching her wrists in his hands.

The coolness of the metal wall on her breasts, on her cheek

made her shiver as something hard was placed around each of her wrists.

"You had handcuffs in your pocket?" She swallowed a squeal as Alex spun her back to face him.

"Only around you." Sliding his hands up her torso, he strummed his thumbs over her nipples, then slid his hands inside her bra and tugged the fabric down until her breasts popped free. The underwire pushed them up like an offering, and Alex bent his head to suck one into his mouth, reaching into his jeans pocket at the same time.

"Hold this for me, babe." From his pocket, he pulled a small bag and a condom. He slipped the foil wrapper of the condom between her teeth, and she had to clench to keep from dropping it, effectively gagging her.

"This is going to hurt for a minute." Pulling on her nipple with his lips until her knees buckled with the sensation, he then clasped it in the fingers of one hand and removed something from the little velvet bag with the other.

"What is that?" Spitting the condom out of her mouth, she tried to shy away, but pressed as she was against the metal, she couldn't go anywhere.

Alex held the item up for Maddy to see. It looked like a small, slender pair of silver tweezers, decorated with a dangling sapphire-blue charm.

"Hold your breath." Catching the distended flesh of her nipple in his thumb and forefinger, Alex slid the clamp onto the heated flesh.

"Fuck!" Maddy forgot about Declan, outside in the car, as a sharp bolt of pain streaked through her. "Who the hell carries nipple clamps in their jeans?" She tried to slide away, to duck under his arms, but found herself trapped.

Arching her back, she whimpered against the discomfort, pulling at her cuffs.

"Maddy?" She heard Alex's voice as if from far away. Her mind was consumed with the sensation of the clamp on her nipple. "What are you feeling now?"

She stopped squirming for a second, considering. It didn't hurt anymore . . . Well, it didn't hurt as much. The pain had melted into an ache, one echoed in the heat between her legs.

"It hurts. But . . . it feels good." Alex took advantage of the fact that she was holding still to bend and suck her naked nipple into his mouth, decorating it as he had done with the first one.

Shuddering in her breath, she glared at him. "What the hell is the point of these?"

"You'll see." His hands dipped to the zipper of her jeans, unfastening them, then rolling them down over her hips. Catching the elastic at the sides of her bikini panties in his hands, he rearranged the fabric so that it rested between the lips of her labia.

Maddy couldn't hold back her moan when he began to toy with the elastic, working the thin cotton back and forth over her clit.

"So wet for me. I love it." Abandoning her panties, Alex slid two fingers inside her slick heat.

"Shh." A wicked grin crossed his face as Maddy cried out. "Declan might hear. He might want to come watch."

She pulled at her handcuffs. With her hands bound behind her back, she couldn't do more than watch as Alex unzipped his own pants, then, retrieving the wrapped condom from where she'd dropped it, sheathed himself in latex.

"I owe you a spanking later for dropping this." Maddy's eyes went round, and then he'd lifted her again, arranging her legs around his waist. Tugging the fabric of her panties to one side, he pressed the head of his cock to the slick entrance of her cunt and filled her in one hard stroke.

"Ahh!" Maddy let her head fall back. With her hands cuffed behind her, her back arched and her breasts were thrust forward. The tips of her nipples, which burned with blue heat from the clamps, rubbed over the bare expanse of Alex's chest and had her eyes rolling back in her head.

"Come for me, babe, unless you want Declan to find us." The idea made her frantic. She didn't want the big man to walk in on this, and yet found the idea of being watched—they were nearly out in the open, after all—so, so hot.

Her breath grew ragged, and her hips braced to accept the hard, strong thrusts of Alex's cock. He filled her to the point of pain every time he seated himself inside of her, making her shudder in response.

"Are you ready?" Maddy barely had to wonder what she was supposed to be ready for when Alex worked a hand in between their bodies and, with sure fingers, removed first one clamp, then the other. She heard the clinking sound of them falling to the floor instants before the blood rushed back into her nipples and set her breasts on fire.

She buried her face in Alex's neck to muffle the shriek. It was incredibly painful, and yet, as the sore tips of her breasts abraded Alex's chest in time to his thrusts, she found that she wasn't focused on pain.

She was overwhelmed with sensation. As Alex began to thrust faster, slamming her into the metal wall, the sound echoing throughout the empty space, she felt her pleasure stretching tighter and tighter, until suddenly it snapped and sent her shooting to the stars.

She tightened her grip on Alex's hips with her legs, and in return he seated himself one final, vicious time, and she smelled the salt of his release on the air.

Shuddering, he emptied himself inside her. He held her weight up, his cock still nestled inside her, until she felt the liquid heat of his semen begin to trickle out of the condom and down her thigh.

"Damn, that felt amazing."

Maddy winced as Alex pulled out. He set her gently on the ground, then removed the condom and wrapped it in a tissue that he pulled from his pocket. He tossed it aside, then turned back to press a kiss to Maddy's lips.

"You never fail to amaze me." He grinned as he situated her bra back in place.

Maddy hissed as the fabric pulled tight over nipples that she knew were going to be sore for days.

"I like that you're going to remember me every time something brushes over your chest for the next week." Alex's smile was smug, yet all Maddy could manage was a shiver as he whispered hotly into her ear, turning her and releasing her from her cuffs. He massaged her wrists, then lifted them to inspect for bruises.

Tracing a finger quickly over the pale pink stripes, Alex bent, giving her a spectacular view of his tight ass. Though he'd just made her come, and hard, she felt her mouth water.

She watched as he scooped up the fallen nipple clamps, then pulled his jeans back up over his lean hips.

"Mr. Fraser?" The sound of Declan's voice was muffled by the metal walls of the car carrier.

Maddy's head whipped around to look at Alex, her eyes wide. For the first time since they'd met, he looked taken aback. She couldn't help it. A giggle escaped her lips.

He turned to her, and a sexy, crooked grin lit up his face. Bending, he helped her step back into her jeans. "Better hurry." Alex grinned at Maddy as he reached for his shirt and pulled it over his head. She cursed the garment as his rock-solid abdomen and ridiculously sexy tattoo disappeared beneath the soft black cotton. "Declan's seen me naked, but I have no doubt he'd enjoy getting an eyeful of you."

Maddy rolled her eyes and grunted as she worked her jeans

up her body. They were snug, and her skin was damp with sweat, so pulling them up her legs left her red faced and out of breath.

If Declan saw her naked—and more important, if he were to show that he enjoyed the sight—Maddy suspected that Alex would punch his lights out.

"When did Declan see you naked?" She could hear the steps of Alex's right-hand man crunching over the gravel. Hastily, she smoothed her shirt down.

Her legs were deliciously weak.

"In the locker room, of course." Alex grinned as the big man who seemed to keep his life running smoothly appeared, silhouetted in the opening of the car carrier. "We like to make insulting remarks about each other's manhood while we hose off from tae kwon do. Isn't that right, Dec?"

Declan actually cracked a hint of a smile. "You make insulting remarks. I don't have to. I'm secure in the size of my manhood."

Holy hell, the Irish giant had made a joke. Then he turned to Maddy, and his expression became unreadable.

"You do tae kwon do together?" It seemed odd to her, that Alex would buddy up for a lesson. Though he was enigmatic, he also struck her as a bit of a loner when it came to close friends.

A loner in the middle of a sea of people.

"Sort of." The two men smirked at each other for a moment. "Declan is my instructor."

"I see." And she did—she saw the reason that Alex kept Declan so close. She would have, too, if she were rich as sin. The knowledge just confirmed her suspicions that the big man was lethal.

"I was a bit worried when I saw the quad back here and couldn't see either one of you." Maddy bit her lip as Alex led her down the ramp of the truck. Her heart rate was still elevated, and she knew the scent of sex must have clung to both of them like a heavy perfume.

"Well, here we are." Alex grinned cheekily at Declan, who shook his head in resignation. Maddy was about to offer up some convoluted excuse when she realized that, if Declan had been with Alex for any length of time at all, he had to be aware of his boss's more . . . unique . . . pastimes.

She caught the big man's eye, and he set his face to have no expression. She winced inwardly.

Declan knew exactly what she and Alex had just been doing.

"Do you require anything else right now, Mr. Fraser?" Declan pulled keys to what Maddy assumed was the car carrier from his pocket.

"No, thanks, Dec. I'm going to drive Maddy home. I think she's had quite enough excitement for one day." She thought of the terrifying yet exhilarating quad ride, and then she thought of Alex pressing her up against the side of the truck, and she wasn't sure which part was crazier.

"In you go, babe." Taking her by the hand, Alex pulled her away from Declan, the quad, and the truck and back to the Turbo. He opened the door for her, helped her in, and even leaned in to buckle up her seat belt. She thought about telling him that she was quite capable of doing that for herself, but really, it was kind of nice to be taken care of.

Moments later, they were on the gravel road, heading back to Paradise.

"You're blushing." Maddy squirmed in her seat, feeling Alex's eyes on her sideways. "Tell me why."

"I—." She thought about telling him that it was none of his business. Then she thought about how it felt to trust him, to put herself in his hands for an hour as they rode the quad.

She wanted to do it again.

"Declan knows we had sex in the car carrier." Maddy twisted her fingers together. Truth was, having sex where anyone could have seen had been pretty damn exciting, but she was still amazed by the fact that she'd done it. Hell, she'd very nearly initiated it.

There was a moment of silence. Maddy turned and saw that Alex was trying not to laugh. A growl slipped from between her lips, and her hands curled into fists. "Why is that funny?"

Alex managed to swallow most of his smirk, though she could still hear the amusement in his words. "Yes, I imagine he knows, Maddy."

She was momentarily mesmerized by the midday sun glinting off of his night-dark hair as they drove, the contrast striking.

"What I find entertaining is that you are so sweetly embarrassed by it. Most of the women I've dated would have invited him on in."

If he was trying to shock her, he'd succeeded. Her mouth hung open, and she was at a loss for words.

"I—you—" Maddy found she didn't care to dwell on the women he'd dated in the past. "And . . . have you ever?"

It was Alex's turn to look shocked. "No! Never." His words were vehement. "Why would you ask such a thing?"

"Because this morning you told me that often in BDSM relationships there can be multiple partners." She was proud that she managed to keep her voice calm. "You said you're monogamous, and I believe you. But you also said that you'd be willing to try it if I were interested in it. So . . . have you?"

Taking his eyes off the road for a quick second, Alex looked at her questioningly. She returned the stare. Maddy thought it was a valid question.

"You know, for someone so sweet and innocent, you sure are curious."

Maddy wanted to say something sarcastic, but he was right. She wanted to know. She wanted to experience.

She waited for him to answer the question.

"Yes, I have. I've done BDSM scenes with another man and my sub, with another woman and my sub, depending on what the sub needs." His voice was matter-of-fact, though Maddy jolted.

Get used to it, Maddy. If she wanted this, then she needed to stop being such a prude.

"But never with an employee." He looked at her sideways to gauge her reaction as he turned the corner to her apartment building.

Her heart was racing. This seemingly innocent conversation had evolved into something heavier. Alex's nonchalant comments about threesomes, as if they were just a part of this "lifestyle," had thrown her right off her game.

It was one thing to play with Alex's little butterfly vibrator and some scented oils in the privacy of her bedroom. Threesomes . . . scenes . . .

What was she getting herself into?

Maddy was silent as Alex parked the Turbo, rounded the car, and opened her door. He let her unbuckle her own seat belt this time, though he did extend a hand to help her from the low-slung vehicle.

Her palm was clammy in his as he walked her to her door.

"Well?" He brushed a windblown strand of her long chestnut hair back from her face. She was struck again by how gorgeous he was. Even in faded jeans and a simple black T-shirt, he exuded the power and confidence that made him a tycoon.

A tycoon . . . and a Dominant.

"You trusted me today, Maddy, out on the sand."

She nodded, her tongue feeling swollen in her suddenly dry mouth.

"And it was good."

She nodded again. She knew what he was going to ask.

"So what do you think? Will you sign the agreement? Will you try?"

Maddy shook, but managed to spit out the word regardless. "Yes. I'll try."

Satisfaction and possession washed over Alex's face as he brushed his knuckles over her cheek. Maddy expected him to pick her up, to take her inside, to demand that she sign the contract right that moment so they could start.

Instead he pressed a hot, wet but short kiss to her lips, a kiss designed to leave her wanting more.

"Hearing that pleases me more than I can say." He nipped at her lower lip, making Maddy moan.

"Come to me when you're ready. But if you take longer than a week, I will come for you."

CHAPTER TEN

The El Diablo Casino was busier than Maddy had imagined it would be, given that it was early evening and a weekday. She had to circle the lot several times before finding a place to park.

Nervously, she twined her fingers in the strap of her purse as she made her way into the lobby. Though she'd gone home to change clothes before driving there and was now wearing a silk indigo-colored sundress rather than the jeans and sleeveless blouse that she'd had on, she still felt plain amid the women in rhinestones and evening gowns, feathers and sequins, leather and lace.

But she wasn't there to hang out. She was there to find Alex.

Walking past the bar where he had bought her that ridiculously expensive first drink, Maddy eyed the brass and chrome elevators that could take her up to the penthouse. They wouldn't do that unless she had the passkey to scan, though.

She was too nervous to call Alex and ask him to come down. Feeling her heart rate begin to speed up, she took a deep breath, then decided to wander around the casino for a bit, buying some time until she calmed down.

It worked, for a few minutes at least, as she wandered among the slot machines. She wasn't in the mood to try her hand at blackjack again—she'd been lucky once and didn't want to tempt fate.

She'd tried her best to keep her eyes away from the balcony on which she'd once seen Alex standing, but after ten minutes, she couldn't help it anymore. Although she'd come here to see him, she hadn't been quite ready to find him until now.

She looked up, her heart in her throat.

He wasn't there.

Disappointment swamped her, though she knew it wasn't overly rational. Just because he wasn't standing on the balcony didn't mean anything. She hadn't even had the guts to tell him that she was finally coming to him.

She'd go have a glass of wine, relax a bit; then she'd call him. She hurried back across the casino floor to the turnstiles through which she had entered. Against her better judgment, she turned to take one more quick look at the balcony.

Alex still wasn't there, but someone was. Squinting, Maddy made out a flash of dandelion-soft blond hair disappearing back through the sliding doors.

Someone was up there with him.

Did it mean he had found another woman? He'd said he was monogamous, and she'd believed him, but . . . well, the man must have had women throwing themselves at his feet all the time.

She felt sick. She needed to leave.

"Miss Stone." The thick Irish accent caught Maddy just before she exited the building entirely. She turned to find Declan standing behind her, a hand to his Bluetooth.

She didn't answer, just looked at him wide-eyed.

"Mr. Fraser asked me to catch you if I could. He saw you on the cameras. He'll be down in a moment." Maddy's heart did a funny little dance inside her chest.

She wondered briefly what Alex would say to Declan if she decided to leave. And then he was there, striding across the marble lobby, seeming not to notice the stares that his looks and bearing drew.

He nodded at Declan as he approached, and the big man returned the gesture before fading away into the crowd. Then Maddy was alone with Alex for the first time in a week.

"Hey." Her voice was soft.

"Maddy."

Her reaction to him was visceral. She wanted so badly to curl up in his arms and to stay there forever. "Alex, I wanted to tell you . . ." She studied him as she tried to work up the nerve to do what she'd come there to do. He looked different. He was wearing his glasses, but she'd seen those on him before. He was dressed far more casually than she'd ever seen him, in jeans that had a hole in one knee and a T-shirt that sported the name of a gym. If it hadn't been for the casual clothes, Maddy might have thought she'd interrupted his time in the dungeon.

"Am I interrupting something?" There was something here that she wasn't quite catching.

"I couldn't let you leave without seeing you."

She noticed that he blithely sidestepped her question, but she could focus on only one thing at a time at the moment.

"Do you have something to tell me?"

"Here." Opening her purse, Maddy pulled out a sheath of papers. Fingers trembling, she passed them over.

His eyes searched her face intently before he unfolded the creased sheets. She watched him read, noted the slight flaring of his nostrils when he got to the part that required a signature.

It was signed, Maddy's name scribbled in her loopy cursive.

"Are you sure?"

She couldn't quite read his expression, but his words lifted her spirits. She took a deep breath. This was it, the moment of no return. "I'm sure, Alex," she replied, and a tremor ran through her. "If you still want me."

Alex's eyes darkened, and next thing she knew, he had pulled her into the bar where they'd met, behind the counter, and into a small room, the door to which she'd never noticed before.

The room was teensy, furnished with a couch and a desk and not much more.

Maddy opened her mouth to ask what purpose this room served, and instead found herself pressed back against the door, her wrists bound by his fingers, her arms above her head. Pressing her into the hard surface with his hips—and his sudden erection—Alex took her mouth in a wet, hot kiss that left her breathless.

"This is how much I still want you." Holding her wrists in one hand, he skimmed his other down her body to her hip. Bunching the fabric of her sundress in his other hand, he pulled the skirt of her dress up until his fingers found skin.

"Alex." Maddy was acutely aware of the busy bar on the other side of the door, which wasn't a thick slab of wood by any means. If they made too much noise, everyone would be able to hear them.

"Be still, sub." Shocked by his words, Maddy froze as commanded. He growled with satisfaction, then slid two fingers past the elastic of her bikini panties and inside of her. She had been wet since he'd pressed her against the door.

"You're going to come for me, Maddy, hard and fast." He slid his fingers in and out, then crooked them several times in succession. Her vaginal walls clenched him like a fist, the sensation intimate and so, so good.

"Alex—" Her hips began to thrust into his hand as the pleasure built, coiling tightly inside of her. His name was a strangled whisper on her lips.

"Not a sound." His expression was intent, focused entirely on her, drinking in the nuances of her arousal as if he wanted to remember them forever. "Come, Maddy. Come for me."

He slipped his fingers from inside of her and rubbed them

in a hard circle over her clit. The orgasm was like a bolt of lightning, short and bright and electric. It left her panting, staring at him wide-eyed.

Before she could say a word, he spun her around. "Put your palms flat on the door, above your head."

Maddy did as he told her, her knees trembling.

"Do not move a muscle."

"Ahh!" She cried out, loudly, when the exposed skin of her ass was delivered a firm, hard spank.

"Quiet." Dominance layered his voice. She was shocked, in disbelief that he would do this then and there, of all places.

Another blow, then another. She kept track in her head as the burn spread over her skin, counting ten in all.

"That was for making me wait." Alex turned Maddy back to face him, kissed her gently on the lips, then buried his face into the long waves of her hair as he smoothed her skirt back down over her hips. She whimpered as he started to pull away.

She liked it. Maddy liked being spanked, since she knew that she richly deserved it.

The taste of pleasure made her greedy, and she wanted more. She wanted him to come while he was deep inside of her, marking her as his own.

"Can I come upstairs with you?" Now that she had him, that things were decided between them, she wanted to lose herself in him in the dark of night.

Slowly, he shook his head. "I'm sorry, Maddy. I wish you could. But now isn't a good time."

Ice water washed over Maddy like someone had dumped a bucket over her head.

Not a good time. Surely he didn't have a woman up there with him. Logically, her brain reminded her of the fact that he just didn't seem like the kind of man who would do that.

But the doubt remained. She had signed his damn agreement. She could see the evidence of his arousal, rock hard and surging out the top of his jeans. She really couldn't think of a good reason that he didn't want her in his home, particularly when she could give him the release that his body clearly wanted.

"All right." She wasn't going to make a fuss. Trust . . . He kept telling her that trust was what this relationship had to be all about.

Still, it stung.

Looking down at her toes, Maddy smoothed the rumpled skirt of her dress over her hips, waiting for him to open the wooden door and lead her out. She thought they were quiet enough, but still, she was embarrassed to look the bartender in the eye on her own.

Her flushed cheeks and messy hair surely screamed of what they had just been doing.

"Maddy." Bending, Alex cupped her face in his hands. They were nose to nose, and she had no choice but to look right into his eyes. "It's nothing sinister. I just have something going on right now that I can't interrupt. But tomorrow . . . Do you work tomorrow?"

Breathless at his proximity to her, Maddy jerked her head up and down the tiniest bit. "I'm done at nine." She grimaced internally. She and Joe had moved on from that one strange evening when he and Alex had all but pissed testosterone in front of her, and they had gotten a bit of their old groove back.

A bit . . . but not all. Maddy was pretty sure that what was gone between them was gone for good, and it both made her a little sad *and* made closing shifts with just the two of them slightly awkward.

Alex frowned a little as she tensed at the thought, but didn't push. Instead he pressed a kiss to her forehead and stepped back.

"I'll come pick you up tomorrow night at about nine thirty."

"What should I wear? Where are we going?" Maddy couldn't help but feel a little giddy.

He smirked as he reached into his pants, adjusting himself so that his erection wasn't as noticeable. When the hem of his untucked shirt fell over the top, she couldn't tell at all, though it surely couldn't be comfortable for him.

"I'll have your clothing for the evening delivered to your house during the day tomorrow. Make sure you're ready at nine thirty. Wear nothing that isn't in the box." With that, he opened the door to the small room, took her by the hand, and led her out as if nothing intense had just transpired between them.

Maddy trembled with eager anticipation at the thought of the next night.

What was he going to do to her?

CHAPTER ELEVEN

"Holy shit."

Maddy had been home from her shift at the diner for less than five minutes. As promised, there was a large box wrapped in brown paper sitting on the woven mat in front of her door.

As Mrs. Wilson from down the hall peeked out of her door with curiosity, Maddy lugged the box inside, placed it on the table, and attacked it with a kitchen knife.

"He's nuts." She couldn't hold back the exclamation as she discovered the contents of the box. The items inside were layered with delicate pink tissue paper, but that didn't soften their shocking impact. "I'm not going out in public dressed like this."

The first item was a bustier. It was constructed of black lace that tapered to a V in the front and back. The slim straps were satin ribbons, far too easily untied.

Maddy would blush wearing this in the bedroom, let alone in public.

Closing her eyes for a long moment, she tried to gather some mojo. It didn't help, but a quick glance at the clock told her that she had only twenty minutes before Alex would arrive.

The next item was a skirt, which soothed her shocked sense of propriety initially. It was almost ankle length, lightweight material, and the prettiest shade of bright blue.

Maddy held it up to the light to get a better look at it . . . and that was when she realized it was completely see-through.

She searched the box rapidly. Surely there were some missing pieces—a cardigan or a slip.

She came up with a set of strings that kinda, sorta resembled a thong, a pair of strappy black stilettos, and a boxed set of
Buffy the Vampire Slayer Blu-ray Discs. The latter made her grin
and melt a bit inside, thinking of him drinking out of her silly
coffee mug, but her nerves still refused to dissipate.

Trapped, Maddy looked at the clock on the kitchen wall.
Alex had been very specific about wearing only what he sent
and nothing more. And he was enough of a control freak that
she knew, deep down, he hadn't made a mistake.

Mortified, she carried the items to the bedroom. A small
part of her considered refusing, considered dressing in her own
clothing.

But there was that trust issue again. She closed her eyes
against the headache that threatened, and after stripping,
pulled on the shreds of clothing that, to her way of thinking,
barely constituted lingerie.

Thong, skirt, bustier, heels. Maddy avoided the full-length
mirror in the bedroom as she hurried to the bathroom to comb
her hair, brush her teeth, and add some mascara and lipstick.

What she saw reflected there stopped her in her tracks.

She looked . . . well . . . She looked sexy. Really sexy. The
bustier pushed up her breasts, which looked lovely and creamy
white next to the black lace. Though the blue of the sheer skirt
wasn't next to her face, it nevertheless managed to brighten her
skin tone.

Maddy was stunned enough by what she saw that she was
able to ignore the fact that she could easily see the entire thong
through the sheer material.

The alert on her iPhone reminded her that she had only five
more minutes. She hastily applied mascara and rosy lipstick, then
scooped her hair into a bun rather than her usual ponytail.

She liked the look of her naked neck, rising above the ribbons of black.

At the door, she contemplated pulling a jacket or wrap around her, since desert nights could get extremely chilly.

Wear nothing that isn't in the box. Maddy had to admit that she was tempted to do it, just to see what would happen. Then she thought of Alex's expression when he was angry and was overtaken with the mental image of a lion devouring a lamb.

She left the wrap. She would behave.

She looked at her cell phone again. He would be there any minute. As the seconds ticked by, Maddy started to feel as though the walls were closing in on her. Her hand was turning the knob of her door when she realized that, given her attire, waiting outside was probably not the best idea.

Her doorbell rang, and she started, even though her hand was already on the door.

"Oh God," Maddy whispered to herself as she looked down and took one deep breath. She might have been nearly naked, but she looked good.

"Wow, Maddy." Alex looked her up and down slowly, and she could see the pleasure in his expression.

Little champagne bubbles of joy bathed her skin. "Hi." She smiled shyly. She felt better about her clothing now that he was looking at her like that. She averted her gaze to the floor, trying one last time to gather up her courage.

When she looked up, Alex's wolf had taken over. Maddy swallowed thickly and her arms twitched, wanting to cover herself, since his avid stare made her feel so exposed. Somehow, she didn't think he would like that, and she was too nervous to deal with the punishment part of the festivities just yet.

"I'm pleased you've followed my instructions so well."

She didn't understand why it mattered so much that he was pleased, but it did. "They weren't that hard to follow." This wasn't exactly true. She still had to walk across the parking lot dressed like . . . she was.

As if sensing her dilemma, Alex shrugged out of the suit jacket that he was wearing. He placed the heavy fabric around her shoulders and buttoned it in the front.

It was way too big, covering Maddy to midthigh. She wanted to wrap her arms around herself to better soak in its warmth.

It smelled so good. It smelled like him.

"That should keep your neighbors from getting an eyeful." Alex surveyed her, and something in his gaze told Maddy that he liked seeing her in his clothing. "But make no mistake, Maddy. Where we're going tonight, the suit jacket won't be allowed."

His words were ominous enough to pull her attention away from the sight of him in his shirtsleeves, the top two buttons of his plum-colored shirt undone.

He was really just too good-looking to be true.

"Where are we going?" Once seated in the Turbo, Alex turned the car back in the direction of Vegas. Maddy had assumed that he would simply take her back to the penthouse until he'd made the comment about not being able to wear the suit jacket where they were going.

But if they were going to the penthouse, she was fairly certain that she'd be naked.

"If I tell you, you'll obsess and worry the entire way and be unhappy by the time we get there. So I won't tell you. I'll show you. By then you'll have so much to look at that you won't have time to think too much."

"Alex." Despite his reassurances, his words made Maddy's heart begin to beat double time. She curled her fingers into the edge of the leather seat as the Turbo sped down the freeway.

"Almost there." They were on the edge of the city, in a neighborhood far removed from the neon lights of the strip. It was filled with businesses and dotted with the occasional house. It was one of these that Alex pulled up to, a monstrous two-level with a sweet Victorian design.

There were no signs, nothing to indicate that it was more than a home beyond the valets dressed in discreet black suits at the door.

"Will you tell me now?" Maddy didn't think that her nerves could take much more.

Alex chuckled as he guided the Turbo up in front of what appeared to be the valet service. He was at her car door before the others could reach them, helping her out.

"Mr. Fraser. It's been a while." The man smiled at Alex, then turned his gaze to Maddy. He looked her up and down, and she suspected that he knew she was wearing something naughty beneath the suit jacket. "Very pretty, Alex."

She felt exposed and somehow as if she should have been insulted, but she wasn't. Instead, that flush of pleasure washed over her, perhaps because something in this man's bearing reminded her of Alex.

"Maddy, this is Julien Knight. He's the manager of this fine establishment." The man, who was lean and lethal-looking as a panther, had flawless golden skin, black dreadlocks pulled back in a ponytail, and an eyebrow ring. He wasn't her type at all, but he managed to exude sex appeal all the same.

"Oh, hello."

Julien took Maddy's hand and kissed it, his mouth warm against the skin of her palm rather than the top. He looked up at Alex with a cocked brow. "She new to this?"

"Very." Alex placed an arm around Maddy's shoulders, and even she couldn't miss the fact that he was staking a claim. "She's visiting tonight. Hands off."

His tone was light, though she could hear the danger behind the words. Rather than scampering away in terror as many would have done, Julien threw his head back and laughed.

"Heard, understood, acknowledged, *el capitaine*." Still chuckling, Julien waved them forward. "Go, go. I have work to do."

Maddy looked up at Alex in alarm. If someone else spoke to him like that, she suspected they'd have found themselves out of a job.

Instead, Alex was grinning, like he was in the company of an old friend.

"Come on, Maddy, before Julien makes a bigger play for you." He was half joking. Maddy was puzzled by the interaction she had just witnessed. The Alex she was seeing right now was more relaxed than she had ever seen him.

Alex pushed the heavy mahogany door, ushering Maddy ahead of him. She blinked at the change from the bright presunset light of outside to the dim, candlelit-enhanced interior.

"Welcome to In Vino Veritas."

"*In Vino* What?"

While she was distracted, Alex placed his hands at her shoulders, pulling the suit jacket away.

She clutched at it. "Alex, we're in public!" She hissed as his insistent fingers brushed hers aside and, to her obvious horror, peeled the jacket off of her.

"No!" Her hands fluttered up, then down, then back up again, trying to cover everything all at once. "Give that back!"

"Maddy." His fingertips never leaving her, Alex circled around until he was standing in front of her, blocking her view of anything but him.

She was new to this, but she needed to understand. When they were in his club—when they were in any club, or in any kind of sexual situation—he was in control.

If he wanted to share her beauty in an outfit he'd chosen for her, that was his decision, not hers. And he'd gone very, very easy on her in regards to the clothing he'd chosen.

"What you wear tonight is not your decision; it is mine. If I choose for you to strip naked and continue the evening in your skin, then that is what you will do. And you will not protest, because this is what pleases me." Maddy opened her mouth, then closed it again, glaring instead of speaking.

Her expression told him that *no way* was he stripping her naked in public.

She was going to be upset.

"What is your safe word, Maddy?" He caught the merest glimpse of a scowl from her. She looked so cute and sexy when she was mad.

"Blackjack," she muttered and fisted her hands at her sides. She was quite clearly not happy with him.

"You are free to use it." His voice was mild, his expression neutral as Maddy's head whipped up to look at him with wide eyes. His meaning came through loud and clear.

He watched as she battled with herself.

When she lifted her chin slowly and returned Alex's stare, she was clearly still not feeling too friendly toward him.

He was proud that she'd won out over her insecurities, but she still needed to understand that, in this situation, she needed to respect him.

"Watch it, Maddy." Although his voice was mild, Maddy's eyes widened slightly with frustration, but he didn't give.

It wasn't enough for her to simply be here. She needed to give it her all.

Maddy forced her lips into a stiff semblance of a smile. Alex nodded, pleased, and ran his knuckles over her cheek.

"Trust me, babe. Remember?" He heard her sigh as he turned and walked down the long hallway, leaving her to follow.

She had to trust him, but it was a process.

"This way." Alex gestured them through a door to the left. Maddy still seemed preoccupied, and it took a moment for her to look up at her surroundings.

"What is this?"

Alex tried to see the room through the eyes of someone seeing it for the first time. At first glance, the room appeared to be an upscale restaurant or bar of some sort. It oozed opulence. An ornate assortment of tables and chairs were placed in what seemed to be a haphazard manner around the room, though they looked too good where they were placed for it to have been anything but intentional. The tables were draped in black, and the chairs were midnight and gold, which matched the great swooping strings of gold lights that adorned the ceiling.

A massive bar of polished black wood stretched along one side of the room. Above it, gold-tinted wineglasses hung upside down from black racks, all neatly ordered and shiny.

The wall behind the bar—in fact, every wall in the entire room—was glass tinted the palest gray. If a person squinted, they could see that the glass was in fact floor-to-ceiling cabinets, displaying as well as organizing their contents.

What they were displaying was wine. Racks of it, rows of it. The entire room was floor-to-ceiling bottles of wine.

Alex approved of the music that was playing, recognized the song "Vampires" by Godsmack. The music combined with the unique atmosphere lent the entire scene a sexy, Gothic feel.

He and his partners had worked hard to make it stunning.

"Let's have a drink." Maddy resisted. He turned, raised an eyebrow at her, and she cooperated by walking forward with him.

He knew that she was embarrassed, but he was about to show her something that would hopefully put her mind at ease.

"Maddy, look." He placed a hand at the small of her back, then urged her forward, gesturing around the room with his hand.

This early in the evening, there weren't many patrons. He saw three couples, one threesome, and one man sitting alone. All had golden glasses and wine bottles, and one table had a plate of grapes and cheese as well.

"Huh." He heard Maddy inhale sharply as she finally clued in to what he wanted her to look at.

He bit back a smile.

Two of the couples were made up of one man and one woman, all regulars. In each the man wore black leather. One of the women was clad in a bustier almost identical to Maddy's, but when she shifted position it was easy to see that she was naked below the waist except for a thong. The other woman was clad in a baby-doll nightgown made of sheer pink.

It was entirely see-through, and she was wearing nothing underneath.

Alex had been in BDSM clubs often enough that he didn't see the choice of attire as shocking. To Maddy, however, it was probably mind-blowing.

The third couple was comprised of a woman dressed in a three-piece suit. Her companion was a slender young man wearing red vinyl pants and a black collar.

The threesome had two men, holding hands and dressed similarly and simply in black leather pants and tight black T-shirts. The woman with them wore a black hobble skirt that reached to midcalf and was so snug that she couldn't possibly have walked in it. It was made of shiny black and had laces that were pulled tight.

In comparison, Maddy was almost overdressed.

"See? I went easy on you." He watched her visibly squelch

the urge to narrow her eyes at him when he waved to Elijah, the only other person in the bar, who stood to greet them.

As always, his friend was dressed impeccably, expensively, and uniquely. He wore a suit of charcoal gray, but his shirt was an eye-searing blue that accentuated the hue of his eyes. His tie was black with a print of white skulls, and the golden waves of his short hair shone in the matching light inside of the bar.

"Alex."

Alex urged Maddy forward to where the man stood. The others in the bar eyed them curiously, probably wondering who the new sub with the owners was.

"Elijah. Great to see you, man." They hugged briefly, a couple of back slaps thrown in.

When Elijah turned his stare to Maddy, she looked terrified. "What have you brought to Veritas, Alex?"

Alex could easily see the Dom in Elijah's bearing and wondered if Maddy would see it, too. From the way she stiffened, she did.

"This is a BDSM club?" Maddy looked up at him with wide eyes.

He smiled at her encouragingly, then gestured back to Elijah with his head. "Maddy, this is Elijah Masterson. He's one of the owners of In Vino Veritas." Alex decided not to tell her that he was one of the owners as well, at least not yet. One bombshell at a time.

She let Elijah take her hand, let him kiss it as Julien had outside. "You're one of the owners, too."

Alex nodded slightly. He loved how quickly her mind worked. Pulling out a chair for her, he got her settled, and then he and Elijah sat. Maddy furrowed her brow slightly.

Elijah caught her puzzled expression, as did Alex. "The typical protocol between subs and Doms is only enforced in the club. In the wine bar, you need to concern yourself only with the limits set by your own Dom, in your personal relationship."

"Protocol?" She narrowed her eyes, showing her irritation.

Alex reached for her hand and gave it a warning squeeze before reaching for the bottle of wine that was sitting in a bucket of ice on the table. "Let's have a drink. Don't worry yourself about anything beyond what I tell you tonight."

She eyed him suspiciously as he filled a glass and handed it to her.

"Château Cheval Blanc. Nice choice, E."

Elijah watched, waiting for Maddy to try it.

Her hands trembled as she sipped. "It's lovely. Thank you."

Elijah smiled at her obvious pleasure in the wine.

Alex smirked. "Maddy prefers the Mouton Rothschild Bordeaux." Maddy's face flushed instantly, and he rubbed his thumb over her wrist, easing her discomfort. He couldn't resist teasing her when she had such a lovely reaction.

"This one is lovely." She didn't glare at Alex, but he noted that she ignored him to smile at Elijah. "Really. Thank you."

"Eager to please, this one." Maddy's lips parted slightly as Elijah fixed her with his brilliant blue stare. "And so pretty. Look at that blush."

"Mine." The claim was knee-jerk, but he'd seen too many women fall prey to his friend's charm.

He didn't think his friend would make a move, not unless he was invited to, but Alex found that he'd needed to put it in words.

Both Elijah's and Maddy's faces reflected surprise, and Alex struggled to keep his expression neutral. He wasn't sure yet of what was happening between Maddy and himself, but his attraction to her had grown deeper.

As if trying to break through the thick silence, Maddy spoke quickly. "You said you're an owner?"

"Elijah, our friend Luca Santangelo, and I started the club five years ago. We were business acquaintances who became friends because of our common interest in the BDSM lifestyle."

Maddy nodded and sipped at her wine, and he could see other questions swimming in her eyes.

They would get to them in due time. He didn't think it would be beneficial for him to tell her right now that he and his partners had created In Vino Veritas with themselves in mind, a place where they could indulge their own desires and yet feel comfortable.

"None of us cared for the clubs that already existed in Vegas. They're all open to the public, without enough safe-guards in place. There's no privacy, little security. And they're filled with people who dabble in the lifestyle on the weekend without any actual intention to dominate or submit." Elijah's expression was serious, and Alex sighed as his friend spoke what he'd decided to hold back.

"So . . . you all come here often, then?" Maddy's voice was clipped.

"Elijah and Luca come here more than I do, since they're more involved in the day-to-day running of it." Alex reached a hand up to Maddy's shoulder and casually trailed it down to her wrist. He needed her to understand that, yes, he'd had relation-ships with submissives in the past, but she was special.

"I've had two exclusive Dominant/submissive relation-ships, Maddy. I consider them strictly to be ex-girlfriends." When she looked into his eyes, Alex nearly forgot that Elijah was there. All that mattered were the two of them.

"I do come to the club on occasion, sometimes because I want to, and more often because the owners need to show their faces from time to time. I brought you here tonight to show you a wide spectrum of things that my lifestyle includes. It doesn't mean I'm interested in them all."

Maddy squirmed in her chair, then masked her discomfiture with a sip of her wine.

"Did you bring the cuffs?" Alex glanced over as Elijah reached into his pants pocket. He withdrew a pair of ice-white leather cuffs and a small key, which he handed to Alex.

"Had to order these specially. We don't use them very often." Grinning at Alex, he stood to go, then turned a more sober face to Maddy. "We rarely allow someone to visit the club and simply observe, Maddy. Participation is what creates the environment here."

"Thank you?" Clearly Maddy didn't know how to respond.

"Enjoy." With a last nod, Elijah turned and left the table, stopping to talk to Theo, Matt, and Allison, the party of three who were still seated across the room.

Maddy turned to Alex warily, eyeing the cuffs.

He caught up a wrist and wrapped the strip of leather around it. The sight of the cuffs against her skin aroused him beyond measure. "The white means that you're new and that no one is to touch you without express permission from one of the owners."

"You mean, if I weren't wearing the cuffs, someone could? Even if I said no?"

Alex locked one cuff into place. They didn't attach together, but there were metal loops where any number of things could be hooked.

As the second lock clicked into place, Alex noted a tremor of excitement that worked through her frame. He curved his lips in a small smile of promise.

"In a BDSM club, saying no is often part of the play. That's why there's a safe word. A commonly used one is *red*, and the club safe word is *vino*. Your Dom also must discuss any personal safe words with you before you start. Yours is *blackjack*. Use any of these three, and we'll stop and talk."

"What if—and I'm not saying you will—but what if the person doesn't stop?" Nerves made her voice tight.

Alex's mouth pinched in a tight, grim line. "Shouting *red* or *vino* will bring everyone in hearing range running. Even if you're shouting a strange word, like *blackjack*, repeatedly, someone will come to check it out. We've tried hard to make this a safe place for those in the lifestyle, Maddy. A lot of people feel that it's a family. Trust, remember?"

She nodded jerkily and looked down at her bracelets. "Will—are we—will we do something tonight while other people watch?"

The Dom in him saw that the idea both scared and aroused her. He filed it away as something to explore later. "No. Not tonight." With firm fingers, Alex stroked through the strands of her hair that had fallen loose from her bun. "Not even if you get excited and decide you want to. You need time to digest what you've seen, and we'll need to talk about it. No, we're just here to watch."

Picking up her wineglass, he held it up to her lips and tilted it for her to drink. She sipped greedily, inhaling a deep breath when she was done.

"One other thing, just to keep in your mind tonight." He set the wineglass back on the table, then traced a finger over Maddy's damp lips. She licked at his fingers, making blood surge into his already swelling cock.

"I don't do public scenes when I'm in an exclusive relationship."

CHAPTER TWELVE

The inside of the In Vino Veritas club was far busier than the wine bar. The room smelled faintly of candle wax and lemon disinfectant.

Maddy's eyes went wide as she took her first quick glance around the room. Then Alex stepped into her line of vision.

"Pay attention to me, Maddy." As if she could do anything else when he looked at her like that. "You're wearing the white cuffs, so no one is allowed to touch you tonight. That said, you need to demonstrate some of the appropriate behaviors, or you will upset people. Do you understand?"

She licked a tongue over suddenly dry lips. "What—what do I have to do?"

He smiled, pleased at her question, she thought. He reached out to toy with her cuffs with one hand, and the other traced a pattern over her collarbone, making her heart thump in her chest.

"Keep your eyes down around a Dom/Domme unless he or she speaks directly to you. Even then, try not to look them right in the eye. Some don't mind, but some will take it as a serious sign of disrespect. Address all Doms/Dommes as *Sir* or *Ma'am*. If you speak with one."

Maddy focused on the beat of Alex's pulse, right below his ear. "I don't have to call them *Master*?"

"Again, some clubs require that all Doms/Dommes are called by that title. You wouldn't follow it with a name though, because that implies that you belong to the person you are addressing." His hand dipped slightly, tickling the space between her breasts. She could feel her nipples pucker against the silk of her bustier. "For instance, you would call Elijah *Master*, but not *Master Elijah*. And it would be proper to call me *Master Alex*, but I prefer *Sir*."

"All right." Maddy nodded faintly. "I can do this."

Alex raised an eyebrow, waiting.

"I can do this . . . Sir." He smiled, pleased.

"I thought that the best way for you to get a taste of this life would be for you to act as a new submissive would here. I've arranged for you to serve drinks. You will do this in a timely and pleasant fashion. You will do what is asked of you by any Dom, bearing in mind that these cuffs mark you as mine."

Maddy could feel her breath starting to hitch as her mind caught up with the rest of her, the sure beginnings of a panic attack. It was one thing to be there while Alex could protect her. She didn't like the idea of being sent off into the wilds of this unfamiliar club by herself.

"Hey!" Alex caught her by her chin and forced her to look right into his eyes. "Breathe. Easy. One, two. In, out. Look at me, Maddy."

He breathed in time with her, and it felt as if he were breathing for both of them, forcing Maddy's lungs to go through the motion. After a long moment, she could feel the suffocating dregs of panic recede.

"Now, what about that scared you so badly?"

Maddy knew she could confide in him. "The whole point of my list is to push me, because I hate new situations." She tried to make it sound as rational as it did when Dr. Gill said it. "But I can do only so much at a time, so that I can still draw a bit of control into the new situation with me. I was okay with coming here because I'm with you, and you make me feel in control."

The corners of his lips turned up in the barest semblance of a smile. "Go on."

"Going out there alone . . ." Maddy gestured widely with her arm. "It terrifies me."

Clasping her by the upper arms, rubbing his hands up and down to ward off her chill, Alex pressed a kiss to her forehead. "It's the responsibility of a Dom to know exactly how far he can push his sub." His face was deadly serious. "So you'll have to give me a little more credit. You'll be serving drinks here, in the lounge around the bar only, for one hour. I'll never have you out of my sight. Is this going to push you too far? Did I misread?"

The relief was instantaneous. She wanted to please him, she did. The thought of walking freely even in the lounge, dressed as she was, made tingles of both nerves and anticipation rumble through her. She was scared, but she thought she could do it.

She was at least going to try.

"All right. Sir." Maddy tacked on the title at the end. "You said an hour. Will we leave then?"

"That depends on you." Tracing his fingers over her cuffs one last time, he turned Maddy to face the bar, which sat like an island in the middle of the club. "If you see anything that interests you, we can go observe. Ultimately, though, I don't care to play in public."

She swallowed, wishing desperately for a glass of ice water. She was glad he didn't enjoy playing in public. It was an interesting fantasy, but she wasn't sure that she was okay with strangers watching her at her most intimate.

"That's Luca." The man behind the bar was massive, clad in faded black leather pants and a biker vest. Gorgeous, with a Latin tinge to his looks, he was at least six feet four of solid muscle.

Ringing his left bicep was a tattoo that matched the one on Alex's arm. While Maddy always had the urge to run her lips over Alex's, she could only objectively appreciate the beauty of Luca's.

"Luca is the other owner?" Alex nodded. Maddy ran her hands over Alex's biceps, where she knew the black ink to be. "Does Elijah have one, too?"

It was ridiculously cute to catch Alex off guard. She thought that his face flushed, though it was hard to tell in the lighting.

"We got them when we opened the club, as an oath to make this a safe haven for people like us." He was embarrassed, she could tell. She tried to smother her grin. "Just don't go spreading that around."

Maddy mimed zipping her lips shut, though she couldn't quite hold back her grin.

He patted her lightly on the butt, urging her forward. "Now go. Luca will tell you what to do."

Maddy's feet hurt.

It had been fifty minutes, and thankfully the sore feet, clad in the strappy stilettos that Alex had picked out, were the worst part. Many Doms, and even a few Dommes, had eyed her up and down, and several had even commented on various parts of her as if she weren't there.

"Pretty sub."

"Gorgeous tits."

"Wonder what's under that skirt."

"Who does she belong to?"

Though several times she had to bite her tongue, she managed to follow Alex's instructions. Head down. Don't speak unless spoken to.

"Sub." Though the male voice could have been addressing half a dozen people in the vicinity, for some reason Maddy was sure he was speaking to her. She looked up to see a slim Dom dressed in black leather pants and a white button-down shirt, lounging in a leather chair.

A beer was in his hand. Alex had told her that the alcohol consumption of everyone at the club was strictly monitored, but this guy looked like he might have started before he arrived.

"Come here." His request was no different than a dozen others Maddy had received over the course of the evening. She couldn't have said why, but a feeling of trepidation rolled through her.

Still, she did what she was told, crossing to where the man slouched. She studied him from beneath lowered lashes.

"You're wearing too many clothes." Before she could do more than squeak, he positioned his thighs between her legs and pushed her down until she straddled his lap.

Greedy fingers reached for her breasts.

"Don't." Maddy slapped his hands away and tried to remove herself from his lap. His hands clasped her waist, holding her down.

"Be nice, little subbie." His breath smelled of beer. "I want to get acquainted with the newbie's hot little body."

She didn't even consider her next movements. She didn't care if she was going to get punished for disobeying an order; she hollered at the top of her lungs.

"Blackjack! Vino! Red!"

"I'm right here, Maddy. No need to yell." Alex's familiar hands found her waist. He wrapped her tightly in a hug, then pushed her behind him, so that he was shielding her.

From the corner of her eye, Maddy could see Luca, still behind the bar, but watching closely.

"Are you new here?" The rage emanating off of Alex was palpable. Maddy could feel the heated waves charging the air.

"A little." The man stayed seated, though he shifted uncomfortably.

"Do you not have an understanding of what white cuffs on

a sub mean?" Alex spoke so quietly, it was almost a whisper, but his words didn't need any more volume.

He was scary.

"I'm a Dom. I'm allowed to touch." The man looked belligerent, like a child who'd had playtime revoked. "She's a sub. What's your problem?"

Maddy watched, fascinated, as Alex pinched the bridge of his nose with frustration.

"What is your name?" He looked like he was about to peel the man's skin from his body—and enjoy it.

Maddy wasn't going to play Xena: Warrior Princess. The big man had been about to grope her in places that she sure hadn't wanted to be touched, and Alex had fixed it. She was just fine with that.

"Kevin." The man slammed his beer bottle down on a small side table. "I don't need this shit. This club sucks."

"How did this asshole get in here?" Maddy heard Alex murmur under his breath.

Still emanating fury, he pointed to the exit. "Out. You're not welcome here ever again. You can leave peacefully, or Luca can escort you. Your choice."

Kevin stood at that, his fists bunched. "You can't do this! I'm a guest! Who do think you are?"

Before her eyes, Alex turned from scary to scarier and at the same time exuded his *Fuck you, peon; I'm a billionaire* attitude.

"You may call me Master Fraser, and I am one of the owners of this 'sucky' club. Now, unless you'd like to lose your teeth and gain a black eye in the bargain, I suggest that you leave."

Kevin looked like he was having a hard time controlling his caveman impulse to lash out at everyone in sight. In the end, though, he stormed away, shrugging off Luca, who had come out from behind the bar.

Once the beastly man was through the exit, Maddy turned

to Alex. His color was up, and he was breathing hard. He devoured her with a heated look.

"Thank you." The words barely left her lips before he cupped her ass, lifting her off of her feet and crushing her against the hard length of his body.

When he possessed her lips in a feverish kiss, she felt the rigid length of his sudden erection pressing in to her with urgency.

His tongue swept over her lips, demanding entry. She opened for him, clutching him around the shoulders with eager arms. He explored her mouth as she arched into him, letting him do as he wanted, because clearly he needed this touch to defuse the anger of only moments ago.

He kissed Maddy until her head spun. When he finally pulled away, they stared into each other's eyes for a long moment. Maddy could feel something funny happening to her heart, and it made her tremble as, gradually, she again became aware of where she was.

"Was there anything else you wanted to see tonight?"

She shook her head vehemently. While serving drinks, she'd gotten an eyeful of all kinds of things that she'd never even imagined before. Some had distressed her, some she was merely curious about, and some . . . well, some definitely aroused her.

But they aroused her because she wanted to go home and do them with Alex.

She told him so, and he rewarded her with another fierce kiss, sliding her slowly down his body. When he clasped her hand in his and they began to walk toward the exit, she heard catcalls and whistles from those who had witnessed the entire scene.

Maddy flushed, and Alex wrapped an arm around her. He bent close to whisper in her ear. "Don't worry about them. Let's go home."

It didn't occur to Maddy until later that when he said *home*, she thought not of her apartment, but of the penthouse. And it was also then that she realized that, for most of the night, Alex had shoved her from one new situation to another, and so long as he was nearby, her panic stayed away.

CHAPTER THIRTEEN

M addy was naked and standing in the middle of his bedroom.

Taking his time, Alex walked around her in a wide circle, keeping his pace deliberately slow. He wanted her to feel exposed and under his control.

His desire for this woman had permeated his entire being. He'd wanted, so badly, to bring her up to the penthouse the night before. If it hadn't been his weekend with his daughter, Rae, he would have.

Against his better judgment, he wanted to introduce them. But he wasn't going to introduce a new woman into the five-year-old's life unless he was sure she was going to stay, and though what was between Maddy and himself was palpable and undeniable, he'd learned quite quickly that Maddy never did exactly as he expected she would.

Her eyes followed him until he frowned at her, shaking his head slightly. Maddy dropped her eyes to the floor, and Alex felt the rush of sexual pleasure that came with a woman's submission.

"I took you to the club tonight to see many of the different aspects that can make up a BDSM lifestyle." Moving to stand directly in front of Maddy, he undid the buttons of his shirt with care, swallowing his grin when she darted a look at his naked flesh and swallowed, hard.

"The things that we do, the things that we don't do—that's entirely up to us." Unable to resist touching her, he grazed the knuckles of his hand over her cheek, savoring her shiver. "There's one form of bondage, however, that you didn't see to-night, and since I'm particularly fond of it, I want to show it to you."

He heard the swift intake of her breath and shifted the ca-ress of his hand to the hollow between her breasts. "Have you ever heard of *shibari*?" He enjoyed the way the word sounded, flowing off of his tongue.

Maddy stared up at him, wide-eyed, and shook her head.

"*Shibari* is a Japanese word that translates as *to tie* or *to bind*." His cock rose at the mental picture of Maddy, laid out before him, the soft, triple-stranded hemp rope laced over her skin in an intricate pattern. "Though the correct Japanese term for beautiful erotic bondage is *kinbaku-bi*, most Western practitioners use the other term. Regardless of what it's called, it's a beautiful practice that binds the submissive in a beautiful way."

"Is it . . . does it bind me more than handcuffs would?"

Alex could hear the trepidation in Maddy's voice. He made sure to keep his tone firm and confident. He was an experienced Dom, and it was important for the growing trust between them that Maddy knew she could trust him to keep her safe.

"It can bind as much or as little as I choose. Since you're still very new to this, I will bind your arms and your legs, but it will be in a way in which I can release you almost instantly if you feel the need to use your safe word. All right?" Her muscles visibly relaxed as he reminded her of the fact that she did indeed have a safe word.

"On your knees." He simply gestured to the floor. He didn't want her to have a chance to overthink it before he started.

Dropping to the floor, Maddy sat up straight.

Kneeling behind her, Alex pushed her knees apart and,

with a hand splayed flat on her stomach, set her weight back so that she sat on her heels. "Hands clasped behind you." Again, he guided her into the position that he wanted. "Don't move."

Alex rose and took a moment to look down at Maddy before he retrieved the coil of soft, thin rope from his dresser.

He'd had two somewhat serious relationships, and he'd had numerous casual affairs. None of the women had ever caught his attention and held it quite like Maddy had. He couldn't quite put his finger on why she was so special.

She had more spunk than most, and was skittish, which was a trait that he wasn't used to. It was more than that, though. And as a man used to having his own way, he highly anticipated the pleasure of her submission.

"I wish you could see how beautiful you look right now." Again kneeling behind her, Alex started the binding by looping the end of the rope around Maddy's ankle.

She started when he pulled the loop snug, then slid a finger between it and her skin to ensure that it wasn't too tight.

"It's all right." He could feel the tension in her muscles. He'd used handcuffs on her, a scarf, but from what he understood, rope made a person more aware of their bonds.

With sure fingers, Alex wound the rope around Maddy's naked ankle, then up and around her wrists. He secured the two together, ensuring that, while the ties would feel snug to her, he would be able to get them off quickly if it became too much for her.

"You're so lovely." For now this was as much as he intended to do for bondage, though one day he knew he would love to see her suspended while in his ropes.

But this was enough to start.

From her wrists, Alex wrapped the rope around her waist. Looping it up over a shoulder, he wound it between and around her breasts, down over her other shoulder and back to her waist.

He threaded it between her legs, making sure to tie a knot directly over the swollen nub of her clit, and then finished by securing the rope back to her ankle.

"Now three deep breaths, slowly." Alex counted with Maddy. He wanted her to get used to the tightness of the rope, to understand that she could still breathe.

With the third breath, she appeared to notice her muscles relaxing just the tiniest bit. Acceptance, submission—it was beautiful.

"Have you ever had a cock in your mouth before, Maddy?" Standing in front of her, he slowly undid the button and then the zipper of his slacks. She jolted slightly at the question, but he saw her incredibly blue eyes widen with arousal as he fisted his cock.

Slowly, warily, she nodded, fixated on his naked erection.

"Open your mouth." She couldn't do much more than that, bound as she was. His cock was in line with her mouth, but he stepped closer, brushing the weeping tip over her lips, looking down at her as he did.

He enjoyed the way the pale ribbons of rope crisscrossed intricately over her rosy flesh. The bonds around her breasts held them up and out, and he could see that her nipples were fully erect.

Slowly he eased the head of his cock between her lips. She moaned softly around his flesh, her tongue swiping over the tip, and he felt a shudder pass through him.

It felt so good, to be inside of her without a layer of latex between them. Since Lydia—Rae's mother—he'd always made sure to take care of protection himself. The feeling of Maddy's hot, wet mouth around his erection was damn near the best thing he'd ever felt.

"Suck." Clasping his shaft firmly, he allowed only the head inside her mouth. Slowly, tentatively, she began to pull, and he felt his testicles draw up toward his legs as the pleasure overtook him.

"Harder."

Maddy hollowed her cheeks as she obeyed; as she did, she gasped and her body jerked.

Alex couldn't withhold his wicked grin. She'd discovered what the knot of rope over her clitoris was for.

"You may move however you'd like to bring yourself to orgasm, provided you continue to bring me my pleasure." He watched her eyes darken as she considered his words. He wondered if she would be brave enough to ensure her own release as well, or if she would stop with his.

As she worked him with her mouth, she tentatively moved her hips. He closed his eyes against the sensation as she inhaled sharply, a jolt of pleasure shuddering over her.

"That's a good girl." He stroked his hand up and down his own cock, a thin stream of precome falling onto Maddy's tongue. She continued to suck, finding a rhythm with the rope between her own legs. Alex looked down through heavily lidded eyes, transfixed by the sight of her.

Her cheeks would hollow, and his fist would move up and down his shaft, slick with her saliva and his own excitement. Then she would tremble as small waves of pleasure passed through her body.

Mouth, fist, tremble. The rhythm continued, and Alex felt his release beginning to build in the base of his spine. Reaching down with his free hand, he cupped Maddy's throat in his fingers, forcing her to rise up a fraction on her knees. It brought her into sharper contact with the knot of rope, and her body stiffened. She cried out as her release broke over her, her teeth grazing him as she shuddered.

It sent him over the edge. Taking care not to thrust himself down her throat, he emptied himself into her mouth, overwhelmed with pleasure when she swallowed, then laved her tongue over the tip.

"Babe." Maddy looked up at him, and the pleasure and contentment he saw in her eyes reflected what he felt himself. Bending, he planted a kiss to her forehead, then ran his fingers lightly over her shoulders. He had to untie her, had to look to her aftercare.

He hadn't set out to feel this way, and he knew that she hadn't submitted to him, not fully, as he needed her to.

He was a man who liked a challenge.

And Maddy Stone was the most delectable challenge he'd ever faced.

After, they showered in Alex's ridiculously large bathroom. His bathtub was as big as a Jacuzzi, and with her muscles sore from Alex's attentions, she had ached to soak in it.

Alex, however, had had other ideas. He had pulled her into his glass-walled shower. The four rainfall showerheads had been a new experience in luxury and pleasure, as had the smaller, handheld one that he had aimed between her legs.

"May I borrow a T-shirt and maybe some sweats to get home in?" Silence greeted Maddy's words, and when she turned to see if Alex had heard her, she winced at his expression, wondering if she had somehow broken one of the unspoken rules of their new relationship.

From the corner of her eye, she caught sight of something bright peeking out from beneath the bed, something that seemed out of place. It was a bright orange rubber ball, its color conspicuous in the masculine room that was all done up in black, gray, and slate blue.

She opened her mouth to ask Alex about it, but the question promptly fled her head with his next words.

"I'd like you to stay the night, Maddy."

Cautiously, she examined the idea and found she liked his invitation to stay with him. Her guilt was currently a small shadow lurking in the back of her mind—present, because it always would be, but for the first time since the accident, she was happy enough that it didn't overwhelm her.

Maddy found that, at the moment at least, she didn't want to retreat to the comfort of her own apartment. She wanted to be wherever Alex was.

"Are you sure you don't want me to go?" Perhaps he wanted her to stay the night because of the thing he'd called *sub care*. He'd described it to her as he'd hustled her off to the shower and held her in his arms beneath the steaming water.

A Dom was responsible for the care of his sub after an intense experience like the one they'd just had. Maybe that care extended all night.

She had now been to a BDSM club, but Maddy still had no idea about so many things in Alex's world.

"I'd actually like you to stay the weekend. You have the next two days off, right?" Maddy nodded, her heart in her throat.

The entire weekend? She didn't have any clothes. She didn't have her toothbrush, or her comb, or the little bottle of her anti-anxiety medication that she used only as an extreme measure.

She could feel the tension growing in her body. Alex dropped his towel and moved closer, clasping the back of her neck and rubbing.

"Easy." As always, his touch calmed her. "I'm not going to make you. But am I correct in thinking that you want to?"

Maddy considered, then nodded.

Yes. Yes, that was definitely what she wanted.

"So you're worried because you're not prepared?"

She frowned a bit. It wasn't always the easiest thing, the way Alex seemed to have a direct line to her thoughts.

But . . . he was right. Again.

"I'm sorry. I know it's anal. I just like having my things. It . . . lets me relax, a bit." It sounded so stupid when she said it out loud. She wanted to hang her head. If Alex had been looking for some simple sex and fun when they'd met, he'd sure picked the wrong woman.

"Hmm." He was considering. "Well, there are two options. You can give Declan your key, and he can go to your place and gather up what you need."

"No way!" Maddy wasn't sending the poor man off to Paradise, Nevada, to retrieve her toothbrush. He was probably in bed with his wife, his girlfriend, someone right at that very moment, and she wasn't pulling him away from it.

"I thought that's what you'd say." Again, his ease at predicting her reactions caught her off guard. They hadn't known each other for very long, but it felt, in a way, as if they'd known each other for their entire lives.

"So here's the other option. I have toothbrushes. I have soap. I have everything you could need, or access to get it. They're not the ones you're used to, but they're yours." Maddy's ever-softening heart wanted to read more into his words than Alex likely meant. "In the morning, I'll send Declan to get you some clothes. Do you think you can make it until then?"

She looked up sharply. His face was sober—he wasn't making fun of her. For that alone, she would say yes.

"I don't have any pajamas." As she whispered this, Maddy stood on her tiptoes, bracing her hands on his shoulders. He was completely naked, and she was wrapped in nothing but a towel.

Her heart began to race for a reason entirely apart from panic.

Alex grinned, then bent to press a light kiss over her lips.

"You won't need any."

. . .

"I need a date." At his words, Maddy looked up from her seat at Alex's feet almost lazily. They had been in the bedroom for most of the lazy Saturday, with the exception of some business calls on Alex's part. She'd finally called a time-out and as a precaution had dressed herself in the jeans and long-sleeved T-shirt that Declan had purchased from heaven knew where.

That morning, Maddy had woken up to find bags of new clothes, toiletries, and makeup at the foot of the bed. She'd protested—she'd thought that Declan would go to her apartment to get her own things.

"It's just money, babe." Alex had shrugged his shoulders in a way that told her he wasn't entirely comfortable with her questioning his generosity. "And it was easier for Declan to do this than to drive to Paradise."

Maddy knew this, but still . . .

"It's too much. Have him return some of it." *Most of it.* She'd picked out a few pieces of makeup, some jeans, and pajamas. "This is nuts."

Alex opened his mouth to say something, then stopped. It wasn't like him to censor himself, but when he spoke again, she understood why.

"Maybe we can just put them in another room here." His words were cautious, and she felt her breath catch in her throat. "You can use them when you stay over."

Relax, Maddy. This doesn't mean anything big. It'll take months to train you properly as a submissive. That's all he's referring to.

It didn't feel like that was all, but she'd shoved that voice away. She'd argued, and he'd gotten bossy. He'd finally shut her up by pushing her back onto his bed.

Now it was late afternoon, and they hadn't done a thing all day except enjoy each other.

"I thought you didn't date." Maddy watched him closely as soon as she spoke, realizing that she may not have said the right thing.

"Hmm." Alex was wearing nothing but a pair of black lounge pants, which sat low on his hips. The sight of the ripples of his abdomen and biceps was a constant distraction.

He ignored her words, instead pulling her closer to him, and she breathed a sigh of relief. Still, she gave herself a little internal lecture.

That's right. He doesn't date, Maddy. Whatever he has in mind, it's all part of his submissive agreement. It means nothing.

"I need a date for tonight. I have an event." Taking her by the hand, Alex led Maddy back over to the bed. There was still one box from Declan's shopping spree that morning, one that Alex hadn't wanted her to open right away.

She'd been curious, but since she'd been protesting the quantity of the purchases on her behalf, she hadn't had much of a leg to stand on in pressing to know the contents.

"It's a formal date." Alex nudged the box over to Maddy. "I'd like you to wear this."

She looked at the box with trepidation. "It's not another bustier, is it?"

Alex stared at her, then threw back his head and laughed. Once it seemed to be out of his system, he pinned her with his Dom look, and she gulped.

"The event happens to be a work function. But if it pleased me for you to attend wearing nothing but your underwear, you would do so. Am I correct?"

Maddy tried to smooth out her features, her sensitive areas still sore. She couldn't handle any more punishment at that moment. Or any more pleasure, for that matter.

"I'm waiting, Maddy."

She bit her lip, hard, in an effort to keep her expression neutral. "Yes, Sir." Part of her longed to tell him, *I'd like to see you try,* but even to herself she couldn't argue with the pleasure she found in submitting to his will.

"Open it." The cardboard was stiff and unwieldy as she tried to pry the lid off. Finally, the stiff golden cardboard gave way, and the lid opened to reveal a mountain of sparkly tissue paper.

Beneath the tissue was one of the most beautiful garments she had ever seen.

"Alex, it's exquisite." Slowly, Maddy pulled the swath of silk and lace out of the box. It was a dress—a gorgeous, amazing, incredibly expensive dress.

At first look, it wasn't much more than a short little strapless dress, cut from gorgeous midnight-colored silk. Sexy, but not overly unique.

But as the eye traveled down and found the lace that began at midthigh and fell in sumptuous waves to the ankle, it became something much more.

Maddy was speechless.

"Alex." She opened her mouth to argue, but as she did, she saw a flicker in his eyes that told her, somehow, that he really wanted her to accept this.

Accepting it made her incredibly uncomfortable.

She wanted to please him.

"Thank you." His face softened into one of those sexy grins. "Are you going to tell me where I'm going to be wearing this amazing dress?"

He grinned again. "You'll find out."

A knock sounded through the closed bedroom door.

"Come in!" Maddy was alarmed by the sudden change as Alex welcomed whoever was on the other side of the door. She'd been enjoying the little cocoon that she and Alex had been living in all day.

A tall, skinny man dressed in yoga pants and with a bright

blue asymmetrical hairstyle bustled into the room, carrying an enormous bag. Behind him was a gorgeous, curvy Latina woman, with sleek curls that fell down past her shapely rear.

"Maddy, this is Rocco and Angelina. They're here to do your hair and makeup." The pair began to circle her like sharks, commenting on her appearance as if she weren't there, and she lost sight of Alex for a moment.

Highlights were mentioned and so was bikini waxing.

"Alex, where the hell are we going tonight?"

Rocco grabbed Maddy's hand and hauled her to the bathroom to wash her hair. There were yet more mutters, these ones about hairspray and eyebrow waxing.

Maddy didn't like how Alex had maneuvered her into a corner, where she didn't have much choice but to attend this party with him. At the same time, she found it sweet that he had thought of things like hair and makeup. She was appalled at how much money he must have been spending on her.

"Alex!"

Like any sane male, he was trying to slip out the door while she was distracted. When he heard the sharpness in her tone, he turned.

Maddy planted her feet in the entrance to the bathroom before Rocco the tugboat could pull her right on in. She raised an eyebrow, fully aware that, for one brief moment, she had a sliver of an upper hand.

"The event. What is it?"

Alex eyed the bowl of purple gel that Rocco passed under Maddy's nose, wanting to know if the scent appealed. He couldn't quite swallow the smirk of amusement over her discomfiture.

"We're going to a party at Massimo Santorini's house."

It took her a moment, and then she remembered. "The man from the casino in Paradise? The one who thought I was a prostitute?" Her mouth fell open, and she shooed Angelina away as she stared at Alex. "No. No way. He's going to think something even worse, especially if I show up in a dress so expensive that you clearly had to buy it for me!"

Not to mention that something about the man made her nervous. She didn't like him and would have preferred to stay far, far away.

When she looked up at Alex again, her protesting came to a halt. He'd gone all Dom on her again, and she knew even before he crossed to where she stood and caught her chin in his hand that this was a battle she would lose.

"He will behave himself, or I will pull from the deal, which to him would be worse than being castrated. Understand that we are only attending this function to sweeten the deal. So you will allow Rocco and Angelina to do your makeup and hair. You will get dressed, and you will meet me in the front entry-way at precisely six thirty."

Maddy pinched her lips together. This time she couldn't help herself, and the glare transformed her face.

It was difficult accepting his orders, when they were so entirely contrary to what she really wanted, which was to kick Rocco and Angelina out of the room and to return to the cozy comfort of the afternoon that she and Alex had spent together, reading, watching *Buffy the Vampire Slayer*, and exploring each other's bodies.

It was strange to feel the discordance, because in the short time in which Maddy had known him, she found that quite often what he wanted was what she wanted, too.

"Keep pushing, Maddy." Alex's voice was dangerous, but she couldn't seem to stop herself.

"Or what?" She gasped when his fingers worked their way between the denim of her jeans and the skin of her hip. Right there, in front of two strangers, he caught the elastic string at the side of her panties and tugged.

The movement pulled the lace over her clit, and pleasure washed over her in a hot wave.

"For the attitude, you lose these." He tugged the elastic one more time, and Maddy had to grab at his shoulder to stay standing. A sadistic smile was on his lips—he knew exactly what he was doing to her.

"What do you mean, I lose them?" She didn't like where this was going.

"No panties under your dress." Maddy recoiled in shock.

She couldn't go to a party at Massimo Santorini's house without underpants. It was just so wrong.

"Do you remember the butterfly vibrator that I used on you, that one night in your apartment?" Maddy's face heated, and she couldn't help but squirm.

"Of course I do." She wasn't likely to forget anything about that night. She remembered Alex tying the straps around her hips, parting her labia with his fingers, and then settling the hard nub of the toy directly over her clit.

Need washed over her, causing her nipples to pucker and dampness to pool between her legs.

"I see that you do." The smile of a predator who had scented his prey made her wish he would throw her on the bed, Rocco and Angelina be damned.

"If you push me any further, you will wear the butterfly beneath your dress tonight. I will have the controller with me. You'll have no idea when I will turn it on, or for how long. You'll wear it all night." Reaching into his pocket, he pulled out the strings that comprised the toy, as well as the remote.

"I'm going to leave it here on the bed as a reminder. Don't even think about hiding it, or your punishment will only get worse."

Maddy had no retort, feeling aroused, nervous, and angry all at the same time. It was a heady mix of emotions.

She watched as Alex moved back to the door, gesturing toward the bathroom with his head to remind her that she had company, before she said anything too outrageous. Just before he left, he tossed one final thing back over his shoulder.

"I should mention, Maddy, that the punishment will only get worse for you. I'll enjoy every minute of it."

Dumbfounded, when Rocco pulled Maddy back into the bathroom, she didn't resist.

CHAPTER FOURTEEN

Despite her ongoing hesitations about spending more time in Massimo Santorini's company, Maddy had survived the makeover treatment and found herself ready to enjoy an evening at Alex's side.

As they exited the vehicle, with Alex commenting, "What a monstrosity," Maddy nodded in complete agreement, transfixed by the sight of the house that Massimo Santorini called home.

It was a Gothic horror show, standing out from all of its blander neighbors like the stereotypical sore thumb.

"It looks like Frankenstein lives here," Maddy whispered to Alex as a valet gleefully drove the Turbo away and they made their way to the entrance of the house. "I'm kind of afraid."

"At least there'll be lots of dark coffins for doing dark deeds." Alex waggled his eyebrows at her in an exaggerated gesture, and she laughed in return.

She wasn't mad at him anymore. No, she had sat through the hair and makeup, grimaced through the eyebrow waxing and firmly declined the matching bikini grooming.

She'd put her dress on and taken her panties off.

But she had one little surprise for him, one that made her feel a whole lot better about the situation. She grinned to herself, savoring the anticipation.

"Speaking of dark deeds . . ." Maddy smiled at the butler who stood at the front door with flutes of some kind of sparkling wine. When she saw that she'd gotten Alex's attention, she reached into the small clutch she carried and removed the tiny object that she'd secreted away. "I have this for you."

Alex studied the small remote control for the butterfly for a moment before it hit him what it was.

The look on his face was well worth the wait.

"You're wearing it? Right now?" Alex took the glass of wine from her hand and downed it in one big gulp. "Jesus, Maddy."

Riding the high of her triumph, she barely had a chance to look around the massive ballroom that their host seemed to have in place of a living room when Alex pulled her to the end of the long entry hallway and, leaning back against the wall, pulled her snug against his body.

"Alex!" The way he'd arranged them, they looked like a couple sharing a sweet embrace on an evening out.

Only the two of them knew that his cock had hardened to what had to be the point of pain. It was pressed into Maddy's belly, hidden from the view of others, but a constant reminder to her.

"You want to play games, little sub?" Grinning, Alex showed her the tiny remote that he had tucked in his palm. She didn't have even a moment to catch her breath before he turned it on, the setting low but continual.

"Alex! No!" Involuntarily, her hips pressed against him. Turning her head to the side, Maddy locked stares with two girls who didn't look old enough to drink and who were wearing dresses that could have done double duty as bikinis. They were making their way down the hallway, all saccharine sweetness for Alex and nasty scowls for Maddy for being with such a gorgeous man.

God, she thought, *if only they knew.*

Her body was rigid, trying to push away the overpowering sensations. After nearly a full minute, Alex turned off the vibrator, and she sagged against him with relief.

"Do little subs get to say no to their Doms, Maddy?"

A soft cry escaped Maddy's lips as he turned the remote back on, the intensity stronger this time, coming in long, steady pulses.

Her cunt was slicked with wetness, and she wanted to rub against Alex like a cat.

She couldn't.

"There's that blush again. I love seeing your skin go pink from my attentions." He stopped the vibrations, then ran a hand over her cheek.

"Please," Maddy whispered to him. The toy made her edgy with need. She pressed her hips against him, and though he had to be nearly as needy as she was, he didn't show it.

"Please what, Maddy?" He let the vibrator start again, but for only one short, hard burst. Her fingers dug into Alex's shoulders like claws.

This was all her own doing. Maddy knew this and couldn't decide if it was the best or worst idea she'd ever had.

"Please let me come." Pressing her hot face into the skin of his neck, Maddy inhaled the scent of Alex's cologne and squeezed her eyes shut, hoping he would have mercy on her.

"Since you asked so prettily." He adjusted the controls on the remote, and the vibrator began to pulse in brutally intense intervals. Maddy could barely keep her face set in a pleasant smile, could barely swallow her cry as the need quickly coiled in the depths of her belly and then exploded.

She tried to swallow her panting as she came down from the high, staring into Alex's eyes. "You bastard."

As soon as she had her senses back, she looked around quickly. People were still coming in the front door; partygoers were milling about with their wineglasses. No one was staring at them. No one seemed to have noticed.

"I wish I'd brought a condom." Alex reached surreptitiously

between their bodies and adjusted himself the way she'd seen him do before, hiding his erection until it faded. "If I had, I'd bend you right over that piano bench for calling me a bastard."

His voice was wryly amused, but Maddy had no doubt that he'd do it. Before he could urge her away from the wall and out into the crowd, she pressed her hips into him provocatively.

"Let's find a room. A closet. Something. Let me take care of this for you." She licked her lips to make sure he got her meaning, surprised by her own daring. "I . . . I've always had a fantasy of that. A closet, someplace public."

Of you.

Temptation flashed over Alex's face, and then he shook his head. "Later. Later I'll strip you out of that dress and take you until you scream my name." His voice was cocky, but she knew very well that he could do it. "I don't want to be caught unawares in Santorini's house. I just want to make nice, try to sweeten the casino deal, and get out of here."

Maddy understood his rationale, but it didn't help the ache between her thighs.

"By the way, my fantasy is you. You, in a sex swing, open so that I can taste every last bit of you while you scream."

Maddy stared at him openmouthed. She had no words with which to respond to that admission. Pulling herself away from Alex's distracting aura, she ran a hand over her hair to smooth it, though the encounter had been so discreet that it wasn't as messy as it felt like it should have been. To clear her head of the lingering effects of her covert orgasm, she snagged another glass of wine from a passing tray and sipped.

The wine was sweet and fairly palatable, but it lacked the . . . finesse of the wines she'd shared with Alex. It was a good analogy for the two men themselves, Maddy thought as they wound their way into the main room, where people crowded tightly, some swaying to music, some simply drinking.

"What a clusterfuck."

She followed Alex's gaze as he looked around the room. Maddy felt a little conspicuous in her fancy dress, which, while the sexiest thing she'd ever worn, seemed like a nun's habit when compared to the clothing of most of the other women in attendance.

Apart from the occasional woman who clearly had more sense than the rest, the women were clad in a very loose definition of formal wear—that is, most were at least wearing dresses and skirts, but they were of the short, tight vinyl variety, paired with bustiers and sheer blouses. The men, clearly business acquaintances of Massimo's, mostly wore dark suits, which made the women stand out like exotic birds.

The attire was not so different from what might have been found at In Vino Veritas. At the club, however, it fit. In fact, the club was far classier than this event, which, while supposedly a business function, was teetering on the edge of the line between dance club and frat party. Maddy tried not to be judgmental, but the entire gathering made her feel dirty.

"What kind of business is Massimo in, exactly? Does he own more than the one casino?"

"He owns the one casino, which is actually quite lucrative. He's eager to sell because, as rumor has it, he's in a little over his head with some people." Alex's words were light, but she didn't for a moment believe that he was interested in a casino solely based on a rumor. "He also owns a hotel. Nothing that would let him afford his kind of lifestyle, which lends credence to the rumors."

Maddy eyed Alex as she thought it over. "If he has dubious connections, then is it smart to buy something from him?" She didn't know the first thing about business deals, but she did know that the man made her nervous.

"Normally, I wouldn't touch him with a ten-foot pole." Alex's voice was flat. Clearly he had no love lost for the man. "When he approached me with the deal, my first inclination was to turn him down. But the more I looked into it, the better the deal looked. He needs cash badly enough to sell for far below value, and the casino itself does quite a steady business. It will need a face-lift, but I think it would do very well, attracting people who are curious about the Vegas experience but don't necessarily want to pay Vegas prices."

"Alex, why do you need another business?" She winced as he raised an eyebrow at her question. "Sorry, I don't mean to pry. But . . . you're already successful, aren't you? Why do you need more?"

Alex artfully pulled her out of the way of a skinny brunette who reeked of rum and couldn't stand without clutching the arm of the man she was with—a man who winked at Maddy and ran his tongue over his lips when he caught her looking.

Maddy recoiled, and Alex pressed his hand to the small of her back.

"I want you to wait right here." His breath was warm on her ear, and she became conscious of the fact that she still wore the butterfly vibrator and that he still had the remote.

Using his fingers to press against the bare skin of her back, Alex guided Maddy to a bookshelf that stood against the far wall.

"I am going to go speak to Massimo quickly. I want you to wait right here. I will have my eye on you the entire time." Alex pressed a quick kiss to Maddy's forehead before approaching a podium on the far side of the room. A large plush chair was on the podium, and Massimo sat on it like he was a king in his throne. A petite redhead was on his lap, her breast enclosed in one of the man's hands.

Shifting his attention from Alex to Maddy, Massimo smiled, and it wasn't a friendly expression. Maddy knew that there had to be something more between the men, but she couldn't imagine what—Alex didn't seem the know the other man outside of the potential business deal.

Maddy shivered and broke eye contact, turning toward the shelf, running her eyes absently over the dust catchers and the single framed photograph that sat on it.

She couldn't wait to get out of there.

"Mr. Fraser." Alex couldn't help but judge the man who couldn't be bothered to rise from his chair to greet him. Then again, Alex thought as he watched Santorini's hand slide up the inner thigh of the redhead on his lap, the man was otherwise occupied. "Welcome to the party. I see you brought your... lady friend."

The girl looked to be barely legal. Contempt rolled through him, and he pinched his lips together with disgust. "She has nothing to do with you." Alex didn't want Santorini's eyes on Maddy, didn't want her to speak to him. He was regretting even bringing her, but he hadn't known that the party would be so quickly dissolving into a drug-fueled orgy.

Santorini looked taken aback; then, rather than trying to make nice as he had been, his lips curled into a sneer. "Let's get to business, then. Will you buy the casino or not?"

Rage curled through Alex's gut. There was only one thing keeping him from upending Santorini from his chair and escorting Maddy from the premises as quickly as he could. And that was his charitable foundation. He wanted the proceeds of the deal to start the foundation for teens whose families rejected their alternative lifestyles. He could afford to start the foundation now, certainly, but if he waited, turned the potential gold mine around, and used those proceeds, it could and would be so much bigger and better.

Delayed gratification. It was a rule he lived by. He would

put up with Santorini's sleaze until the deal was signed for that reason alone.

"I want another fifty thousand knocked off the asking price."

Santorini's eyes narrowed, and Alex could have been fresh out of business school and not missed the rage that entered the man's demeanor. Alex held up his hand, effectively silencing the other man. "Your gambling debt has cast a shadow over the business. It's not worth what you're asking. Also, I'll be paying you cash up front. We both know that was one of the reasons you came to me in the first place."

"You owe it to me." The other man spat the words out; then, as if trying to demonstrate that he thought Alex was beneath his respect, Santorini lifted the skirt of his companion and bestowed his attentions on her.

Alex swallowed a grimace, making sure to keep his expression set, even a little scary. As one of the owners of In Vino Veritas, he wasn't a stranger to public sex, but this wasn't one with pure intention. This was Santorini trying to show Alex that he wasn't worth him interrupting his pleasure.

All Alex saw was the poor girl, who was clearly high on something and was being used as an object, but Santorini wouldn't see it the same way, he knew.

"Fifty thousand, Santorini, or the deal is off." Turning, Alex stepped down from the podium, wanting Maddy in the safety of his arms. He shouldn't have brought her here—he should have known.

"Take a look at the photo your *lady* is looking at!" Santorini shouted after him. Alex ignored the man, moving unerringly toward the woman who had somehow become the center of his world. "You'll see why you owe me."

Santorini's words slurred a bit, and Alex shook his head, wondering if the other man was high as well. Hell of a way to do business.

"Let's get the hell out of here." Though he didn't want Santorini to know that his feelings for Maddy ran much deeper than the sexual, he needed to touch her. He settled for lacing his fingers through hers, enjoying the warmth of her skin.

Maddy was studying the shelf, which carried a vase that, unless Alex was unusually wrong, was a knockoff Ming vase. It also held a photo in an ornate, gaudy rhinestone frame.

Maddy gestured to it before allowing herself to be pulled back into the crowd.

"Is that Massimo's wife? She's too pretty for him." Though he wanted to get Maddy out of there, something about the photo, a posed glamour shot, caught his eye.

The woman in the picture was a beautiful blonde, though a slightly hard edge painted her features. It had been years, but the woman's face tugged at something in Alex's memory.

"Fuck." He didn't realize he'd stopped, but he understood in one big rush why Santorini had always been so aggressive toward him—why the other man had approached him in the first place, why he whined whenever Alex cut down the ridiculous asking price.

Years earlier, Alex had met the woman in the photo, Alessandria. She'd been a member of In Vino Veritas, one who had briefly caught Alex's eye. They'd had a short affair, in which she'd never wanted more than sex. Alex had respected her wishes and hadn't gone digging into her past, since she hadn't made moves for anything beyond what they shared in the club.

"Alex?"

Beside him, Alex felt Maddy tense. He felt out of control, off balance, having had this thrust upon him. Why hadn't he known about it?

"We're leaving." Urging her ahead of them, Alex held his breath until they were outside the house.

Alessandria had had scars on her body, ones that she

wouldn't tell him the cause of. He understood now that she was tied to Santorini. She must have been his wife, or his longtime girlfriend. He was likely responsible for those scars, and Alex hadn't done anything about it.

He waited until the valet brought the Turbo back up to the house. Then he crowded Maddy against the passenger's-side door, boxing her in with his arms.

She looked up at him, eyes wary, as if she'd picked up on his agitation.

"The scars on your legs, Maddy. The picture in your locket. What are you keeping from me?" He wanted to punch the car with frustration when her eyes shuttered and her lips pinched together.

"I'm not going to talk about that." Not *I don't want to* but *I'm not going to.*

"Maddy, I'll give you one more chance to answer my question. Tell me what you're keeping from me."

Alex fisted his hand in her hair and tugged, exposing her throat. He ran a finger down the length of the chain of her locket. She shivered, trying to hold still, before flinching away, her hand flying to cover the pendant protectively.

"I see." His voice was dark.

To his surprise, instead of opening to him, Maddy's eyes sparkled with tears, but it was the outrage in her voice that jolted him.

"What about you? You have secrets, too, like why I couldn't go upstairs with you the other day. And just now, what was that? You're not going to tell me, are you?"

This time it was Alex who glowered in the face of the pointed questioning, not accustomed to being questioned or having to account for his actions.

It was a strange sensation, one he wasn't entirely certain he was comfortable with.

"You expect my life to be an open book, but it goes two ways. Trust, Alex. Remember preaching that?" A flush of anger rose in Maddy's cheeks, and Alex slowly backed away, knowing better than to try to touch her in that moment.

He had nothing that he could say. His biggest secret wasn't one he was willing to share with anyone. For her safety, he couldn't.

"Well, then." His heart gave a strange thud, and he frowned at the physical pain.

"I guess there's nothing more for us to say."

CHAPTER FIFTEEN

Maddy was an emotional wreck by the time she arrived home. It felt like days had passed since facing off against Alex outside of Massimo's house.

She'd tried to take a cab home, but though he'd just ended their relationship, Alex had threatened to handcuff her to a pole if she didn't voluntarily wait for Declan to come get her.

She hadn't had the energy to argue. Now she stood in the front entry of her apartment, looking down at her fancy clothes, wondering how in the hell the evening had gone so wrong.

Something had set Alex off—but what? Had she done something? Said something wrong?

She'd started the day as happy as she'd been in a long time. Now she was far worse off than she'd been before.

Drawing in a great ragged breath, Maddy wished she'd saved some of the wine that Alex had sent her weeks earlier. She needed some. And that wasn't all that she longed for a taste of. Alex had opened up new worlds to her.

From inside her tiny evening bag—the one Alex had chosen for her—came the ring of her cell phone.

She thought it might be Alex. Suddenly furious, she tore into the bag, ready to answer the phone, to scream and yell.

Instead she froze.

Impossible as it was, her night had just gotten worse.

She wasn't in any frame of mind to answer the phone, but as always, her guilt wouldn't let her ignore it.

"Hi, Nate." She suppressed tears that came at the sound of

the familiar voice on the other end. God, but she could use someone to lean on. For so long, she'd forced herself to go it alone.

"Maddy!" Her heart sank when she heard the slight slur in his words. "S' good to hear your voice, honey."

Maddy forced her own tears back. Next to what Nathan had gone through, her problems were trivial. "How are you doing, Nate?" If he'd had a few too many beers, then she knew he wasn't doing well. Nathan drank only to combat the blues.

"Little lonely tonight, Maddy. You know?" Oh, did she ever. "I'll think I'm moving on, think I'm doing okay; then out of nowhere it hurts all over again."

Maddy winced and let Nathan go on a bit about Erin, about her smile and her laughter. It actually felt good, for a moment, to talk about the things that they both missed about her sister— to share the pain.

But when she managed to end the conversation and hang up, the guilt rolled in like a fog that never quite lifted. It chilled her from her bones out, making her fingers numb, prickling her skin with gooseflesh.

On top of the debacle with Alex that evening, it was too much.

She needed to alleviate some of her guilt, which was building up inside of her like carbonation in a bottle. She needed a release.

Punishment.

She thought of In Vino Veritas and of the things she'd seen there. Could she go without Alex?

The idea terrified her; still, she was angry enough to do it. Narrowing her eyes as the idea took root, Maddy lifted her fingers to her locket.

Her secret wasn't even a *secret* so much as it was something she simply didn't want to revisit ever again. Alex, however—

whatever he wasn't telling her affected him in the here and now. Affected her.

She could understand his frustration. But if nothing else, he had taught her to stop overanalyzing everything she did.

She wanted to go to In Vino Veritas. That was exactly what she was going to do.

Julien whistled as Maddy stopped her car at the front of Alex's club and stepped out.

"Damn, girl." His blatant approval lifted Maddy's spirits an inch, though that meant they still were close to rock bottom. He gestured to her car, then held out his palm for her keys. "Alex meeting you here?"

Nervously, Maddy tugged at the hem of her ridiculously short black skirt. She didn't possess anything that would even closely resemble fetish wear, so she'd gone for a sexy secretary look instead, as best as she could manage with the meager contents of her closet. Short black skirt, plain white blouse. The daring came from the seamed black stockings, the high heels, and the fact that she'd left a few buttons on the blouse open.

Any one of those items would have felt daring for Maddy in a normal circumstance. Altogether, they made her feel like she had when she'd worn the bustier and skirt that Alex had chosen for her.

She felt like a different person entirely. That was good, because regular Maddy wanted nothing more than to lock herself in a closet and cry over her breakup.

This Maddy had something else entirely in mind.

"Alex and I aren't together anymore." Though the dominance that Julien exuded, so similar to Alex's own mannerisms, made Maddy want to keep her eyes down, she looked defiantly up as she spoke.

He whistled again, then took her keys from her hand, his fingers lingering to dance over her palm.

"Is that the truth?" Tossing the keys high in the air, he caught them behind his back, making her smile. Then he tucked a finger in the neck of her blouse, tugged her close, and ran his finger over her collarbone. Maddy stiffened, and though his touch didn't light her on fire the way Alex's did, she still responded to his dominance and found that she liked the feel of his fingers on her skin.

"If that's still the case in a few hours, when it's time for me to play, I'll come find you." Gesturing toward the steps that led to the building, Julien released Maddy with a devastating grin and a swat on the behind, which made her jump.

"Inside, sub. I have work to do."

Maddy frowned and stomped down on the urge to rub her behind. That hadn't been a gentle pat, but more of a hard spank.

Suddenly she found herself second-guessing her decision to enter the club. Without Alex at her side, her old reservations came back, and she felt exposed, naked, vulnerable. And she really didn't know the first thing about protocol at the club.

Were all the Dom/mes this . . . handsy?

If she walked in there, was it like dropping a lamb into a cage full of lions?

Slowly, Maddy pushed on the heavy wooden door of the building. The interior was exactly as she'd remembered it— dark, Gothic, and sexy as hell. The music of Metallica seeped out of surreptitiously placed speakers in the entryway, and the angry notes appealed to her and the mood she was in.

"Miss Stone." Startled, Maddy looked up to find Elijah, the golden god of a man Alex had introduced her to, looking down at her with concern. Dressed in a pale pink dress shirt opened at the collar, with expensive-looking black dress pants hanging from his hips, he was sexy as hell, yet seeing him still didn't give her the same jolt that seeing Alex did.

She felt almost guilty, as if she'd been caught someplace she shouldn't be.

She was allowed to be here. At least, she was pretty sure she was. His quick appearance, however, told her that Julien had likely contacted him to let him know of her arrival. She tried to hold her head up high as she greeted him with a hello.

She waited for the lecture, since the attention she was receiving was clearly because of Alex. But she wasn't his property—after this disastrous night, she wasn't even his submissive.

"Are you sure you want to be here?" Those blue eyes studied her intently. It was all he asked.

"Yes." Maddy spoke before she could lose her nerve. "Yes, I . . . I want . . ." Her voice trailed off.

It was so hard to say out loud what she wanted.

"What do you want, little one?" Elijah's bearing was so similar to Alex's, Maddy trusted him on a gut level.

"I want punishment." Her voice was scarcely more than a whisper. She trembled as she spoke, but swallowed down her nerves. "I want to be here."

"I see." Elijah looked her up and down in much the same manner as Julien had. His stare came to rest on her face, his expression contemplative. "And why do you feel you need to be punished?"

"I'm not going to talk about that." Maddy's words left her mouth in a heated, angry rush. "I won't. I just . . . I need a release."

Elijah pressed his lips tightly together, considering. "You'll do this with me, then."

Maddy wasn't sure about the idea of partnering with one of Alex's business associates. Surely a stranger would be better.

She opened her mouth to argue, and he seemed to grow larger, more dominant.

"I don't recall asking for your permission, little sub." Reaching into his pocket, he drew out a pair of fleece-lined leather cuffs, similar to the ones she'd worn the other night, though these lacked the tint of virgin white. "Hold out your wrists."

He may not have made her heart race, but Maddy still found herself responding to his commands. She held out her wrists and soon was buckled into the leather bracelets. Like the first pair, these weren't linked, but had fastenings that could be connected to all kinds of bonds.

"Remain still." As if she were no more than a piece of artwork, Elijah pulled his iPhone from his pocket and, his movements leisurely, sent a series of texts.

Maddy found herself twitching with impatience.

"Do you have someplace you need to be, sub?" Finished with his texts, Elijah slid his phone back into his pocket and, looking up, raised an eyebrow at Maddy. "I was under the impression you were here to be punished."

Maddy's heart gave a great thud, and she felt tears prickle at the backs of her eyes. Yes, she wanted to be here, but she wanted to be here with Alex.

Not an option anymore, Maddy. Steeling herself, Maddy raised her chin, though she made certain to keep her eyes on the floor. "Yes, Sir. I'm sorry, Sir. Please punish me, Sir."

Though her eyes were on the ground, she felt Elijah studying her. Then she felt a tug on one of her cuffs.

"Follow me. Stay behind me. Do not look up."

Maddy swallowed against her suddenly dry throat as she followed Elijah down the hallway. She could tell when they passed through the entrance to the club, because the lights dimmed, the music became louder, and the sounds of pleasure and pain filled the air.

"We'll stop right here." Elijah left her side for a moment, and Maddy felt a twinge of panic, though she assumed that a friend of Alex's would keep her safe. Still, she didn't trust this man on a gut-deep level the way she did Alex.

God, she wanted Alex.

Get over it. He'd made it clear—she couldn't have him, not unless she told him her secret.

Still, he'd awakened a need deep inside of her, and this was the best way she knew to fill it.

"Come." When Elijah returned, he carried a leather bag similar to the one Alex had had the night he'd used the oils on Maddy. Despite her upset, she found her curiosity was piqued.

Did all Dominants have a bag like this, a bag full of toys?

Maddy followed Elijah across the floor of the club. He stopped next to something that looked like a wooden sawhorse, though it was padded with leather the color of wine.

Each leg had a thick metal loop with a length of chain. Two of the chains ended in more cuffs, ones slightly larger than the ones on Maddy's wrists.

She felt her pulse kick into overdrive as she looked down at the cuffs on her wrists and realized what the chains were for.

"Unfasten your blouse."

Startled, Maddy looked up at Elijah. Surely he didn't think . . . *Well, what the hell else did you expect, Maddy?* From what she'd read, a BDSM scene didn't always include sex, but it wouldn't be a strange assumption for Elijah to make.

"What's your safe word, sub?"

When Maddy failed to unfasten her blouse as quickly as he wanted it, Elijah stepped forward, unfastened the buttons with nimble fingers, and peeled the fabric over her shoulders. He tossed it to the side and then reached for the zipper of her skirt.

Soon she wore nothing but her black bra, thong, pantyhose, and heels.

"Very nice." He nudged her to one end of the bench-type contraption. "Safe word. Now."

"Blackjack." Maddy almost used the word for its intended purpose when Elijah ran his hands over her ass and down her calves.

He made her repeat the club safe word as well. As she stood, nerves making her tremble, the man knelt behind her, his long fingers closing around one ankle.

"I'm cuffing your ankles to the bench now, Miss Stone." Maddy's entire body tensed as she heard the cuffs snick. Elijah ran a finger between the metal and her skin, checking, she thought, to make sure the bonds weren't too tight.

"Breathe." Huffing in and out, he demonstrated what he wanted her to do. Standing, walking around to the front of the bench, Elijah fastened his intense blue stare on her. Maddy found she had no choice but to do as he said, her breath slowing and deepening until her body relaxed.

"Good girl." Maddy gasped when Elijah slid his hands into her bra, cupping her breasts and strumming his thumbs over her nipples. Still caught in his stare, she felt confusion flood throughout her as her nipples bunched beneath his touch and wetness slicked between her legs.

She responded to his dominance, and her body enjoyed his touch. But otherwise he left her cold.

She missed the connection that she had with Alex.

Elijah's cell phone chimed the note of an incoming text, and Maddy felt infuriated when he slipped his hands from her bra to answer it.

"Seriously?" She sputtered out the word, incensed that he would leave her half-naked, bound body to check his text messages right in front of her. "You're a bastard."

The glare he gave her made her tremble, but she couldn't hide her scowl.

"I may not be the Dom you want, Miss Stone, but that kind of behavior is not acceptable in this club." Tucking his cell phone into his pocket, he leaned forward, his lips brushing her ear with heat. "Especially not when I have what you need."

Dom or not, Maddy was about to tell him that he wasn't what she needed at all. But then he stepped out of her line of view, and she saw what he had been referring to.

Alex. Alex was here.

CHAPTER SIXTEEN

Maddy looked beautiful, the black lace of her bra and stockings setting off the cream color of her pale skin. She was aroused—aroused by Elijah's hands, damn it—but she wasn't even close to trembling with surrender as she did with him. And Alex couldn't deny that his heartbeat quickened as soon as he laid eyes on her.

"Elijah." Crossing the floor of the club, Alex nodded to his longtime friend. Though he wasn't sure how he felt about someone else's hands on Maddy, there was no one he trusted more.

He was so bloody angry with her—with himself—and when Elijah had texted him to say that she was at the club, he hadn't thought, had simply come.

He still wasn't sure what he would say to her. Though he was more tempted to confide to her than he'd ever been with anyone, he didn't tell people about his daughter, especially not his lovers. He didn't want them using her affection as a tool to his bank account, his heart, as Lydia had done. As she still did.

So he did the only thing that felt natural in the moment. Alex approached the spanking bench. Making sure to keep his expression masked, he placed a finger under Maddy's chin, lifted her face so that he could study it intently.

She was angry. She was shocked. She was aroused.

As he stared down into her eyes, her gaze dropped. She was such a natural sexual submissive, yet was so spunky otherwise, that her submission was a beautiful thing.

If she told him what she was hiding—if she trusted him and bared her soul—then he would do the same.

For now, he would remind her of what was between them.

And he would enjoy himself at the same time.

"It's time to play, little sub."

Maddy shivered at Alex's words. What was he doing here? It was clear that Elijah had let him know when she arrived at the club, but after his parting words to her earlier, she never would have thought he'd come.

Was there still hope for any sort of future between them?

"Elijah, prepare her for me, if you would."

Maddy's attention was jerked straight back to the present. "What do you mean, prepare me?" Her body tensed as Elijah opened his toy bag. "Excuse me?"

"Silence." The word reverberated in air that suddenly felt still and hot. Maddy couldn't do anything but look at Alex. "I do not normally care for public scenes, as I've told you. In this case, however, it pleases me, just as it pleases me for Elijah to prepare you for my attentions. Therefore, it will please you as well."

Maddy opened her mouth, expecting to tell them both to go to hell, but at that moment, from behind her, Elijah unhooked her bra and, in one swift movement, slid it right off.

She tried to speak but was quelled with another commanding look from Alex.

Her nipples pebbled as, with a hand splayed flat on her back, Elijah pressed her down onto the bench. Her stomach pressed lengthwise along the leather, which warmed beneath her skin. Quickly, he secured her wrist cuffs to the remaining lengths of chain.

She was bound and open, and she could do nothing about it.

"Her hair."

Maddy looked at Alex as he spoke quietly. Elijah quickly ran skilled fingers through the long ribbons of her hair, braiding it neatly so that it was out of her face and she could see.

Then she felt his hands at her waist, warm and sure. Slowly, slowly he peeled her stockings down until the elastic snugged the skin beneath her ass. Her thong followed. The flesh of her bottom plumped out over the top, exposed completely, and the tightness of the elastic created an interesting pressure between her legs.

"Beautiful." Elijah smoothed his hand over her ass, and Maddy shivered, though this time it was with more pleasure than tension. It was as if, since Alex had given his permission for Elijah to touch her, she was free to enjoy the sensation.

She didn't have to think, didn't have to worry. She simply had to feel.

From his leather bag, Elijah drew a small jar. Maddy eyed it warily, remembering the mint and cinnamon oils.

"This might sting for a minute." Unscrewing the lid, Elijah dipped his fingers in and came back up with a thick white cream.

Maddy opened her mouth to ask what it was, but a small shake of the head from Alex told her that she didn't have permission to speak. She pressed her lips tightly together as Elijah splayed one hand flat on her stomach, then slid his other hand between her legs.

Next his fingers separated her lower lips, then spread the cream unerringly over the hard nub of her clit. It stung, as he had warned her, and then . . . then she felt blood rush to that small spot, drawn by the sensation-enhancing cream.

She couldn't stop the wetness that followed immediately after.

"Very nice, sub." Elijah slid a finger inside her heat, testing

her wetness. Maddy clenched her inner walls and looked help-
lessly up at Alex.

"Soon, babe." His face was dark, his expression wicked.

Maddy drew a great, shuddering breath, closing her eyes
against the sensation.

Something wet drizzled over the crack that divided the
cheeks of her bottom, and the eyes she'd just closed flew back
open.

"No!" She jerked against the restraints, looking up at Alex,
wide-eyed. "Not there."

Moving until he was directly in front of her, he squatted
down onto his heels. "Trust, Maddy, remember?" Then he held
her gaze as he ran his fingers over her locket.

She tried to pull away and found that she was restrained
tightly enough that she couldn't.

"You've made it clear that's a hard limit, Maddy. I won't
open your locket." Alex's voice cooled off, and Maddy felt a
trickle of unease. "But when we're done tonight, I want you to
look back at what we did, think about the trust you felt, and
then think about keeping secrets from each other."

Maddy's anger faltered at the flicker she saw in Alex's eyes.
Was he going to tell her what he was hiding from her?

She had only a moment to wonder about it before she felt
Elijah's fingers explore her sensitive skin.

"You can use your safe word," Alex reminded her as he
stood up and stepped out of her line of vision.

One set of hands took hold of the cheeks of her ass, holding
her open, exposing an area that had never been exposed before.
Another hand worked cold liquid through the crack, concen-
trating on the tight pucker that lay hidden between.

Oh, no. No. Not there. She tried to pull away and couldn't.

"Be still." The one set of hands continued to hold her open;
the other pressed something hard against her pucker.

When she resisted, a firm hand smacked across her ass, stinging sharply.

"One more sound, and I'll gag you." Alex's voice was matter-of-fact. "Now relax and it will hurt less."

Maddy wasn't sure she wanted anything that hurt at all. She couldn't quite stifle her cry as the hard object pushed against her entrance, fighting to work its way past the tight ring of muscle.

"Push back against it, Maddy."

Squeezing her eyes shut, Maddy did as she was told. The plug burned as it was worked in, in and out in increments, twisting back and forth, waking nerves that Maddy hadn't even known she had.

Then her muscles gave, and it was inside of her, burning her from the inside out.

She lost track of time, conscious only of the discomfort. She whimpered as one of the men pulled on the plug, making her nerves sizzle. A hand was worked between her legs, strumming over her clit, and suddenly the burn merged with the heat of pleasure, melting her lower half with suddenly searing heat.

"I think she's ready for you, my friend." At the loss of sensation, Maddy lifted her head to see Elijah walk around to the front of the bench. Bending, he caught her cheeks in his hands and pressed his lips to hers for a slow, deep kiss.

Maddy ran her tongue over her lips as he pulled back, confused and needy all at the same time.

"He's a lucky man, Miss Stone." As he ran his lips over her ear, she shuddered at the intimacy of his whisper. "He's also a very good one. Make sure you keep that in mind."

Elijah stood and turned to walk away.

"Would you like to stay and watch?"

Maddy tensed as Alex asked his friend the question. Her search for pleasure and punishment had brought her to the club, but now she wanted to seek that pleasure with Alex alone.

The front of Elijah's dress slacks was tented with his arousal, and temptation crossed his face before he shook his head.

"Thank you, but no. This, I think, needs to be between the two of you." The other man walked away, and Maddy found herself alone once more with Alex.

Maddy was clearly confused and off balance, and that was exactly what Alex had been hoping to draw from her. He didn't want her able to think, to analyze things in that busy little brain of hers.

He just wanted her to focus on how he could make her feel.

"I wish you could see yourself right now. I've never seen anything so beautiful as you, bound and helpless. The lace of your stockings makes your skin look nearly white. Your ass is plump and pale and waiting for my touch." Alex circled the bench, checking the color of her hands and feet. They were still healthy and pink, so her circulation was good—the cuffs weren't too tight.

From the leather bag that Elijah had left behind, Alex drew an item that had a very small ivory handle from which cascaded ribbons of golden brown leather. It was a very small flogger—the smallest one he'd ever used, technically called a *pussy whip*.

Alex held it out for Maddy to see. He expected her to question him, and he wasn't wrong, though much of the anger had seeped from her tone.

"What is that?" Her voice was soft, husky.

Alex's erection jerked in his pants in response. He wanted to sheath himself in her heat right that moment, but reminded himself that it would only be better if he waited.

"This is a martinet, Maddy. A very small flogger." He flicked it through the air with a small snap of his wrist, letting her see the way the strands swished. "I'm going to discipline you because I'm upset with you. Do you understand why?"

The softness from her expression fled quickly as she stared up at him. "I'm upset with you, too. Do I get to beat you after you're done with me?"

Alex swallowed a chuckle. Damn, but he liked her sass, her spunk. The way she pressed her lips together, however, reminded him that they still had secrets from each other.

Squatting in front of her, he ran a finger over her cheekbone. "I've done you wrong by not sharing with you, and I'm sorry for that." He let the strands of the martinet dance over the exposed nape of her neck, and she shivered. "If you can find it within yourself to trust me, to share with me, then I will happily do the same." He felt his pulse speed up as he spoke, but he knew that he was doing the right thing.

This was a woman with whom he could share the secret of his daughter. He felt certain that Maddy would never use that knowledge against him or, heaven forbid, against Rae.

He waited, giving Maddy an out. He watched intently as myriad expressions passed over her face, fear and guilt taking hold.

He felt his heart sink as, reaching a conclusion, she pressed her lips tightly together and shook her head. She wasn't ready.

"Very well." Tamping down his disappointment, Alex circled back to stand behind Maddy. She didn't feel she could trust him yet. There was still hope.

Smoothing his hands over the globes of her ass, he savored her startled jump. And oh, how he would enjoy doing it.

"I'm not going to give you a set number of lashes, Maddy. You've got me in a mood, and I'll stop when I'm done." She began to tremble, but when he checked her over, he concluded that she was more aroused than scared, though there was a fair amount of trepidation as well. To send her fears fleeing, he tugged on the plug still nestled inside her tight opening, smiling wickedly when she cried out.

"Hold on tight, babe." Stepping back, Alex lifted his hand and brought the flogger down in the first blow.

"Oh!" Maddy tensed and cried out, but he knew that it was more with shock than with pain. The martinet wasn't big enough to cause much damage, even in the hands of someone inexperienced, which he definitely was not. Besides which, he intended to keep his blows light.

He wanted her to feel a wide range of sensation, but he didn't want to hurt her, not unless and until she decided that erotic pain was something she enjoyed.

"What's your safe word?" He grinned as she growled the correct word out.

She was pissed. She was fine.

He didn't count in his head, simply raining a series of short, soft blows over her skin, alternating placement so that no one part of her would be too sore the next day. Her soft moans drove him forward, releasing a flood of endorphins as he admired the pretty pink hue that painted her skin as the result of his handiwork.

Only when Maddy began panting for breath and he felt himself entering that euphoric state reached by a Dom during some encounters did he toss the flogger aside.

He ran his hands over the skin of her bottom, the heat all the more intense under his fingers with the exaggerated senses of top space. Taking up the bottle of gel that Elijah had left behind, he poured a liberal amount over her hot skin, enjoying the way she jumped back, snuggling her ass against his rearing cock.

"Not just yet, babe." He worked the extra lubricant around the plug that was readying her for him. Reaching between her legs, he ran his slick fingers over her clit, working it until her body tensed and he could tell that she was on the edge.

Perfect. He wanted her to associate pleasure and not just pain with what she was about to experience.

"Come for me, Maddy." Getting a firm grasp on the wide base of the plug, he pulled it out as he worked her clit with expert fingers. He felt her drawing tight as a rubber band and pushed the plug back in.

Her cry was loud and sharp edged as the extra sensations in her ass made the rubber band of her arousal snap. He continued to work the plug in and out as he milked every bit of sensation from her clit at the same time. Her fingers clamped down around the legs of the bench, holding on as she rode out her pleasure.

He wanted her relaxed, limp when he pushed himself inside of her.

"Don't move." Undoing the buckle of his belt, Alex freed his cock from the confines of his jeans. Though he normally preferred to dress as a businessman for his visits to the club, he'd had no time when Elijah had texted him. Not caring at all for the idea of his little doe in the club without his protection, he'd asked his friend to stay with her and had left without bothering to change back into a suit.

Denim wasn't as forgiving as wool, and he sighed with relief when his throbbing erection was free.

"I've never seen such a gorgeous ass." He couldn't wait to be inside of her. Sheathing himself in a condom, he applied a liberal amount of lubricant to his length and rubbed his hand up and down the shaft, closing his eyes at the sensation of his own hand.

"Brace yourself, babe. This is going to be uncomfortable for a minute." She clenched and moaned invitingly as he spoke and then again grabbed the base of the plug, wincing as he pulled it out, her body pushing back against him as he entered her, making him see stars when her heated flesh pressed against his erection.

Their groans mingled together in the air, his with pure plea-sure, Maddy's with desperation. He knew how she felt—she wanted more, wanted to reach that same place he occupied, where the mind ceased to function and all that was left was sensation.

Rubbing her clit with one hand and grasping her hip with the other, Alex slowly worked his way into her body, which re-sisted him all the way.

"What a good girl." His words were a murmur when, after she drew in a deep, shuddering breath, Maddy's muscles finally gave way, and he slid in to the hilt, his balls coming to rest against the curves of her ass. His breath was ragged as he tried to keep himself in check.

He'd never felt anything so good, so right, as the insanely tight heat of her ass locked around his impossibly hard cock. The stockings she had worn, wrapped just below her ass cheeks, added an extra layer of snugness that felt like a little bit of heaven.

"Okay?" He listened to make sure she was still breathing regularly, waited for her nod. "Hold on."

Sliding back, he again worked his way inside of her. Fuck, but he wasn't going to last long. She felt too good, too right.

Slide out, work in. Again and then again. He tried to be gen-tle, knowing she'd never done this before. His hand gripped her hip harder as he tried to keep his strokes even.

"Fuck." He wasn't going to last much longer. He began to again work his fingers over her clit, determined to pull one last orgasm from her before he lost himself in her body.

When he felt her muscles again start to flutter, he slid two of his fingers inside her dripping cunt. He hilted himself inside of her, jerking in and out in tiny strokes as his fingers worked in-side, pressing against the thin membrane that separated her cunt from her ass.

He could feel his cock moving with those fingers and knew how intense it must have felt for Maddy.

This time she came with an excited scream, making the flesh that held his cock impossibly tighter. One more thrust and he was lost, his orgasm starting at the base of his spine and shooting through his entire groin so hard that he shouted.

It was a long moment before he again became aware of his surroundings. In his peripheral vision, he saw that several club goers had gathered to watch the scene. He didn't deny them the pleasure, but as always, he felt exposed as he pulled from Maddy's body and drew the condom up and off of his cock.

She winced as he pulled free from her body. He knew that she would be sore for days, and he liked knowing that she would remember him, remember this every time she moved.

"Here." Elijah moved forward, holding out a soft, warm blanket.

Alex shook his head. "I'll need to ask that one more favor of you, my friend."

Elijah eyed him, his expression unreadable, before nodding.

Standing to the side, Elijah watched as Alex knelt and released Maddy's chains, then pulled her stockings back up over her tender flesh. Scooping her limp, exhausted form into his arms, he carried her to Elijah, who wrapped her in a blanket and held her close.

"Alex?" Those big doe eyes blinked at him sleepily, and Alex felt her tugging at his heart strings. He wanted to gather her close, to hold her in *his* arms.

But he had a point to make. He'd decided to trust her, but she hadn't done the same for him, not yet.

"Elijah is going to take care of you until you're ready to go home." The betrayal in her eyes made him feel like a first-class shit, but he just didn't know how else to get through to the stubborn woman.

Leaning forward, he pressed a soft kiss to her lips, then tapped a finger on her locket. She looked up at him warily, and he knew he'd made his point.

Even knowing that, it killed him to turn around, to walk away, leaving her in the arms of another man, even if that man was one of his closest friends.

She needed to learn to trust him, because without trust, what they had was worth nothing.

CHAPTER SEVENTEEN

Maddy winced as she bent to gather dishes from a table. It had been nearly twenty-four hours since she and Alex had been at the club, and if anything, her bottom was more sore today than it had been the day before.

Carrying the dishes back to the kitchen, Maddy ground her teeth together with frustration. She still couldn't quite believe that Alex had left her in the care of another man, even if that man was someone he trusted. And she chastised herself for wanting more of Alex's ministrations with a kind of desperate longing she'd never known before.

When he'd tapped his finger on her locket, she'd gotten his meaning loud and clear. She needed to open up to him—no more secrets.

Damn it, why couldn't he just understand? She was ashamed. No matter what Dr. Gill said, no matter what Nathan said, she would always feel guilty for the accident that had killed her sister. She would always be ashamed that, somehow, she was the one who had cheated death.

She would rather die herself than see the disgust she knew she deserved on Alex's face.

And yet . . . unless she was very much mistaken, he had decided to trust her. Tit for tat.

Could she be brave enough? Or had all of her courage died in the car wreck with Erin?

"Just seated someone who asked for a table in your section."

Susannah's statement caused Maddy's heart to thump heavily inside her chest.

Was Alex here?

"Not bad-looking, but I like the other one better." Susannah grabbed plates for her table from beneath the warmer, then scurried back off across the diner to her section, leaving Maddy with a sense of dread.

The other one?

Smoothing her hand over her ponytail, she made her feet carry her back out to her section. The man had his back to her, but when she saw the long dark hair, the dark suit worn stubbornly despite the heat outside, the arrogant posture, she knew.

Anger flooded her as she crossed over to him, confronting the man with her glare.

"Miss Stone." Massimo Santorini smiled up at her, his expression pleasant, though she saw that he watched her with those shark eyes. "I had hoped you'd be here."

Maddy swallowed down the distaste. Maybe if she just served him a meal, if she didn't antagonize him, he'd go away.

"What can I do for you?" Her voice was sharp, clipped, and she knew that her meaning was clear. Do what you came to do; then go the hell away.

"I'm actually here to do something for you, Miss Stone, though I will accept some coffee while I'm here." The look he gave her made Maddy feel dirty, and she longed for a shower to scrub away the greasy sensation of his eyes on her. "I assume it's fresh?"

"Of course it is," she snapped, turning his cup over with a slam. How dare he come here, to her place of work, insinuating that the venue was beneath him.

From what she'd seen of him, he was in no position to judge anyone.

"I'll take two sugars. I like it sweet." Massimo sat back as if he expected her to sweeten his coffee for him. She slid the bowl containing the packets of sugar and Splenda across the table, raising her eyebrows as she did.

This man was nothing but a bully. She wasn't going to let him push her around.

"Sit, Miss Stone." Irritation flickered over the man's features, though he quickly smoothed it away. Massimo gestured widely with his arm, as if Maddy were a guest in his home rather than his waitress in a diner.

"I'm working." She could smell his aftershave, the scent spicy and strong enough to make her gag. She wanted to take several deliberate steps back, to put space between them, but didn't want to give him the satisfaction of knowing that he'd intimidated her.

"Don't make this difficult. I'm here for your own good."

Maddy felt a sinking sensation in her stomach, knowing that whatever brought this man to her place of employment, it wasn't going to be good. "Say what you have to say; then go."

Massimo chuckled, and the sound lacked all mirth. "Do you know, Miss Stone, that Alex Fraser phoned me this morning and told me that he was no longer interested in purchasing my casino?" The man watched her with an expression as intense as that of a hawk as Maddy blinked, stunned.

Why would Alex have done that? He'd wanted that property.

"As you can imagine, I am most displeased with this turn of events. I chose Mr. Fraser because he had done me a great disservice in the past, and he owed me."

Maddy furrowed her brow. As far as she knew, Alex and Massimo hadn't known each other before the one man had approached the other with the casino deal.

Massimo, watching her so intently that she felt naked, laughed at her confusion, the sound laced with bitterness. "Yes, your lover has secrets, as I'm sure you're aware. This one, though . . . this one was not a secret that he tried to keep. Instead it was the result of sheer arrogance." Massimo reached out and encircled Maddy's wrist with his fingers. She tugged against his grasp to no avail.

"Sit down." Massimo spoke as if he were commanding her. This was a man who was trying his hardest to be dominant—a man who wanted to dominate *her*. She understood now that the trait had to come from deep within—she had no compulsion to do as this man said, no urge to please him as she did with Elijah, with Julien, and especially with Alex.

"Take your hand off of me." Sexually submissive or not, she didn't have to do anything she didn't want to, not for this man, not for anyone. "I could scream and get help, but I'd much rather pour this pot of scalding coffee on your face. It's your choice." She waved the pot in the air, grimly satisfied when Massimo removed his hand, though his expression became openly nasty.

"Your *lover* couldn't have told you that he cuckolded me with my wife, because until two days ago, he had no idea."

Maddy tried to hide her shock, but then she remembered Alex's face when he'd caught sight of something that startled him at Massimo's house—the shelf holding the single photo of a beautiful woman. It was only after that that his manner had changed so drastically.

"He didn't care enough about her to find out that she had a husband. I'd assumed he would know and that when I went to him asking for help, he would make it right. He considers himself an honest man." Massimo's bitterness made his words sour. "Even then, he didn't think me important enough to dig very far into me. He didn't look hard enough to find out that the woman who used to be my wife was once his submissive. That's the term for all of you little sluts, isn't it?"

Maddy's mind whirled. Massimo's anger came across like he was a child having a temper tantrum. And yet she was certain that none of it was her business. Not anymore.

"I would like you to leave now." She'd had enough emotional highs and lows in the last few days to last her a lifetime. Planting her feet, she pointed at the door. "Coffee's on the house. Just go."

Massimo stood, and Maddy had long enough only to think that it had been too easy when the man spoke again.

"I'm not done. Alex Fraser drove my woman away from me, and I came here to return the favor. I know his secrets, and I'm going to tell you." He grinned, and Maddy shook her head, trying to stop him before he could tell her what he seemed so desperate to reveal.

"No." She wanted to know, but she wanted to hear it from Alex.

He leaned forward, close enough to get in her space, but not enough to touch her.

She grimaced at the sensation and sought desperately for a way to escape him.

"Alex Fraser has a daughter. He fucked his shrink and knocked her up." He grinned maliciously, seeming to savor the expression of shock on Maddy's face.

"Didn't know that, did you? You might think you're special to him, but in his eyes, you're just like Alessandria.

"You're nothing to him, and you never will be."

After work, Maddy found herself driving to El Diablo. She didn't believe that she was nothing to Alex—she knew better than that. She had seen how much she mattered to him. But the fact remained that she now knew that Alex had a daughter, a child he hadn't told her about.

She hadn't been completely open with him herself, but this—well, if he truly cared, this was something he should have told her about.

Why had he kept such a secret from her?

As she parked in the large lot, she thought back to the night at the club. He had said that if she shared her demons with him, he would do the same. Had he been telling the truth?

Maddy felt sick. The situation had been made all the worse for the fact that Massimo had been the one to impart the news. He considered things even now. Maddy hated him for telling her something she hadn't wanted to hear from him.

"Miss Stone." As she'd expected, Declan was waiting in the lobby for her. She'd texted to tell Alex that she was coming over, that they needed to talk.

She'd planned to ignore him if he'd told her not to come. He hadn't.

Silently, Maddy followed Declan into the elevator.

The big man kept glancing at her, something he normally did his best to avoid.

When Maddy could ignore it no longer, she sighed and looked him in the eyes. "What is it, Declan?" Though she'd never have believed it if she weren't seeing it, he shifted uncomfortably and then actually blushed.

"The boss, he's been hell on wheels since the other night." Declan pinned her with a look that told her he thought it was her fault for his master's bad attitude. "Just go easy on him, would you? He might come across as indestructible, but he's human, too."

Alex waited with anticipation for the elevator to arrive at the penthouse.

He'd been startled to get the text from Maddy. He'd hoped,

waiting with bated breath, that she'd decide to take that step, to share everything with him.

He'd never dreamed it would happen so soon.

The elevator door *ping*ed and then there she was. She was dressed in torn jeans and a plain blue T-shirt, but to him she always looked lovely.

"I'm glad you're here." The words were simple, but a true expression of how he was feeling. "Why don't you come in and sit down. We'll have some wine and talk."

Before he could turn, he saw in her body language that something was wrong.

"What is it?" He stepped toward her, wanting to wrap her in his arms, but the expression on her face told him that would be a bad idea. "Maddy, what's going on?"

"Why didn't you tell me about your daughter?"

It wasn't often that Alex found himself taken aback, at a loss for words, but in that moment he felt as if Maddy had hit him in the head with a brick.

His first thought was of Rae.

"How did you find out?" He wasn't ashamed of his little girl—the farthest thing from it. But the way in which she'd been conceived had made him all kinds of wary about women trying to trap him into commitments. He'd die before letting anyone use his daughter to get to him. There was also the issue that he was a very wealthy man and that Rae could be a target to those without scruples because of it.

He found it best to keep her existence close to his chest.

"So it is true? He didn't make it up?" Maddy looked suddenly weary, as she raked her hand through her hair. "Were you ever going to tell me?"

Alex felt a flash of anger streak through him. This misunderstanding between them took two. "I was going to tell you, as soon as you'd decided to share your mysterious past with me."

Maddy's expression froze, her eyes wide. As always when he brought it up, her expression became tinged with guilt.

Frustrated, he realized that she hadn't been coming here with a mind to share, not at all. "How did you find out?" He repeated the question. For the sake of Rae's safety, he had to know.

Maddy tucked a strand of hair behind one ear, looking up at him with an expression that was both tired and sad. "Massimo Santorini came to the diner specifically to tell me. I'm not sure why he's so focused on me. But he was looking to get revenge on you for pulling out of the casino deal."

At her words, Alex felt his temper rise. No matter how upset he was with her, the thought of that scum Santorini near Maddy made his blood boil.

Though Alex had had no idea about Alessandria's personal life—he'd honored her wishes in that respect—it didn't make the other man less of a cuckold, at Alex's hands. He couldn't completely blame the man for wanting revenge for his loss.

And the man knew about Alex's daughter. The idea made Alex shudder, though if he had judged him correctly, the Italian would now consider them even.

Fisting his hands in his hair, he tugged in an attempt to release some frustration. This sense of maladroitness didn't happen to him often.

"In my early twenties, I was worried about my interest in a certain lifestyle. I decided to seek help. I began to see a therapist named Dr. Lydia Tanner." He ground his teeth together, just thinking about what an easy target he'd been. "I'd just made my first million. I felt alone. She had more power over me than I knew."

Maddy regarded him warily. He wondered if she knew that she was holding her locket, protecting her secret.

"She decided that I would make a better husband than patient. She seduced me, lied about birth control. She wanted a ring." And though he hadn't given her that, because of the daughter they shared, she would be in his life forever.

Alex eyed Maddy. She looked stunned. "That night in the club, I decided that I would tell you, that I could trust you. But I wanted your trust in return." He eyed her locket, making sure that she saw what he was looking at. "The deal still holds."

She looked as if he'd struck her.

Anger and frustration washed through him, and he tamped down the urge to kick the wall. Why wouldn't she just let go? He wouldn't let her fall. But until she did, they had nothing.

"I see." More hurt than he cared to admit, Alex deliberately walled himself off behind a mask of indifference. "In that case, I don't think we have anything more to say to each other."

"You don't understand!" Her voice was slightly frantic. "You'd be disgusted with me. You'd hate me. I couldn't stand for you to see me that way."

His curiosity was piqued, and he knew that, with a little searching, he could find whatever it was that she hid from him.

That, however, wasn't the point. He needed to hear it from her. Even if trust hadn't been such a necessary, integral part of a Dominant/submissive relationship, ever since Lydia, it had been painfully important to him.

Without it, there was nothing, at least for him.

"Maddy, you could never disgust me, no matter what you told me. If you refuse to believe that, there's nothing left for us." He heard her harsh intake of breath and braced himself, waiting—hoping—for her to speak.

Instead he found only silence. His heart hurt.

He did the only thing he could to save himself—he turned to walk away. "Declan will show you out. Goodbye, Maddy."

"Wait!"

Alex stopped, then slowly turned back around as Maddy spoke.

"I . . . Just give me some time. An hour. Can you meet me at the club in an hour?"

Alex didn't speak, but he did nod before he again walked away.

CHAPTER EIGHTEEN

Maddy entered the club area of In Vino Veritas with her heart in her throat.

Get it together, Maddy. You can do this. Looking down at her new bustier, which was the color of crimson, and the matching sheer skirt, she felt her stomach do a slow roll.

This would be so much easier if she knew either way.

Crossing the room, she sat on one of the plush velvet couches where Elijah had told her that the unattached submissives tended to congregate. Once she'd gotten over the weirdness of the fact that the man had had his hands in several very intimate places on her body, he'd been easy to talk to when she'd called and asked for a favor.

Looking around at the club that was still fairly empty, she knew that it might very well be too late for her and Alex. Still, unlike her sister, she was among the living, and she'd discovered something that helped her remember that.

"Madeline." Looking up with her heart in her throat, Maddy swallowed her disappointment when she saw that the man who had called her name was Elijah, not Alex. She forced a smile to her lips for the sake of the man who'd welcomed her back that night, though he certainly hadn't been obliged to.

"He's a stubborn bastard." Holding out a hand, he helped Maddy to her feet. "But I think you'll win in the end. Come with me. Let's get your wine."

Maddy took several slow, deep breaths as she followed Elijah to a back corner of the club. Her pulse beat fast enough with nerves that she felt nauseous, but she fought her way through them.

Elijah had set the scene exactly as she'd requested. The worst that could happen now was that Alex wouldn't show up.

And if he didn't, she would survive. She'd even come back here, to the club, after a while.

She couldn't fool herself into believing that she wouldn't be devastated.

"Do you want me to help you into the swing now? Or do you want to wait?" Elijah's face was serious, but showed no judgment as Maddy searched it.

"I . . ." The thought of being bound in the swing, of being so exposed while she waited for someone who might never show up, was terrifying.

It was also the best way to prove that she was ready to trust.

"Help me in, please." After a long, hesitant moment, Maddy reached for the sideways zipper on her skirt.

She didn't want to hide.

This was terrifying.

"Sit on this wide part here." Catching her by the waist, Elijah settled Maddy's bottom into the seat of the sex swing. It swayed with her weight, the sensation disconcerting. She wasn't entirely sure that she liked it, but she remembered Alex's words.

My fantasy is you. You, in a sex swing, open to me.

She looked up at Elijah for courage, trying to ignore the fact that her lower half was covered with nothing more than a red lace G-string.

"Lean back." A strap went around her torso, under her breasts. It held her in place and made her feel more secure.

Then Elijah clasped one of her ankles, lifting it up to his waist and securing it in another band. Her other leg followed, and suddenly she was suspended, the swing swaying slightly back and forth.

"Oh my God."

Elijah chuckled as Maddy tensed with apprehension.

"This is . . ."

"Incredibly sexy." The man looked her up and down, and Maddy thought she caught a hint of wistfulness in his gaze. It was gone before she could be sure.

"The wine is right here. I'll have a dungeon monitor keep an eye out to make sure that no one bothers you who shouldn't." Elijah's eyes flickered over the swells of Maddy's breasts, the shadows visible beneath the sheer lace of her thong.

"If he says no to this, to you, then he's an absolute idiot." Nodding, Elijah walked away, leaving Maddy as alone as she could be in a public club, her legs splayed and vulnerable.

Minutes passed. To Maddy, it felt like hours. Other club members passed by, stopping to admire her, to comment on how pretty her cunt was, her breasts.

After Alex's very public claiming of her, none of them did more than that.

As the time crawled by, Maddy checked out of her own head. Leaning back, she closed her eyes and simply let herself drift, aware of nothing outside of her own body.

She had no idea how much time had passed when suddenly firm hands clasped her inner thighs.

She jolted, the swing swaying beneath her as she struggled to sit up and couldn't because of the way she was positioned in the swing.

"Alex." Relief threatened to drown her. He didn't take her into his arms like she wished he would, but still, he was here.

That had to mean something.

"What is this, Madeline?"

She winced as he used her full name, something he hadn't done since they'd first met. Recalling how he'd opened himself to her and how she'd thrown his trust back in his face, she licked dry lips.

She would have to work for it. That was fine. He was worth it.

Reaching behind her neck, she undid the clasp of the locket she always wore. With trembling fingers, she opened it, then handed it to Alex.

Surprise flickered over his face, but he still said nothing.

"This is a picture of my sister, Erin." She studied the sunny blonde in the photo at the same time Alex did and found that grief still ripped at her heart.

It always would; she understood that now.

But Erin would have been angry as all hell to find out that for the last two years her sister had all but stopped living along with her.

"Two years ago, the two of us were in a car accident. We were both talking; we weren't paying attention. We crashed, and I walked away with some cuts and bruises."

A hot tear trickled down her cheek, infuriating her. She was trying so hard to be strong, but damn it, it still *hurt*. "Erin died in the hospital the next day, from head trauma. She had a fiancé. They were supposed to get married that summer."

Alex's fist closed over the locket, hiding it from her view as Maddy shuddered.

"I was the one driving. It was my responsibility. I've carried that guilt around with me for the last year. I've tried so hard to run, but no matter what I do, it stays." Though she was terrified that she'd see disgust on his face, Maddy forced herself to look into Alex's eyes. "It's my fault. I don't tell anyone because I can't handle their disgust on top of what I already feel for myself."

Alex was silent for a long moment—too long, Maddy thought. Then he reached for her legs, tracing his fingers over the silvery scars that the accident had left.

She squirmed in the swing, suddenly desperate to cover herself, to hide from that penetrating gaze.

She cried out when, reaching above their heads, Alex twisted the swing so that she faced away from him. With a cupped palm, he spanked the curve of her ass, slow and deliberate, though she could hear his harsh breath and knew that he was holding back.

One, two . . . nineteen, twenty. Maddy's own breath shuddered out of her lungs when, finally, Alex turned the swing back around and glared down at her, fury on his face.

"I should repeat that a hundred more times for what you've put me through."

Maddy tried to catch her breath, the air rasping in and out of her lungs. Her ass was on fire, her skin too tight for her body.

"Don't you understand yet, Maddy? I could never feel disgust for you. I love you."

Her mouth fell open as he ground his teeth in frustration. "You . . . but you . . ." Maddy's mind whirled. "You left me!"

"I've told you from the beginning what I needed, what I wanted. I don't play at dominance, Maddy. I need your submission, and that means that I need your trust."

Shame worked its way through the cautious joy as Alex continued to scowl, his temper up.

"Is it too late?" She heard the hope in her own words and hoped that he did, too. She didn't know if she were truly capable of submitting to him as deeply as he needed, but she knew that she wanted, needed to try.

"That depends on you." Releasing the swing and stepping back, Alex raked a hand through the dark tangles of his hair. "Damn it, if ever I needed a drink, it's now."

Her own mouth felt like cotton, so Maddy gestured to the bottle of wine that she'd requested from Elijah.

"I bought some wine, in case . . . in case." She felt so silly, having this conversation while her legs were open wide in a display for him. "Mouton Rothschild, Bordeaux Red—1943 was an excellent vintage."

Alex cocked his head—she'd clearly caught him off guard.

"You bought a bottle of the Rothschild? How on earth did you pay for that?" Crossing to the small table where it stood open, breathing, waiting to be drunk, Alex poured the ruby red liquid into one of the waiting glasses.

He crossed back to Maddy, held the glass toward her but just out of her reach. He was waiting for her answer.

"I scraped together my tips and asked Elijah if I could purchase just one glass of it." It was mortifying to admit that to a man who could have purchased cases of it without making a dent in his bank account. "He gave me the bottle on the house."

"I bet he did." Alex's small smirk reminded Maddy that Elijah had had his hands on her body at Alex's request . . . and that she'd liked it.

She gulped thirstily when he finally lifted the glass to her mouth. "Aren't you having any?"

Alex had lifted the glass to the light and seemed to be considering. "I think I will." Without warning, he grasped the skimpy strings that made up her thong and ripped it off of her body, then upended the contents of the wine over Maddy's cunt.

She cried out as, grasping the swing on either side of her ass, he pulled her lower lips to his mouth and licked at the crimson liquid.

"Tastes much better this way."

Maddy's fingers slipped on the straps of the swing as Alex

began to rock her gently back and forth, licking away wine from her cleft, her clit at the same time.

"Oh my God." Her hips arched, but she couldn't gain any ground. All she could do was lean into Alex's clever mouth as he sipped the wine from her flesh, then continued to taste her long after the wine was all gone.

"Damn it, Alex. Please!" Approaching the peak only to have him remove the sensation as fast as it had started, she knew that he was working her deliberately, withholding her release.

"Please, what?"

Feeling the thrust of his tongue inside her heat, Maddy felt her eyes roll back in her head. "

Say it. Say my name. Tell me what you want."

"You!" Her cry was close to a scream, and for the first time, she didn't care who heard. "I want you! Alex, make me come. Please!"

Holding her labia open wide with one hand, Alex closed his teeth very deliberately over her clit. Maddy sagged, then tensed as she shuddered through the long, hot orgasm.

When she was again able to see, she found Alex shirtless, his cock freed from his pants. When he saw that she was again focusing on him, he pressed his erection to her wetness and seated himself inside of her.

Something was different.

"Oh." He wasn't wearing a condom. Did he realize?

"I haven't been inside a woman raw since Rae's mother." His teeth were clenched, his face showing that he was as overwhelmed with the sensation as she was. "But you are *the* woman. You're mine. I've never wanted a woman to be a permanent part of my life, of my daughter's life. But with you, it's not something I want; it's something I need."

Setting his feet shoulder width apart, Alex pushed the swing away from his body, then pulled it back, hard. Maddy gasped as the momentum caused him to slam inside of her, hitting her womb with his length.

It felt so good. It felt right.

With Alex, she felt complete.

"I want to be a part of your life." She moaned as he moved the swing from side to side, forcing her to twist on his cock. "I love you, Alex."

Releasing the swing with one hand, Alex reached into the pocket where he had put her locket. He handed it back to her, twining their fingers together over the piece of jewelry as he continued to move inside of her. "You can put this back on, as long as you promise that it will remind you of happy memories, not shackle you with its guilt."

Maddy heard his breath begin to quicken and felt the insides of her thighs begin to tighten with another impossible release. "I'll try." Her voice was husky, making her feel sexy in a way that she never had before.

"And you have to wear my ring, as well." Shocked, Maddy stared up at Alex at the same time that her orgasm broke, and the bliss of what he was asking combined with the physical pleasure into the purest sensation she'd ever known.

"I will. Of course I will." She panted, not willing to wait to get her breath back. "Anything you say. I've always been yours."

As Alex grinned and lost himself inside of her, Maddy stared up at him and felt more peaceful than she'd ever been.

She never would have guessed that she'd find strength in submission, but now that she had, she was never going to let go.

EPILOGUE

Maddy wiped her damp palms against her jeans as Alex turned the Turbo off the main road and into a quiet residential neighborhood.

As she did, the glint of the ring on her left hand caught the light, and a jolt went through her. It happened every time the classic diamond solitaire caught her eye.

Six months earlier, she would never have believed what was in store for her. She'd been working through her list of new things with Dr. Gill, item by item, day by day. Now she communicated regularly with Nathan. Alex had helped her to open her own optician's office. She was planning her wedding, of all things . . . though Alex was more interested in their honeymoon.

She still struggled to work through her guilt over her sister's death, but Alex had helped her find herself again. And though she still found it crazy when she stopped to think about it, it was submission that had helped her to regain control over her life.

A small smile played over the corners of her lips, and she shifted on the leather seat. The soreness of her body was a reminder of just how happy she was.

"What's that smile about?" Alex gave her a quick glance as he turned the Turbo into a small gated community. Maddy felt her nerves ratchet up a notch, but swallowed the sensation. She was about to meet Alex's daughter, the child he held so dear.

"I'm just thinking that none of this seems real." And yet, in a strange way, it did. Though the curl of Alex's lips still made her pulse speed up, they had settled into a comfortable rhythm—as comfortable as a dominant billionaire and his submissive fiancée could get.

Alex pulled the car up in front of a large house with classic lines. Though it wasn't ostentatious, it was clear to Maddy that Alex wanted his daughter to have the same standard of living with her mother as she did with him.

"Are you ready?" Turning, Alex unbuckled Maddy's seat belt, his fingers skimming across the skin exposed by her T-shirt, which had ridden up during the car ride. If he had had his way, Maddy knew that she would have met Rae months ago.

But though Alex had trusted in her from the start, it had taken a much longer time for her to accept that they were ready to make this step.

Twisting in her seat, Maddy pulled the large purple teddy bear from the backseat. Its furry limbs—and the wry shake of Alex's head—made her grin.

"I still can't believe that you, of all people, have resorted to bribery." As he exited from the car, then rounded it to open Maddy's door, Alex's eyes twinkled. "You really don't have to worry. Rae is as excited to meet you as you are her."

"It's not bribery." Maddy tried to look indignant, and failed, instead rising on her toes to press a kiss to Alex's chin. "It's an insurance policy."

She was about to meet the child who would become her stepdaughter. Though she was definitely nervous, the knowledge also filled a hole in her heart.

"Well?" Alex clasped Maddy's hand in his, his thumb tracing over her ring. She'd noticed that he always smiled with satisfaction when he looked at or touched the diamond jewelry that marked her as his. "Are you ready to meet the other girl in my life?"

The nerves vanished as Alex lifted her hand to his lips and brushed a warm kiss over her skin.

"I'm ready."

Lauren Jameson is a writer, yoga newbie, knitting aficionado, and animal lover who lives in the shadows of the great Rocky Mountains of Alberta, Canada. The author of the serial novel *Surrender to Temptation*, she has published with Avon and Harlequin as Lauren Hawkeye and writes contemporary erotic romance for New American Library.

CONNECT ONLINE

www.laurenjameson.com
www.laurenhawkeye.com
www.twitter.com/LaurenHJameson

Continue reading for a glimpse of

SURRENDER TO TEMPTATION,

a six-part serial novel by Lauren Jameson.

Available now wherever e-books are sold!

H e was watching me with eyes at half-mast, and he looked so damn sexy that I actually trembled. He opened his mouth as if to speak, but whatever he was about to say was interrupted by the arrival of the dessert that I hadn't wanted, and wasn't sure I could stomach, not with my internal upheaval.

I couldn't help but notice that the scarlet color of the strawberries was enticing against the stark white of the bowl. I caught the eye of the waitress, who winked at me knowingly as she added a separate dish full of soft whipped cream.

I felt my skin flush, the same hue as the berries, with mortification. For something to do, I took a berry in my fingers, toying with it so that I didn't have to look Zach in the eyes.

He had to know how attracted to him I was feeling, I was certain of that. There wasn't a woman in the small restaurant who wasn't watching him at least out of the corner of her eye—and that included Suzanne, the owner, who had looked at least eighty when my parents had first brought me here twenty years ago.

"Let me." Zach's voice had dropped in timbre, sounding even more alluring to my ears than it already had. Reaching across the cheerfully checkered tablecloth, he took the strawberry from my fingers.

The small patch of skin burned where his fingers brushed my hand. Inhaling sharply, I jolted, forgetting that now wasn't a good time, forgetting that I'd just met this man. His expression mirrored mine in intensity. I had no idea what had just happened, but unless I had been robbed of all of my senses, he felt it, too.

"Open your mouth." Zach swiped the berry that he had nipped from my fingers through the mound of whipped cream before pressing it against my lips. I opened my mouth, my tongue flickering out to lick up the cream.

He moaned softly. Emboldened by forces that mystified me, I took a small bite of the juicy berry, chewing slowly, licking my lips after I'd swallowed.

His eyes followed the motions of my mouth, entranced, before flickering back up to look me in the eyes.

"What is going on?" I regretted the words the moment that I'd said them—how naive was I? I knew exactly what was going on, but I didn't have the sophistication to make the next move.

Though my better judgment was screaming at me, I was praying that Zach would ask me to come with him to his hotel, to his house, to his tent, if that's where his bed was. My flesh felt swollen, full to bursting with need.

With a brief thought of the dark blue negligee that was still in its bag in my car, I told myself that I deserved one night of pleasure.

My words might as well have been a slap. Another persona entirely came over Zach, one who was calm, in complete control, and who washed away all traces of the sexual creature who'd been in his place only moments before.

"I must go. I have an early morning." He shifted on the chair, pulling a wallet from the pocket of his snug jeans. The movement made the muscles of his arm tense, and I was entranced, as well as confused.

"Oh." That had been abrupt. I blinked, my mind sorting furiously through the last few minutes.

Had I said something wrong? Done something strange?

I didn't think so, and I had just enough wine left in me to be irritated by the sudden withdrawal of this fascinating man.

"Well, thanks for the company." My voice was heavy with sarcasm. "Always lovely to meet a new person."

Zach had been in the process of standing, and he straightened as though I'd struck him. I again got the impression that he was not at all accustomed to being questioned.

"Agreed." He peeled a bill out of the folds of a wallet that looked to be made of hand-tooled leather and placed it on the table without checking the denomination.

"Before you go, tell me something: What's a man like you doing in a tiny beach town like this?" I had nothing to lose by asking. Clearly I was not going to have all of my desires satisfied, so I wanted at least to have my curiosity quenched.

Apparently I'd asked something either very insulting or very personal, since a hint of anger flickered over his strong features. He didn't answer, just nodded in my direction before striding away to the front door.

Watching him walk away was like having a limb amputated. I tried to convince myself that the melancholy was because of the recent turn of events in my life, but I knew better.

I'd found something that I wanted desperately, something that made complete and total sense in the chaos that was my life.

It had stayed just long enough to tease me with what I could never have.

Growling with frustration, I tipped my head back and downed the last inch of wine in my glass, wiping my mouth with the back of my hand when I'd finished. As I lowered my chin I caught the stare of two girls who were barely out of high school, if at all. They wore tight, sheer tank tops and shorts that rode up high on the thigh. Though one was a blonde and one a brunette, their faces were nearly identical, smirking with amusement at my predicament.

My face flushed. I was already embarrassed enough. And then I did what it seemed I was becoming very good at doing.

I ran.

"I own a house in Cambria. I've come here since I was a child." I gasped as the voice came out of the velvet night. Turning toward the man who had spoken, I glared, hands on hips.

"How lovely for you." Suddenly furious, and angry at myself for the burst of joy I'd initially felt at encountering him again, and for finding that the mere sight of him did strange things to my insides, I moved briskly off down the quiet street. My motel was only a block or so away.

Main Street was close enough to the water that I could hear the water lapping at the shore. The sound usually soothed me, but tonight it grated at my nerves. I'd gotten nearly all the way back to my motel when I felt a hand on my shoulder, turning me.

Then Zach's hands were fisted full of my hair, his lips a whisper away from my own. My breath caught in my throat, and my body pressed itself into his.

My entire being was drawn to his heat, to the smell of soap and musk and man.

I opened my mouth to say something, and gasped when he tugged on my hair, drawing my head back until I had no choice but to look up into his eyes.

Wetness surged through my cleft. I'd never been held this way, never been looked at with torment and desire at the same time.

I loved it.

"I am a very successful man, Devon. I've had to be ruthless to make my way." His eyes narrowed, judging my response, but I found that his harsh words only made me tremble with need.

"That ruthlessness applies to all areas of my life. I am not a nice man." His expression dared me to argue with him. I wasn't about to. He seemed like a lot of things right in that moment, but nice wasn't one of them.

"I don't care." It was naive, I knew, but I truly didn't. Part of me thrilled at his violent words, a part of me that I would never have guessed even existed.

Something flashed through his expression, gone so fast it was hard to believe that it had even been there, but I knew what I'd seen.

He liked the way that I responded to him. Liked it a lot.

"I'm not for you." I was about to speak, about to object, and instead found myself moaning when he slowly, deliberately closed his teeth over the pulse beneath the line of my jaw. He bit just hard enough to sting and, I imagined, to leave a mark, his actions those of an animal asserting dominance over his prey. As he bit, his hand found the soft mound of my breast. He pinched my nipple through the fabric of my top and bra, then pulled, then pinched again.

A short, hard burst of pleasure rocketed through me and I cried out loud, right there at the end of Main Street.

Then I was trying to stay upright on legs that were trembling ferociously. I stared up at Zach with what I knew was raw need and confusion in my gaze.

I watched as he pulled that second Zach back over himself like a cloak, the Zach who was calm and reasonable and not governed by desire. I opened my mouth to say—well, I don't know what I would have said. He cut me off before I could try to frame a sentence.

"Stay away from me."

And don't miss the return to the sexy
In Vino Veritas club in
Lauren Jameson's upcoming

BREATHE

**Coming from New American Library
in 2013.**

Under her prickly exterior, glass artist Samantha
Collins hides a woman who yearns to submit to the
right man. Billionaire Elijah Masterson travels to
Mexico as a routine check on his chain of resorts. He
instead finds himself fascinated by the emerald green
glass sculpture that he finds at a small market . . . and
by the fiery temptress who created it. The attraction
between them is instant, but Elijah resists, not sure
that a woman as strong willed as Samantha could
ever submit in the way he needs her to.

Samantha sees everything she wants in Elijah,
but apart from one steamy night in paradise, he
seems determined to keep his distance. Refusing to
let go now that she's found the strong man she's always wanted, Samantha makes Elijah an offer that
he can't refuse—a month of complete submission.

But will one month be enough?